NELL'S WAR

A story of friendship, love, and tragedy in Swansea during WW2

K.A.Hambly

Nell's War
Copyright © K.A. Hambly 2018

Dedicated to Francis and Ellen

It's Swansea, 1939, and having said goodbye to three brothers and a boyfriend, nineteen-year-old Nell is faced with an uncertain future on the home-front.

From dealing with a wandering grandmother to witnessing the deaths of her friends, she is determined not to let the war beat her down. She joins the ARP and becomes a local heroine, but behind the smiling face hides the private anguish she could never speak of. Despite the toils of war, the only thing Nell lives for are the letters from abroad and the hope of a better tomorrow.

978-0-244-71094-1

Part One

1939

Chapter One

Nell woke, shaken by a nightmare that show reeled around the back of her eyes. It took her a moment to compose herself while the flurry of images faded out to her paint cracked ceiling.

Hoicking herself up against the wooden headboard she turned her attention to the little window covered with a black-out blind and opened it, letting in the early morning sunlight. She acknowledged the brown taped cross affixed to the glass and rubbed away sleep from her eyes before looking again at the horrid reminder of the precarious times she lived in. If this was a glimmer of the future, she didn't want it. She sighed heavily, pushed her eiderdown away and swung her legs off the bed, taking a moment to enjoy the warmth of the sun on her face. As the only girl out of four children, she had her own room, the one facing the back of the Victorian terrace. Though small and fitting only one wardrobe and a dresser it at least offered a reasonable view from the window. Above the rooftops and the lines of washing flapping in the breeze, she could see the grimy docks full of ships and beyond that, the Bristol Channel. Sometimes there would be a cheeky pigeon that would perch on the window ledge, but not today. It usually meant that Mam had no spare bread to feed them. At this thought, she felt a slight unease in her belly and reached to her bedside cupboard to stop the alarm from ringing. Lack of money worried Nell, in fact, these days, a lot worried her. For the last few weeks, she had taken to her room as a retreat from a house full of males and dire conversations, mainly about the phoney war. But since her youngest brother left for the Merchant Navy she had been spending more time with her eldest brother Alfred who was on leave from the RAF. Now all but one of her brothers remained at home, the thought of him going played on her mind, not that she'd tell anyone. Everyone had problems and everyone's brother, father or uncle was leaving for the military; so what made her any different? Not much. Thinking herself silly for getting upset over a nightmare, and knowing that today was the beginning of a new chapter in her own life, a smile formed on her face. She eyed her new dress lying folded on the wooden chair and pushed the idea of war out of her mind, at least for now.

The excitement of what the day held bubbled inside her. She sprung off the bed, slipped on her dress and painted on her pillar-box red lipstick, sure to apply a small amount as everything had to stretch these days, even with the decent wage she'd be earning. Smacking her lips together she stepped back from the mirror to appraise her appearance. The green floral dress her brother Alfred had bought her fitted her lanky, petite frame perfectly and she twirled around on the bare floorboards until she felt dizzy. It wasn't often she'd get anything new to wear, but today she was starting a new job as a wages clerk at Woolworths in town. According to her friends at the secretarial college, she'd recently graduated from, it was *the* place to work in Swansea.

She smoothed down her dress. 'You're ready, Nell,' she whispered and picked up her brown leather handbag off the foot of the bed. She headed out of her room and walked across the landing. The door to the room her brothers shared was ajar and she closed it tight, pushing down a lump in her throat. She tucked a lock of dark hair behind her ear and pounded down the stairs. Her heart did a little leap when she saw sheets of corrugated steel propped against the wall in the hallway. The sight of it only made her more nervous about the actuality of war.

'Morning, Dad. Is this the shelter you were talking about?' she asked as she walked through the living room to the kitchen at the back of the house.

'Morning, Nell. Yes, it was delivered earlier. Cost me an arm and a leg it did,' he said, sitting in the armchair at the corner of the room. He had one leg crossed over the other; holding the newspaper up to his face. The smoke from his pipe billowed from behind the spread of the *Daily Mirror* with the headline:

"BRITAIN, FRANCE MOBILISE: POLES INVOKE TREATY"

The wireless played low in the background that had pride of place on the folded dining table backed against the wall. To the side, three rigorously polished framed pictures of her brothers in their military uniforms stood next to a vase of cornflowers picked from the garden. For many years the table had served the family at meal times and there was many a happy memory associated with it, but now, as there were only three of them at home, they had taken to using the small breakfast table in the kitchen. Everywhere she looked in the house there were little reminders of how things used to be before the threat of war hung over them. When she walked past him, she did a double take, wondering how he could do both, listen and read, but what with the phoney war business, she knew he didn't want to miss anything. Especially since three of his sons were now serving their King and country.

'How much was it, Dad?' she asked, thinking she would buy the groceries this week when she got paid on Friday. It was the least she could do to ease the financial burden they were having.

'Seven bloody pounds to be exact,' he replied, clicking his tongue in disgust.

Due to the council not ordering enough shelters, he had panicked and bought one before he lost his job otherwise he wouldn't have had to pay for it. For the past eight years he had been a dock labourer but since he got laid off a few days ago he had to prepare the garden for the shelter, hence the mud over the terracotta tiles in the kitchen. Normally, the kitchen would be busy at this hour, and Nell thought it was strange for her mother to leave the dirty breakfast dishes piled next to the white glazed double sink that she would otherwise keep spotless. On the wooden table, next to the gas stove was a plate of toast and a pot of tea. She pressed her hand on the teapot to check it was warm and then poured herself a cup, wondering what disaster she had been called upon to help now. Her mother had been a member of the WVS for a while and prided herself on helping the community when she could, even if it meant she had to drop everything at home.

'Dad, where's Mam?' She asked, spooning sugar into the cup.

He didn't hear her. She sipped on the warm, weak tea and went back into the room.

'She's over the road talking to Winnie,' said Gran, giving her a fright. The dainty woman, with a kind, round face sat down on the sofa wearing her flannelette dressing gown and picked up her ball of knitting. Granny Adams was Dad's mother who had come to live with them three years ago when she could no longer look after a house on her own. 'You know what they're like, don't you? They'll gasbag for hours.'

Nell chuckled. 'Yes, you're right there. I really should've guessed that's where she'd be. Has anyone seen Alf, today? I want to thank him again for my dress.'

'No idea, petal. He did say he had to make an urgent call, but whatever he said after that I don't know. My hearing isn't as good as it used to be.'

Nell smiled.

'Okay, Gran, no worries. I'll see him after work. If you see Mam, will you tell her I've gone to work and I'll see her later.'

She looked up at Nell and smiled.

'Will do, love. You've done us all proud, hasn't she, David?'

'Of course she has. I never expected anything less from our Nell.'

'Thanks, Gran, Dad.'

As Nell was about to head back into the kitchen, a shadow passed the pane of glass on the front door, blocking the shafts of sunlight of the hot, hazy day. She wondered who it was as she wasn't expecting her friend for another twenty minutes at least. Before she had got down the passage to open the door, a heavy-set woman with blonde curly hair had let herself in.

'You're early, Bess. It's only seven,' she figured and looked at the clock in the front room for confirmation.

'It's hot out there,' she moaned as her handbag slid from her shoulder to the floor. She made no effort to pick it up and slouched against the doorframe, already shattered having only walked across the road. 'I know it's early, Nell, but Mam said it's the hottest day of the year so far.' She fanned her face with her hand then reached for her bag, taking out a bottle of perfume and spritzing it over her.

'Well if it's that hot out, perhaps we ought to get ourselves a taxi or maybe the tram?'

'I can't, Nell. I'm broke until payday. I gave Mam the last I had to pay the milkman.'

Nell thought about the contents of her purse and her heart sank when she realised that she too also had nothing. This was typical of everyone she knew lately.

'Okay, well I suppose we'll have to leave a little earlier.' It was then she noticed Bessie's plain blue A-line dress with a white lace neckline. 'Oh, that's a gorgeous dress. Is it new?'

Bessie smiled and gave a twirl.

'Yes, it's new, came all the way from London.'

'I forgot to ask, how was London?'

'Apart from Will leaving, it was absolutely fantastic, Nell. I wished you could've come along. We went to Hyde Park for a romantic picnic and then he took me to a fancy little boutique on Oxford Street and bought the dress as a parting gift. As you can imagine it must've cost him a week's wages.' She laughed and twirled around once more. 'Is yours new as well?'

'It is. Alf bought it for me for getting the job. He's such a good man. He'll make someone a lovely husband one day.'

'He will do. All the girls around here love him. I think we'll all miss him when he goes back to base.'

Nell didn't answer. The thought of him leaving made her feel physically sick.

'Do you want a drink before we go?' she asked, deliberately changing the topic of conversation.

'Yes, please, Nell. A glass of water will do.' She said and followed her out to the kitchen. She bid good morning to Gran and Dad as she passed and then pulled out a chair. She exhaled as she sat down and gratefully took the glass Nell handed her. 'I was thinking of popping to the beach after work, do you fancy it? Sarah in work owes me a few bob, so if she pays me back we could get chips.'

'Yeah, I'd like that,' she said, remembering the letters she had to post to her brothers. She reached over the sink to the windowsill, picked them up and flipped through them. 'I don't half miss them, Bess. The house is terribly quiet.' She put them down on the worktop next to her bag and picked up a clean glass from the draining board.

'All this phoney war business will blow over, you watch.'

As Nell filled herself a glass from the tap, she gave Bess a sidelong glance, thinking how she didn't sound convinced of her own statement.

'We can only hope.'

Aware the time was getting on; Nell slipped the letters in her bag and picked up her gas mask that hung in a box at the back of the kitchen door. She grimaced as she slipped it over her shoulder, hoping she'd never need to wear it.

'Shall we go, then?'

Bessie guzzled down the rest of her drink and nodded. 'Come on then, Nell. I bet you can't wait to start, eh?'

Bessie had worked at Woolworths as a sales assistant for the last year. She had put Nell's name forward for the job, which would earn her a shilling an hour. Not only could she afford to help her family now, but for the first time, she felt she had transitioned into adulthood.

'I can't wait. I know it's going to be great,' she beamed.

'Good luck, Nell, I'd better get on with things. There's no telling when or if we're going to need that bloody shelter,' said Dad, getting up from the chair. He folded his newspaper and passed it to Gran. At fifty-two he still had a full head of hair that now had silver streaks running through it, but the toils of working in hard labour were clearly evident on his face.

'Thanks, Dad and don't work too hard. See you later.'

She went over to her gran and gave her a kiss on the cheek, but the woman quickly pulled back with a horrified expression.

'What is this sticky thing on my face?' she wiped away Nell's lipstick mark and gave her a disgusting look.

Bessie found it hilarious and laughed.

'It's my lipstick, Gran. Do you like the colour? All the girls are wearing it these days.'

Gran's eyebrows creased into a frown. Nell thought she was going to puke and tried not to feel offended. Gran was averse to change and thought it was improper that women should "tart" themselves up to go out.

'Oh no, sorry Nell, it feels rather ghastly on the skin. I honestly don't know why you wear it.'

Nell rolled her eyes, thinking it was best not to say anything. Granny Adams wasn't a woman you wanted to get into an argument with unless you wanted a headache. Bess was still laughing.

'Come on, Bess,' Nell said, motioning her out of the house. 'And it's not that funny, surely? You're wearing the same colour.'

Chapter Two

The instant Nell stepped onto the front porch the scorching heat poured over her pale skin. Bess was right; it was the hottest day so far and she feared she'd end up looking like a lobster by the end of it. It was then she heard the loudest voice imaginable from across the road.

'Good luck, Nell,' the male voice hailed.

She needn't guess who it was as there was only one voice in the street capable of shattering windows and that was her old school friend, Francis who lived with his mother, Edna.

She looked up at the row of pale bricked terraced houses with raised gardens and saw him sitting on his steps smoking a cigarette. Despite their friendship being platonic, he had been trying to get her on a date for as long as she could remember. She refused every time. However, today she saw something mature in his rugged face and floppy brown hair that reached into his blue eyes. She often wondered if they could be more than friends, but why spoil a beautiful thing when she had it?

'My interview was last week, you silly sod. I got the job.'

She followed Bessie down the steps and stood on the pavement; shielding her eyes from the sunlight that reflected off the bay windows.

'So do I get to take you out to the Empire Theatre for a date then?' he asked, cheekily. 'Or, if you'd like we could go for a celebratory drink at the Naval?'

Nell wasn't sure if he was serious or being silly. He had a wicked sense of humour which is why they got on so well. She waved a dismissive hand and chuckled, hoping he'd forget he even asked if she just ignored him. But who was she kidding?

Bessie, who was getting impatient, butted in. 'Oh for God sake, Nell just say yes to shut him up, will you?'

Nell glared at her but before she could respond, Francis had heard and stood up. He was tall and handsome and was never short of female company.

'Listen to Bess, Nell and come with me. You know I'll treat you good. I'm a gentleman,' he doffed an invisible hat at them and took a bow.

The girls laughed, but Nell wondered why he was being like this today as she hadn't seen him around for a while.

'Ask him to come to the beach, it'll be like old times,' said Bess, urging her so they could get moving.

The heat was getting to her now, and she couldn't hang around for much longer, so she reluctantly agreed.

'I'm off to the beach later why don't you come along?' she said, now rather hoping they would have a chance to catch up.

'It sounds great. I'll meet you both there around five 'o clock.'

'Five is fine,' said Nell. 'We'll meet you at the slip bridge.'

Nell waved him goodbye and went to catch up with Bessie walking down the street.

'You've got to laugh at him, haven't you?' Bessie said, nudging her arm.

'Oh yes, he's hilarious,' she replied dryly.

'But you like him though?'

'I've always had a soft spot for him, but he's my best friend, Bess. I've known him since school.'

'Well nobody is telling you to marry him, Nell. Just go and have a good time and see how it goes, eh?'

Nell agreed but hoped she'd heard the end of it today. When it came to men, Bess could talk all day long. Besides, at nineteen, she hadn't had a proper boyfriend yet, unlike Bess who had been dating their old school friend, William for the past two years.

They'd only been walking a few minutes and in that time Bessie had kept a cheerful monologue going, barely pausing for breath. She mentioned something about a dance at the Naval the following weekend. Nell, who was finding it hard to concentrate because of the heat, kept tuning out of her conversation and thinks that she may have agreed to ask Francis to go along, but she couldn't be sure. Even if she did, she only had one decent dress to wear, and that was the one she had on.

'You're not listening to me are you?' Bess said as they rounded the corner, passing Danygraig Railway on the opposite side of the road. The chug and a hiss of a steam train went past, almost deafening them.

She pretended at first she couldn't hear her over the racket, mainly because she didn't think a party at this time was such a good idea. Bessie repeated herself, and Nell thumbed to the train that slowed to a stop.

'I am, something about a dance is it?' she raised her voice over the piercing sound of the whistle. She knew how Bessie loved parties and wouldn't give up asking until she agreed to go along with her. And no doubt she would be asked to sing, she thought. Even though she loved to sing, these days it was strictly for herself and the mirror in her room.

'Yes, that's right, a dance and a party. Jack and Alice are celebrating one year as landlord of the Naval, but what with this shitty war news looming over us, he said the whole community should get together to make plans to move forward in the face of adversity…or something,' she said, her face positively beaming.

'That's very nice of him. So we'll either be celebrating or commiserating,' she responded; a little annoyed at how she wasn't taking the threat of another world war so seriously.

Bessie glared at her, her cheeriness drooped. 'Don't be so depressing, Nell. We all could do with this whatever the outcome.'

'But, Bess, what do you expect me to say?' she snapped. 'You can't look at this phoney war through rose tinted glasses. Half of my family is serving away. God knows what I'll do if Alfred leaves too,' she blurted and then regretted being so harsh.

She noticed how quiet Bessie had become and felt guilty about quashing her happiness. But then, Bessie was an only child, so she couldn't possibly understand how she felt at her whole family breaking apart. Or could she?

'Sorry, it's this damn heat that's making me grouchy. I can't stand it.' She sighed, stepping off the hot tarmac onto the wooden Tawe Bridge that linked the town to their area.

'Oh, don't worry, Nell. How could I be annoyed with you? You know all my deepest, darkest secrets,' she grinned.

The early morning traffic rushed by and Nell looked up to see a car passing with two young kids sticking their tongues out at them from the window.

'Little buggers.' Nell laughed it off, thinking she'd give anything for a ride now, but what with the heat, she wasn't sure what would be worse: packed in a cramped sweaty car unable to breathe or blisters. Turning to Bessie, who was busy wiping her face with a tissue, she nudged her arm.

'I need to stop for a minute, it's so hot and my feet are aching.'

'Oh no, don't stop now,' she whined like a petulant child. 'I'm in desperate need of a cold drink.' She licked her lips then linked her arm in Nell's. 'I suppose we'd better carry each other, come on.'

They both laughed and joked as they walked along the river. Nell looked down, at the sun reflecting on the calm water masking its filth and drew her eyes upwards to the fishing boats and ships in the docks. Seagulls squawked and arced overhead. A man, whose face was covered in coal dust waved at her from the back of his boat and shouted good morning. Bessie waved back, chuckling to herself.

'You just can't help yourself, can you, Bess? The first sight of a bloke and you're weak at the knees,' she joked and gave him a wave too.

'Hey now, you've got Francis, madam,' Bessie said, winking at her.

'I don't actually have Francis yet, Bess, and I'm not sure how that could even work out. We're friends, and besides, I was only having a laugh like you. I suppose we'd better stock up on that what with this threat of war.'

Bessie nodded.

'You're absolutely right, which is why I think the party at the Naval will be a good boost for morale.'

Reluctantly, Nell had to agree.

'Yes, I think you're right, too. I'm sorry about what I said. I do understand why you think this party is a good idea. So that's why I'll come along, on the condition that nobody asks me to sing.'

'I'm glad you're coming around to my way of thinking,' she squealed. 'So why aren't you going to sing for us? You know you love it, Nell. Remember our old music teacher, Mrs. Holmes? She said you could have a bright future on the stage.'

'I'd just rather not right now, Bess. I don't feel like singing these days. Anyway, I have more important things to do like earning a wage.'

'You're such a spoilsport, do you know that? Just imagine how much you could be earning if you chased after your dreams.'

'Maybe when things are more settled at home, I'll think about it.'

They walked along the cobbled pavement on Wind Street that was busy with shoppers. Nell shook the top half of her dress, already drenched in sweat.

'So do you think they'll make an official announcement soon?' she asked Bessie. 'Scary isn't it?'

'Well it is scary, but I'm hoping that it'll never happen. I don't want anything to spoil a glorious day like today. Sweat or no sweat,' she lifted her arms, revealing a large dark patch under her armpits. 'Because if it's spoiled I don't think I could ever look at the summer in the same way again, could you?'

Nell agreed though she didn't feel too confident about the results especially since blackout was introduced a mere two days ago. The first night it had been enforced, she felt claustrophobic and spent the evening sitting in the front room with a dim light and a book for company.

'What do you think life would be like if we were to go to war?' Bessie pondered, staring straight ahead, at the remains of the Norman castle looming into view.

'I've been trying not to think of it, but Dad went on and on last night about the first war and I ended up having nightmares. As for guessing what it'll be like to live through one, personally…I don't know. I don't think it's something we can imagine if I'm honest. Maybe the best answer you will get is when we have survived it.'

'Do you think we'll survive it?' asked Bessie, rather gloomily.

Nell threw her a scornful look. 'Of course we will, Bess, how could you even think otherwise?'

'Sorry. I didn't mean to sound so depressing. I was just trying to look at it from all angles, you know. Honestly, there's no telling which way it'll go.'

'Let's keep our thoughts positive then, shall we?'

Nell's thoughts turned to her mam. She knew she'd be terrified too if the war was declared, especially after losing three brothers at the Battle of the Somme in the Great War. Although her mother would scorn her for calling it great as there was nothing great about men losing their lives, as she would say. As they reached the Woolworths building on the corner, opposite the castle, Bessie wrapped an arm around Nell.

'Let's have no more talk about it, agreed? We'll get on with today's job and what will be will be, as my mam says.'

Nell laughed.

'Strange, that's my mam's saying as well,' she smiled, remembering the day she had first met Bess. Bess and her mam had just moved into number 88 across the road, and no sooner had Bess turned up on her doorstep asking for help to move the piano from the pavement into the house, both of their mothers had formed an instant bond over several glasses of whiskey. Even to this day, neither women can remember any of it, but it is still embedded in the minds of the rest of the residents of Jersey Terrace who had to listen to Winnie and Mary singing around the piano all afternoon.

Nell looked up at the Georgian building with its red sign across the door. She felt proud that Woolworths were her first employers. Bessie tugged her arm.

'We'll go through the back entrance, Nell, so I can get a sneaky fag before I have to clock in.'

'Hey, Bess,' said a woman standing outside the back entrance of the shop. She was tall, rake thin with long auburn hair that curled at the bottom. She smiled pleasantly when she saw Nell.

'Morning, Sarah, this is Nell, the girl I was telling you about…'

'Oh, so you're the new girl who's going to work with me?' she said, stubbing out her cigarette.

'Yes, that's right, nice to meet you.'

'You too, love. I'll take you to the office in a moment.' She then turned to Bess. 'Oh, Bess, you'd better go and help Sylvia with the deliveries, the poor woman came into work today with a sprained wrist. She said she couldn't afford time off work what with her hubby away an' all.'

Bess turned to Nell. 'It all happens at Woolworths. I'll have a fag later then and leave you in Sarah's capable hands, Nell. Speak to you at lunchtime.'

As Bess headed inside, Sarah echoed her words. 'It all happens here for sure, you'll soon find out,' she said with a cheeky wink. 'Come on then, let's get to our desks before battle-axe Crawford comes looking for us.' She turned around, stepped inside the building and led Nell through the stockroom and up a narrow staircase.

Nell thought back to last week when she had been called in for an interview.

'Crawford? I was interviewed by a Mr. James. He was a nice fellow, but seemed unprofessional for want of a better word.'

'Oh, him,' Sarah laughed. 'He was sacked a few days ago,' she said in hushed tones. 'He got caught stealing a box of Bronco's toilet paper last week. Can you believe he had the audacity to sell the stuff onto his neighbours? It turned out that one of his neighbours is the niece of the general manager. Silly bugger didn't know that when he turned up on her doorstep and he answered.'

Nell laughed.

'I don't think we've ever had a roll. Dad still pins the old newspapers to the back of the toilet door, but at least we have an inside toilet.'

'Gosh, you're lucky. My father still pins the paper to the door too, he's an old miser though, mind you.'

With that, Bessie came around the corner wearing her maroon uniform. 'Meet you in the canteen for a cuppa later,' she said as she passed her on the stairs. 'I must dash.'

'Okay, if Sarah doesn't work me too hard I'll meet you at lunchtime,' she laughed.

Sarah snorted with laughter. 'Oh, it isn't me you've got to worry about, Nell.' She pushed open the office door and gestured Nell to her desk under a small window. Nell feigned delight, but the thought of sitting in a pokey room with a window not big enough to crawl out of made her uneasy and terribly claustrophobic.

'I've put the accounts on your desk. I trust you know what you're doing but if I can help at all, don't hesitate to ask.'

Nell nodded and took a look at the documents on her desk. 'Thanks, but do you think we can open the window a little more?' she asked, shaking the top half of her dress that was drenched in sweat.

Sarah rolled her eyes. 'No can do, Nell. I've been asking for a new room but they won't give me one. All I can do is to leave the door open and hope some bugger walks past to create a draught.'

Nell laughed and leveled out the platen knobs on the typewriter. 'I'm sure we'll survive then.' She flexed her fingers. 'So here goes, let's earn some money.'

Once lunchtime came, Sarah showed Nell to the canteen and introduced her to a group of women sitting around the table eating their lunch. The girls gave her a warm welcome with one of them shouting that they had to be nice to the wages clerk or she'd fiddle their pay packet. Not that Nell ever would. She saw the humour and joined in with the banter. The oldest woman in the group, who was called Wendy, got up from her seat and reached for Nell's hand, shaking it enthusiastically.

'Welcome, love. Do you sing, by any chance?'

'A little, why?' she asked, thinking Bess had put them up to something.

'We're organising a farewell party for Jim,' she pointed in the direction of the kitchen, at a skinny man with blonde hair mopping the floors. 'He's leaving for the army, poor bugger. His mother is old and doesn't have any more children to take care of her, so we thought we'd give him a little send-off on Friday to raise a bit of cash to help her when he's gone.'

Nell thought he looked too young and thin to be fighting. Three of her brothers were quite strong having all trained at the local boxing club. It's how she imagined all soldiers were, so she was taken aback when she saw poor Jim.

'Oh,' Nell felt awful and knew she'd feel even more awful if she refused the woman. She saw Bess concealing a grin behind a lock of hair and swiftly turned to the hatch. She knew she had put the woman up to it. 'Then, of course, I'd like to sing for you, count me in.'

'Thank you, my love. Bess really sang your praises, pardon the pun. None of us here can hold a bloody tune.'

There was a murmur of agreement from the table.

'It's really no bother. I look forward to it,' she said through gritted teeth. Ever since the time she lost her voice on stage at the church's Christmas concert, she had been reluctant to sing in front of people.

She went to the hatch, digging around in the pocket of her cardigan for loose change. There was nothing, so she checked the bottom of her bag. She quite fancied the mash and stew that was on offer and got excited when her fingers latched on to a couple of coins. She counted the pennies in her hand and rather glumly asked the woman for a cup of tea with one sugar. Bess sidled up to her.

'Before you say anything, or stop speaking to me for a week I told them you sang because you have the most amazing talent. Plus, it's all for a good cause. Don't throw your gift away, Nell.'

'I'm not throwing it away, Bess. I've got to be realistic and keep two feet in this world, not in a fantasy that won't help pay the bills. But, I'll let you get away with it this time because, like you say, it's for a good cause.'

She thanked the woman for her tea and took it to the woman at the till handing over her two precious pennies.

'Is that all you're having?' asked Bess.

'It's all I can bloody afford and I was lucky to find the change for it at the bottom of my bag.'

'Oh yeah, I forgot, me too, but we're having chips later, so there's something to look forward to.'

'It's going to be hard to get any work done today on an empty stomach though, isn't it? I'm a little paranoid people will hear my stomach growling.'

Bess laughed and then made a gurgling noise that made Nell spill her tea in the saucer.

They went to take a seat at a long table. Two women who had just vacated their seats said hello to Nell and welcomed her to the store.

'So where's this fundraiser taking place then?' she asked, then sipped on her tea.

'Ah, well I'm glad you're alright with it because there's something I haven't told you.'

'Here it comes. What is it you neglected to tell me? And why shouldn't I be so surprised to hear this?' she gave her a knowing look.

'You see, it's not just for the staff at Woolworths, it'll involve singing downstairs on the shop floor in front of the customers.'

Bess held her hands up in defence, laughing hard, but Nell wasn't bothered. She loved to sing, always had. She just had to find the confidence in herself again to stand in front of an audience.

That afternoon, in the midst of the unbearable heat, there was a tap at the office door. Nell looked up from the typewriter, surprised to see Crawford standing in the doorway looking flustered. Her face was red and shiny.

'I need a favour, Miss Adams; I need someone to work on the flower stall. Now I know it's not in your job description, but the girl who was in charge of it has been taken sick, heat exhaustion they tell me. Meet me downstairs in five minutes.'

'Certainly, Mrs. Crawford.'

Once the door had closed, Nell got to her feet and let out a relieved sigh. 'I thought she was going to sack me on my first day then,' she laughed. 'Does she ever smile or is that miserable face stuck there permanently?' she asked Sarah who had her head down at the desk, laughing so much she could barely formulate the words coming out of her mouth.

'You should've seen your face, Nell. What a picture.'

'Thanks.' She replied sardonically, but it was lost on Sarah who was still in hysterics as she left the room.

She made her way across the busy shop floor to a stand by the main doors. Above the table was a huge hand-painted poster.

"GET YOUR LUMINOUS FLOWERS FOR BLACKOUT. ONLY SIXPENCE"

Mrs. Crawford stood with her chubby arms folded across her generous chest. 'Ah, there you are. It's quite simple really, just take their money and give change if needed. Come on, there's a queue starting to form already.'

Nell did as she was asked, and went to the table to start serving the customers. She loved the buzz and excitement on the shop floor and wondered if she would be better suited to this type of work.

By the time she was meant to clock out, she'd already sold half her stock and met up with Bessie on the cosmetics counter as she made her way back to the office.

'It looks like you've done well today,' said Bess, handing over the change to the last customer of the day.

'It made a nice change from the office. Fancy swapping jobs?' she joked.

'I wouldn't mind, Nell. You earn more than me anyway.'

'Here you go, Nell,' Bessie stepped out of the fish and chip shop and handed her a hot bag of chips wrapped in old newspaper.

'Aw, thanks, Bess, I'll get them next time.' She inhaled the aroma of vinegar trying to remember the last time she had chips from the chip shop. It had been a while that's for sure, as it had become a rare treat in her house what with her parents being out of work.

'Shall we go and see if Francis is waiting for us then?' asked Bessie.

Nell had a mouthful of chips and just nodded. She was hoping to get a bit of colour on her milk-bottled legs today, but the sun was slowly setting to the west of the town now, heading towards the Mumbles. As they walked along the street, they pointed out the dresses in the shop windows they liked and could ill afford until they came to the main road. A tram was making its way towards them.

'How do you like it in the office?' Bessie asked as they stood on the curb, waiting for it to pass before they crossed Oystermouth Road.

'Stuffy but the girls are great, especially Sarah. Thankfully she's so nice, what with the office being the size of a shoebox,' she replied as they crossed over; dodging a few cars as they went by. The smell of the salty sea air now became apparent as they neared the seafront. They stood on the pavement and Nell looked up and saw Francis waving at them from under the slip bridge.

'Bloody hell, I wouldn't mind betting he's skipped work and waited here all day,' Bessie laughed.

'It wouldn't surprise me if he did either. He seems different today though, don't you think?'

'Yeah, he does a bit. I wonder what's up with him, especially asking you out on a date like that this morning. That was very bold of him I must say. I'll put it down to the extremely hot weather we're having. It can make people do all sorts of funny things.'

'Yeah,' replied Nell, clocking Bess's cheeky grin. 'Let's put it down to the weather, eh?'

'Hey,' Francis yelled, waving at them. He ran towards them wearing a white shirt that was rolled up at the sleeves and trousers that were hitched a quarter way up his legs. 'I didn't think you were going to show,' he said, nicking a chip from Nell's wrapper.

'Hey, get your own,' she laughed, and jokingly slapped him on the hand.

'How did the job go?'

'It went well, thanks. Here you can have them.'

She handed him the rest of her chips and then noticed her inked stained hands, thinking she'd wash them in the ocean. They walked together down the concrete steps onto the beach. Nell took in a lungful of the sea air, feeling calmer now she had got her first day over with.

'Here's a nice spot,' said Bessie, and she lay her cardigan down on the sand to sit on. 'Oh I think I could stay here for the rest of the day,' she wittered on, but Nell's mind was on Francis who sat down next to her.

Happy to feel the warm sand between her toes, Nell lay back, hands propped behind her head. She looked up at Francis as he was quiet now which wasn't usually like him. He sat, looking wistfully at the Mumbles in the distance. As if he sensed her eyes upon him, he turned to face her with a small, weak smile.

They held their gaze for a moment and as Nell was about to ask if there was something bothering him, Bessie chimed in.

'So how have you been Francis? We haven't seen you around much lately.'

'I'm not too bad, Bess.' He took a slow exhale.

Nell thought he was about to say something important, something that had been weighing heavily on his mind a moment or two ago.

'Work is demanding and tiring in this weather, but that's what you'd expect on the railways. Anyhow, I've actually got something important I need to tell you both,' he said but directing it towards Nell.

Nell exchanged an uneasy glance with Bess, and both of them sat up, eager for a bit of idle gossip. At least, that's what Nell was hoping for, but her gut said otherwise.

'I'm glad you asked me here today because I've been meaning to tell you that I've signed up for the Merchant Navy. I thought I may as well go for it before I'd get conscripted.'

Nell's eyes widened at his news. No, it wasn't like Francis at all she thought. It was the last thing she expected him to say as he wasn't the bravest boy she knew, but then again, he wasn't the type to shirk from responsibilities either.

'Have you really? You didn't tell me you were thinking about this,' cried Nell.

'I've been trying to tell you for a while but I could never find the right time.'

'Is that why you've been so busy, so you could avoid telling us?' she asked, feeling deeply hurt and saddened that he was leaving. She secretly hoped that any minute now he'd say that he was joking with them, but she saw how serious his face was and, besides, if it was a joke it had dragged out too long for it to be even remotely funny. Gosh, she thought, he really did mean it.

He ran his hand through his hair. 'You could say that. I only told Mam this morning.'

'Did you really only tell her this morning? How did she take it?'

'Not good, but I'm a man now, I have to do what I think is right and serving my country is the right thing to do at times like these. Don't you agree?'

'Of course, so when do you leave?' asked Bessie, lifting up her sunglasses.

'I leave for Newcastle in a couple of weeks' time.'

Nell didn't want to show it, but her heart sank at the words. She almost felt guilty for thinking that everyone was leaving *her*, but everyone who was important *was.* She didn't know how much more she could take.

Nell pushed a lump down in her throat.

'Well, I'm proud of you for doing so,' she said, and leaned over to give him a hug.

Francis noted the sadness in her eyes and gently caressed her arm. His eyes softened.

'I need to do my bit, Nell. Just like your brothers. I'm not leaving you or anyone else on purpose, you know that yeah?'

'I know,' she said softly.

He got to his feet, dusted the sand off his backside and painted a smile on his face.

'Come on, the last to the water is a stinker.' He offered his hand to Nell that she took and he pulled her up to her feet. Bessie was already sprinting across the golden sand to the crashing waves. 'I didn't know she was that fast,' he said, surprised, and looked back at Nell with a smile that melted her heart.

He looked long and hard at her, and for a moment she thought he was about to kiss her. She didn't think she'd mind if he did, but then Bessie hollered for them to hurry along and the moment was lost between them.

'I'll give you a head start.'

She placed her hands on her hips. 'Oh, so you think you're faster than me, do you? No, go on, I'll give *you* a head start,' she said.

'Okay, but don't say I didn't warn you.'

As he ran across the sand, he undid his shirt, flinging it to the elements. It was then Nell gave into her resolve; watching him as if for the very first time with her breath caught in her throat. She realised she was a fool to think they could only ever remain as friends.

War was far from their minds as they casually strolled home, sopping wet, laughing and joking about their school days. It was just like old times, thought Nell, wishing every day could be like today. Francis had his arm around Nell's waist for most of the way back which she didn't seem to mind, and as they came to Nell's front door, he slipped it away and gave a naughty peck on the cheek before he ran across the road to his house.

'Did you see that?' Nell gasped. 'What a cheeky sod, eh, Bess?'

'Yes, he's definitely a cheeky sod, Nell, and I think he likes you a lot.' She winked at her.

Her cheeks went the colour of scarlet. 'So, are you going home or coming to mine first?' Nell asked, ignoring Bessie's last remark as she felt embarrassed. She had just mounted the steps to the front door when she heard Winnie calling them from across the street.

'Nell! Your mother is over here, love.'

'Looks like we're going to mine,' answered Bessie, concerned.

Not one to raise her voice, the cry of Winnie sent panic through Nell. Both girls immediately ran over the road and pounded up the concrete steps.

'What's happening?' Nell asked, but judging by the old girl's red-rimmed eyes, she already knew the answer. Winnie gripped her arms tight, about to say something but a sob caught in her throat and she began to cry. She took the corner of her apron to dab her tears then ushered her inside.

'Go through, love, your mam is in there.'

Nell didn't know what to think and stormed through the door and down the green painted hallway in a haze, her temples throbbing and her ankles burning where the leather rubbed against the broken skin. A hub of conversation became evident from the front room. She pushed open the door and entered; her stomach leaden with worry. Half the street was already gathered, mingling and chatting with each other; the tone of the conversation was depressing from what she could make out. She looked around the room for Mam, finding her short thin frame beside the bay window talking to her eldest brother, Alfred. At once, her eyes focused in on his clothes, his smart, official-looking navy suit and when she drew closer she felt sick at the base of her throat. Alfred was taller than anyone in the family. He was also the brightest and had been training to become a pilot when news of the imminent war surfaced. Did this mean what she had been dreading, that Alfred had to leave? This nightmare was not about to end anytime soon, she thought. If anything it's only about to begin. There was no point avoiding the inevitable so she made her way across the room, excusing herself to get past.

'Nell, you're home.' Mam cried, rushing toward her. She flung her arms around her then quietly sobbed onto her shoulder.

'It's all going to be okay, Mam,' she said all the while looking up at Alfred, at his RAF uniform. 'Isn't it, Alf? Tell Mam it's going to be okay.'

An uncontrollable sob escaped her lips. She didn't want to believe what her eyes were seeing, but his cool blue eyes, usually smiling, now filled with uncertainty as he looked down at her. She found this unnerving so looked away. Her mother pulled back, gave Nell a kiss on her cheek and fell into the arms of Winnie.

She had an inkling of what this was about and poked Alf's arm.

'Where are you going?' she asked him sternly and folded her arms across her chest.

Alf drew a long, deep breath and took Nell's arms. She noticed his lips quiver with emotion and the tears welling up in his eyes. He then took a calm breath and smiled tight-lipped.

'I'm so glad you're home, Nell as...' his voice cracked with emotion. 'We're in fragile times and I don't know if I'll get to see you again.' He held back the tears that were threatening to fall and cleared his throat.

Nell searched his face.

'*If?* I'll have none of this defeatist talk, Mr. Adams. The word you wanted was "when".

So, you were going without saying goodbye, were you?'

'You know I'd never do that to you, Nell. But look, some things are the way they are, and I have no control over them.' He took her hand. 'We knew this day would come eventually, didn't we? I told you the day I came home that I'd have to go back.'

'Why today of all bloody days, though? And more importantly, Alf, why didn't I know you were leaving today?' She whined, raising her voice. She noticed how quiet the room had become and watched how Alf nervously ran a finger around the collar of his shirt.

'I've had my papers for a couple of days or so but today my commanding officer demanded I get to Biggin Hill. Pronto,' he paused. 'You must try to understand, Nell. How could I tell you about this when you had news about your job? You were so happy and I didn't want to spoil that for you.'

Tears streamed down her face. She nodded that she understood, but wished he had told her sooner, a lot sooner. If he had then she wouldn't be standing here dealing with two life-shattering pieces of news, first Francis and now Alf. She playfully thumped his arm again.

'It's all falling apart, Alf. Why can't things stay the same? Why do things have to change so bloody much around here?'

'I think life would be very boring if it stayed the same, wouldn't you agree?'

She sighed. 'It's taken a phoney war though, but I do see what you mean,' she said indignantly.

'Listen, Nell, you've got to look after Mam and Dad for me. You'll be okay, sis, everything is going to be okay. When has your big brother ever let you down, eh?' His voice faltered once more and he pulled her in for a tight hug. She nestled her head onto his chest where the brass button on the breast pocket pressed against her cheek. Every second really did count now. How she wished they were just children again, taking the dogs for a walk up Kilvey Hill, or blackberry picking, or playing hide and seek on the streets whatever the weather. But life happened almost unexpectedly; they grew up and the world became a dangerous playground. He pulled back from the embrace, lifted her chin with the tip of his finger and then gave a big toothy smile as he propped up his cap to reveal his thick dark curls.

'Here, I want you to have this.' He reached into his jacket pocket, took something out and concealed it with his hand. 'I wonder if you remember this,' he said, taking her right hand. He placed a small object in her palm. She looked down with a big smile on her face at the sight of a silver whistle. 'And do you remember how you always wanted a turn and I'd never let you?'

'I can't take this. It's your lucky whistle.'

'Of course you can take it because I'm giving it to you. Now you're the leader of the pack, Nell.' He saluted her.

'Thank you, Alf. I'll promise to return it when you come home.'

'Nell,' said Mam with Gran standing by her side, 'would you do me a favour and help Gran over the road, please? You know how she gets when there are so many people about.'

She wiped her eyes with the sleeve of her dress and nodded. 'Okay, Mam.' She turned back to Alfred, reached up on tiptoe and pecked him on the cheek, her lips wet with his salty tears.

'Come home to us. Please.'

'Don't worry, Nell. I will write to you as often as I can.'

'You'd better,' she smiled. 'I'll be waiting for the postman every day; you mark my words, Alf.'

'I promise you, Nell,' he said, now quite serious. He then turned to face Gran who was wiping her glasses with the sleeve of her cardigan. He stooped down to hug her, but she didn't respond. 'I'll see you soon, Gran,' but she looked up at him with confusion. The words he spoke literally went over her head.

'Yes, make sure you're home in time for supper, Alf. It'll only get cold and you wouldn't want to do that to your poor mother, would you?' she said, putting on her glasses. 'She slaves away in that kitchen, you know.'

'No Gran, I wouldn't want to be late at all,' he replied and gave her a kiss on the cheek. He looked at Nell, who was doing her best not to laugh. He shrugged. 'She's old,' he said, hugging Nell again. 'I don't think she quite understands unless she does and is trying not to think about it too much.'

'That's maybe it, and if that's the best way she can handle it, I don't see any harm.' She turned to Gran who was looking around the room as though she had lost something. 'Are you ready to go home, Gran?' she asked, tugging lightly at her sleeve.

For such a short woman, she could be quite fierce and outspoken, but lately, she had become rather forgetful which had been a great worry for everyone.

'Oh come on then, Nell,' she pointed her stick towards the door. 'Let's sort this phoney war out, shall we?' She turned to leave, barging her way through a group of slightly irritated people.

Alfred snorted with laughter.

'She's funny. I expect she'll be keeping you on your toes from now on.'

'Yeah, like she doesn't already.'

'I think you can handle it. You can handle anything, Nell.'

'Take her indoors and make her a pot of tea. I think the news has hit her quite hard,' Mary said, watching her mother in law beat her way out of the door.

About to make her way home, Nell turned to face Alf once more.

'Promise me you'll take care, Al,' she said, wishing they had more time so she could say all that she needed, but then figured she'd tell him when he came home for she had no doubt he would.

He saluted and smiled back at her as she stood by the living room door, she saluted back and left, squeezing her eyes closed for a second, trying to imprint his last smile in her mind. Leaving the house, Bessie bounded forward from the front garden puffing on a cigarette.

'I'll be over later after I've helped Mam with the blackout. The ARP will be around tonight, mind, Nell. It's a ten bob fine if you're slacking.'

Bessie had always been a worrier, so Nell just nodded that she'd heard and then turned her attention back to Gran, swooping her arm around her as she walked down the steps, one slow step at a time.

'I'd wrangle those Nazi bastards, you watch, Nell,' she pointed her stick and shook it furiously in front of her.

'Gran, just concentrate on the steps for now then plot your revenge, please. I don't want any accidents.' She groaned, relieved to get her on the pavement in one piece.

Nell held her arm as she stepped off the curb, but due to Gran's constant talking, it took Nell's mind off the road.

'Nell, hang about,' Bessie hollered. 'Alf said he'd be leaving in fifteen minutes if you want to see him off.'

Nell stopped to look back at Bess, not realising that Gran had slipped from her grasp.

'Okay, Bess, I'll come and see him off. Thanks.'

As she turned back, Gran had walked out onto the road without looking, and a black car that had been coming down the street came to a screeching, grinding halt.

Nell looked on, open-mouthed, unable to move from where she was standing. She wanted to shout, to ask if her Gran was okay, but no words would come out.

Gran pointed her stick at the stone-faced driver.

'Let them bloody wait, Nell. I'm gasping for my cup of tea,' she shouted, loud enough for the people in the next street to hear. Unafraid, and unscathed, Gran walked on with a slight swagger to her step towards the house.

'Oh my God,' Nell pressed a hand to her pounding heart. 'You could've got us killed then, Gran,' she said through gritted teeth as she followed her across.

'Walking was invented before the wheel, Nell, come on.' She marched on, across the remainder of the road and up the concrete steps to the house.

Nell thought about the driver and looked back to see if they were okay. The car was now parked outside Bessie's, and when she got a proper look at him she saw he wore an RAF jacket, too. He saw her looking and waved her over.

'I hope the old lady is alright,' he said, popping his head out of the window. 'She just came out of nowhere.'

'Yes, she's okay, thank you. I think she scared you more.'

The man laughed. 'That she did. I'm waiting for Captain Adams. Do you know when he'll be ready?'

'He shouldn't be too long. He's just saying goodbye to everyone.'

'Okay, thank you, miss,' he doffed his cap.

'Not a problem and sorry again for my gran.'

When she mounted the steps, her heart rate settled back into a normal rhythm. It was then she turned back from the porch and saw everyone coming out of their homes ready to wave Alf goodbye, as they did with everyone in the street who had joined the forces.

'Damn Hitler, damn it all,' she huffed to herself and went inside the house.

She got inside, helped Gran into her armchair which she had brought with her from her house and made her a cup of tea. The old dear had fallen asleep giving Nell a moment to rush out the door to wave Alf one last goodbye. He was about to open the passenger door when Nell sprinted down the steps calling after him.

He heard her calling and looked over. 'Nell, come here,' he said and ran over the road. He lifted her up and swung her around. 'I'll be back as soon as I can, okay? It's not a goodbye, you hear?' He gave her a quick peck on the cheek, doffing his cap as he ran back over the road. The crowd that had gathered on the pavement whooped and cheered as the car pulled out.

Choked with emotion, Nell stood on the road watching the car pass the school at the bottom of the street until it turned the corner, disappearing out of sight. The warm, salty tears she held inside now flowed freely down her cheeks.

'Nell,' said her mother walking toward her. 'I need to go and help Sally for a bit, so can you sort out the supper?' she asked, teary-eyed.

It was then Nell noticed Sally's eight-year-old twins, Jimmy and Charles, running amok on the pavement. The dark-haired boys were dressed smartly in matching navy tank tops and grey shorts that exposed their scabby knees, but it was the sight of a brown tag that dangled from their necks that struck Nell. She'd heard about children being sent to the country but now she saw it happening for herself, she could hardly believe what the world was coming to.

'Are Sally's kids being evacuated?'

'Yes, love. She decided it was a good thing. Poor bugger is heartbroken so I'm going to help her get them on the train. Judging by how hyper they are now, I can tell you it's not going to be bloody easy.'

'Do they know what's happening then?'

'She did try to explain to them last night but,' she turned around to look at them and sighed, 'I don't think they fully grasped what she was telling them. More than likely, it'll hit home when they're at the station.'

'I'd rather you than me. I don't think I could bear to allow my kids to go off to God knows where.'

'Makes no difference if they're eight or eighteen, love. I've just sent three boys to God knows where. The only difference being is we can be almost certain these two will come back.' Mary sniffed back the tears and leaned forward to give Nell a kiss on the forehead. 'Thanks for sorting out the tea, love, I'll be back as soon as I can.'

As Mary went to round the kids up, Sally came out of the house carrying two suitcases. A tatty brown teddy bear with a missing ear dangled from the handle of one. Nell met the woman's tear stained eyes and instantly felt as though she was intruding on someone else's pain. About to look away, Sally acknowledged her with a weak smile and started to walk down the steps, calling after the boys who were giving Mary a hard time. Once the boys heard their mother's voice, they both stopped abruptly on the pavement with quizzical expressions. They had now clocked the suitcases and were asking where they were going. Nell watched it all unfold from the opposite side of the street. Sally knelt beside them and explained; probably for the hundredth time that they had to leave for their own safety. Upset, with tears threatening to fall, Nell turned away and began walking up the steps to the house when she heard the boys wailing that they wanted to stay with their mammy.

'We'll be good, we promise,' cried Charles.

It was all too much for Nell, who couldn't help but feel useless. War was looking possible by the second. Walking down the hallway to the kitchen, she passed an old coat hanging on a hook under the stairs given to her by a friend who'd joined the ATS and it put an idea in her head. She decided she would do something that would make a difference. She wasn't sure of what but knew it didn't involve Woolworths or sitting in an office all day. It was the time for sacrifice, and if she had to sacrifice her dreams of being a singer so be it. She passed Gran who was still asleep and blissfully unaware of the chaos around her, and slipped into the kitchen. As she got on with clearing the dishes from the table, she heard someone coming up the front steps and popped her head around the door. David shuffled through the front door, head hung low. He didn't acknowledge her when he passed and quietly went out to the back garden. He wasn't a man of many words, or of expressing his emotions well. In times of trouble, he'd normally be the one who sorted things out, the voice of reason, the strong one they could all depend on. His current state had Nell worried.

Nell put the dishes in the sink to wash, ready to prepare supper when she thought she heard someone crying. She dropped the dish she was washing into the soapy water and glanced out of the window. She had never seen her father cry so openly but there he was, sitting on an upturned metal bucket with his hands pressed against his face for the world to see. The dog from next door, Blackie, was sitting on its haunches beside him.

Knowing he wouldn't want a fuss made she left him alone, stacked the plates and put them in the cupboard. She turned her attention to preparing the supper and opened the pantry door. She stared inside, not really looking for anything in particular as she didn't have much of an appetite now.

Chapter Three

Nell splashed cold water on her face and unplugged the sink. It was then she heard chatter from outside the bathroom window and looked up. The hoarse, raspy voice, from smoking fifteen cigarettes every day since she was seventeen belonged to Florrie from next door. She was telling Mary about the state in which she walked home from the pub last night. According to her, the blackout wasn't helping her nightly jaunts and this morning she found two bruised knees and grazes across her palms.

'People are going to think my old man is beating me up at this rate…'

Mary suggested she cut the amount of alcohol down or leave the pub before it got dark but she wasn't having any of it.

'The war isn't going to dictate how I live my life, Mary. I'm fifty-two years old and I'm not going to change now.'

'*If* there's a war, Flo,' Mary reminded her.

Nell laughed, wiped her face with a towel and went downstairs, glad for her day off. Florrie, who had lived next door to the family for many years, leaned over the fence also smoking a cigarette. She'd often chat with Mary when they were busy with the washing.

'Alright love,' said Florrie, when Nell appeared by the back door. 'How's it going at Woolies?'

'Morning,' she replied. 'It's great there, Flo. I'm really happy.'

'It's afternoon,' said Mary, sitting on the back doorstep smoking a cigarette. 'Enjoy your lie in?' There was a basket of wet clothes by her feet and the mangle she used for getting rid of the excess water before she hung them to dry by the fence that partitioned off the neighbouring garden.

Nell took one look at the shelter and wrinkled her nose at it. 'Yeah, Mam, I couldn't sleep what with this racket going on,' she nodded towards her dad fixing a wooden bed inside the shelter.

He stopped hammering and poked his head out the door. His face was red, and glistening with sweat.

'It has to be done, Nell,' he shouted, having overheard her. 'There's an announcement on the radio at 11.15 today from the Prime Minister. I have a feeling this is the big announcement we've been expecting,' he said gravely and went back to work.

Worried, Nell looked at her mother for answers.

'Why?'

Mary shrugged her shoulders.

'I guess we'll find out soon enough, love.'

'I reckon he's gone back on his bloody word and sent us to war, you watch,' said David. 'These politicians are all the fucking same, pardon my language.'

'Don't be so pessimistic,' Mam spat and shook her head. 'Don't listen to him, Nell.'

The news didn't sit well with Nell and she went to finish peeling the potatoes her mother had left in a bowl on the table. While she got on with things, she heard Winnie calling from the front door that was left open.

'Yoo-hoo, it's only me.'

'Come in, Win. Mam's out the garden having a cigarette on the back step.'

'What do you make of this broadcast then?' Winnie asked, pulling out a chair.

Mam stumped out her cigarette and got up to put the kettle on.

'No idea, Win, whatever will be will be, I suppose.'

Nell poured the potatoes into the saucepan on the stove and then took a box of cornflakes from the pantry for her breakfast.

'It's all very scary though. I mean, just hearing Dad talk about the Great War was bad enough, but to actually live through one...'

All went quiet around the table and then Bessie came in with Mr. Greenwald, the local ARP warden. He was a tall, broad-shouldered Irish man who came over from Cork for a holiday but ended up staying when he met his wife. Nell had never met his wife as she left him a year after their marriage. He had greased back grey hair and wore a pair of round spectacles on his hooked nose.

'Morning all,' he said, taking the seat next to Winnie.

'Alright, what brings you out this morning?' asked Mary already getting another cup from the cupboard.

'I came by to see if David wants to catch rabbits later on. My pantry is almost half empty.'

At that moment, David appeared by the back door, resting his hand on the wall; in the other, he held his pipe which he sucked with vigour.

'If I get that bed sorted, I might do,' he said. 'How's the night patrol going?'

'We could use more help if truth be told, but it's alright. Don't have me giving you a fine now, Mary,' he laughed, wagging his finger at her. 'Make sure every nook and cranny is covered. Ten bob fine if it is and I don't do bribes. I take my job very seriously, I'll have you know.'

Mary scoffed and shook her head in amusement at him. She then handed David his cup of tea.

'What time is it?' he asked her.

'It's 11.05,' said Nell.

'Right,' he said, walking into the house. 'Let's get the radio warmed up then, shall we?'

'No you're not,' said Mary. 'Get those stinking boots off first.'

She already had a mop in hand and was pushing him out the door. He reluctantly took them off, muttered something under his breath in Welsh and then ordered everyone into the living room.

'Come on, you lot, come and hear what he has to say.' He drank his tea as he hurried up the hallway to the front room.

Nell exchanged a worried glance with Bessie who then walked out of the kitchen clutching her mug of tea. Nell picked up her cup from the table and followed everyone into the front room.

Winnie and Mary sat on the edge of the sofa looking anxious, and Greenwald paced the floor around the radio, puffing heavily on a cigarette. Nobody said a word and watched as David turned the knob on the radio, which then cackled. David stood back, rested his hand on the fire surround and chewed his lip. At that moment, the atmosphere in the room became thick with anticipation. The clipped tone of Mr. Chamberlain then came on, addressing the nation.

"This morning the British Ambassador in Berlin handed the German Government a final note stating that, unless we heard from them by 11 o'clock that they were prepared at once to withdraw their troops from Poland, a state of war would exist between us. I have to tell you now that no such undertaking has been received and that consequently, this country is at war with Germany.'

Nell thought perhaps she had misheard the entire thing. It couldn't be true, could it? The thing she feared the most was happening right now, right at this very moment.

She felt shaky and sick. Ice cold chills ran down her arms to her trembling hands. Bessie broke into gulping sobs and grabbed Nell's arm. Nell pulled her in close and was about to offer words of comfort but couldn't muster the energy. Besides, she wasn't sure what good her words could do now when *she* didn't even have faith in what she was going to say.

'Well that's that,' said her mother, obviously stunned by the news. She went to the kitchen offering everyone a fresh cup of tea. Greenwald asked for a drop of gin in his, and the way Nell felt she thought she'd skip the tea and just have the gin.

'I guess we will just have to get on with it then, eh?' said her dad, anguished and pale looking.

'It was inevitable,' said Winnie, standing up and draining whatever was left of her tea.

Unable to comprehend what had just happened, Bessie and Nell left the house in silence and somberly walked out onto a near-deserted street. It had never been so quiet, so still. They walked around the street corner to the back lane.

'Here, have a fag,' said Bessie pressing a cigarette into her friend's hand. 'So much for a phoney war, eh? I knew this would come, Nell, I just knew it. I could feel it my bones,' she said bitterly and stomped her foot on the ground.

'Yeah,' Nell muttered, placing the fag between her lips. 'I'd better not let Ma catch this on my breath, you know what happened the last time, don't you?' she said, wanting to hang on to the semblance of normality which existed prior to this news, but the words kept churning around in her head.

We are at war.

'A bucket of dishwater over your head,' Bess sniggered and then cried again.

Nell comforted her as they slumped down against the brick wall. So far, she hadn't let any tears fall, thinking that she had to remain strong, but for how long she wasn't sure. She kept hoping this had to be a lie and it'll blow over by tomorrow. She thought herself rather silly for thinking it and turned to Bessie.

'Have you heard from your William, yet?'

'Not for a while. The last I heard the Merchant Navy was making a man of him. The cheeky beggar asked if I'd marry him when he comes home. You do think he's going to come home, don't you, Nell?' she asked, her eyes teary and round like saucers.

Nell pushed down a lump in her throat, her eyes now blurry with tears. Everything at this moment seemed uncertain, so bleak.

'Of course, Bess, of course he will. Let's just get back to the house, shall we?' She pushed herself up from the floor and linked Bessie's arm, turning the street corner.

'Where have you been?' cried Francis who was standing on Nell's front porch. 'I can't believe the news, can you?'

'No, but it was expected wasn't it? Anyway, we just went for a fag,' replied Nell, wondering what he wanted.

'Nell,' said Bessie, patting her arm. 'I'll see you later, alright? I need to see if Mam is okay.'

Nell nodded.

'Will you meet me in a little while, Nell, on the corner like we used to?' asked Francis.

She could see he was serious for a change and thought she ought to see what he wanted. It might take her mind off the war for a while.

'Okay, I'll be back out as soon as I can,' she said, needing a moment to gather her thoughts.

When she went upstairs, she overheard her Dad talking to her mother in the bedroom next to hers.

'Don't think it'll be just London that's going to cop it, Mary. I reckon we will be in for a rough old time of it too. It's best to be ready, that's all I was saying…come on, no need to get upset…'

He then went on about needing to find a job as soon as possible. Nell couldn't listen to anymore. She pushed open her bedroom door, closed it and sat down on the edge of her bed. She took a deep breath and stared longingly at her dressing table mirror. The reflection it threw back at her was a sharp contrast from yesterday morning when she started at Woolworths. Now yesterday seemed like a lifetime ago and, instead of the happiness she felt there was nothing but sadness. She sniffed back tears that threatened to fall and took her brush from the dresser to fix her hair. There was no way she could let Francis see her looking puffy eyed and with her hair out of place. She found it oddly amusing that she should care about her appearance in front of him as they had known each other since childhood. If anyone had seen her at her worst, it was Francis.

When she came out of the bedroom, she popped her head around her parent's door. Mary was sitting on the bed folding clothes. Her father had already gone downstairs.

'I'm just going out for a minute, Mam,' she said, closing the door a little after her. She waited for a reply.

'Okay, love,' replied Mary, sniffing back tears. 'Just be in before black-out.'

A cool, welcome breeze blew a strand of hair across her face. She half expected him to be at the corner, but he wasn't there and she wondered where he was. It was then she heard a whistling rendition of Glenn Miller's *Wishing Will Make It So*. She turned to her side and saw the back of Francis sitting on the end terrace wall, his attention drawn to a couple of pigeons walking along the road. She didn't feel like walking down the steps, so she checked if Doris, the neighbour wasn't in her window and made a dash for it across her garden. Francis was still whistling and she gave him a tap him on the shoulder.

'It's such a lovely afternoon, isn't it? It's a shame we have to blot the stars out tonight, eh?' she mused, looking up at the sky. The day was closing in; sky now a bluish-grey with scuds of clouds passing over.

He had stopped whistling and looked up affectionately at her.

'It will soon pass, Nell, everything does. We'll see the stars again, I promise.'

'I wish I could be as optimistic as you, Francis.' She sat down next to him. 'But we've just entered into a world war. Who knows how long the darkness will reign this time around?'

Francis took her hand, and Nell stared down in surprise. He hadn't held her hand like this since they were kids and that was only to pull her up the hill when she decided she couldn't walk any further. Her heart began to beat a little faster. They weren't children anymore so did this mean what she suspected all along, that he did truly love her? She wasn't sure if she was ready to change their relationship, but her heart was saying otherwise.

'We'll get through this war together, you and me. It feels like the end of the world now, but once we win, it will shape a better one, I'm sure of it. It's not being optimistic Nell, its faith, a belief that good will always rise above evil.'

'When did you become so grown up?' she asked, as in all the years she had known him; she had never seen this serious side before.

'11:15 a.m. this morning,' his mouth curled into a smile and then became serious again. 'Its times like these that make you think about what's important in life, Nell, and you're important to me, always have been. If you'll be my girl, I'll always treat you right, you know that,' he said with a passion she was not familiar with when it came to Francis. He wasn't the type to talk about his feelings. Ever.

Though she had suspected his feelings towards her had changed recently, it still took her a little off-guard. It had been many years since she had a crush on him and it had occurred to her that maybe the uncertain times they found themselves in had scared him a little. She felt confused. Could they make it work?

'I know, Francis. You've always been so good to me in the past but… we've always been such good friends…'

'I know, Nell. We're such good friends, and that's why I think we should take a chance on something more. I'm sorry, it's taken so long to admit how I really feel about you. The timing was never right, and I never wanted to mess up our friendship. And believe me; I'm not saying this out of fear of everything that has happened today. My love for you has always been real.'

Her mouth slacked open. She looked him in the eyes, saw the intensity, the love they emanated and knew he meant every word.

'Come here,' she cried, caressing his cheek. 'I'll be your girl, Francis, but promise me when you go away, you'll write to me. The last few months have been so horrible with everyone leaving.'

'Of course I'm going to write to you, Nell,' he drew closer to her and squeezed her hand. He looked into her eyes, 'I love you, Nell, and I know you love me. Just say it. Let me hear those words.'

Without hesitation, she replied that she loved him too. She moved closer to him and felt a release when the words escaped her lips, thinking how silly she had been for not saying anything sooner.

Slowly, he lowered his head towards her and pressed a soft, lingering kiss on her lips. She responded back, wrapping her arms tightly around him. They held each other in a loving embrace until he slowly backed away.

'I'm so glad I have you, Francis.' She opened her eyes and looked into his, feeling a deep, soul connection she had never experienced with anyone else. If this was her true love, she was glad it was with her best friend. She sighed happily and looked up at the darkening sky.

'We'd better get back inside, it's getting late and the wardens will be around soon. I'll wave you off to work tomorrow, shall I?' He asked, taking her trembling hand.

Nell didn't want this moment to end, and asked if he'd stay out a little longer but then she could feel cool drops of rain on her shoulders.

'I look forward to it but don't you have work too?'

'Yes, I need to be at the railway at seven so I'll meet outside about six?' He gave her a cheeky wink and took her hand as they walked back down the street. When they came to Nell's front door, Nell looked up and saw the last of the sun settle to the west, behind the Mumbles Head across the bay. Dark, thunderous clouds were now rolling towards land.

'Goodnight, Nell, see you in the morning.'

'See you at six, then,' she said softly as they unlocked hands.

Chapter Four

Nell was too excited to sleep. Until the early hours, she played the radio low, singing and reading sheet music to prepare for the fundraiser in the morning. Despite the news of war, she was happy and so in love; the idea of singing in front of hundreds of strangers didn't seem to bother her like she thought it would. In fact, she was looking forward to it. She dozed off around 4.30 a.m. sitting on the bedroom floor. The sound of a cockerel that belonged to someone on the hill woke her up at just gone six.

'Oh no.' She pushed back her hair, groaning in agony as she got up from the hard floor. She didn't have much time to make herself look decent so she went to take a quick wash, got fresh clothes on and went downstairs, grabbing her cardigan from the balustrade and quietly let herself out of the house.

Francis was already sitting waiting for her on the garden wall. 'I thought you may have changed your mind about everything,' he whispered, getting to his feet. He gave her a kiss on the forehead and handed her a small bunch of daisies he had taken from next door's garden. Nell laughed when she saw them.

'Don't be silly. I didn't sleep much last night. I've been practicing my singing for the fundraiser at work.'

'I didn't sleep at all. I missed you even though you were only across the road.' He reached out, wrapping a soft tendril of her hair around his finger. Nell shivered at his touch.

'That's a sweet thing to say,' she shied away.

'I'll tell you what, why don't we go to Vee's café for a cup of tea; my treat? She's always open early.'

Nell shrugged. 'Okay, but I look like I've just rolled out of bed.'

'You do look like you've just rolled out of bed,' he laughed, tucking a lock of hair behind her ear. 'But you're still very beautiful.'

'You may want to save the compliments.'

'I have plenty more to give. What do you think I've been doing since we left school, eh?' he asked as they walked down the street. 'Every day when I'd see you out and about, I'd come up with something wonderful to say about you, but I could never pluck up the courage to actually tell you.'

'You're very sweet, you know,' she replied, taking his hand.

'So this means that we are now official?' he winked, linking her fingers.

'I think it does.'

Vera was leaning over the counter smoking a cigarette when they walked in. The aroma of frying sausages made Nell's mouth salivate.

'What can I get you, loves?' she asked, tightening her head scarf that covered a mass of blonde curls.

'Two cups of tea please,' said Francis counting his change.

'And a sausage sandwich for me, too, Vera, I'm starving.'

'You two are out early,' she said, setting down two mugs on the counter.

'Just trying to make the most of our days,' said Francis, handing over the change.

'Don't blame you what with this war business and before you know it you're fifty like me, wondering where the years went.'

'You haven't had a bad life, eh, Vera?' asked Nell.

'Good gracious, no. But I'll tell you a little secret. It got better when they banged my old man up. That's when my life began, and getting this place which has been my saving grace.'

They took their tea to the table by the window. Nell yawned and sat down.

'I don't know how I'm going to manage a full day of work on no sleep.'

'I wish I could come and see you sing. I remember you singing in all the school productions thinking you had the most amazing voice I've ever heard. So why aren't you doing anything about it?'

'I don't know of anyone from here that has ever done anything exceptional with their lives, apart from the ones gone off to serve our country. And let's be honest, most only signed up because they had no choice in the matter. I can't see a way out of this situation right now to pursue my dreams even if I wanted to.'

'I'll make sure you do, no matter how long it takes, I'll get you out of this place, Nell. It'll be you and me against the world one day.'

'Sounds like fun. I'll be waiting.' She sipped on her sweet tea when a thought occurred to her. 'Are you afraid of what may happen when you go to sea?' she asked. She never got to ask her brothers before they left and wondered what could be going through his mind at a time like this.

'I'm petrified to tell you the truth. I mean, look what happened to your Edward on that ship. It's a miracle he survived after that German submarine attacked them. But what choice do I have? What choice does any man have right now? Nah, I'll be okay Nell because I have a reason to come back home, don't I?'

Nell reached for his hand across the table and held it tight.

'You know you do.' She noted the time on the clock hanging on the wall and hurried him along. 'Come on, drink up or you'll be late for work at this rate.'

'Have you told Bess about us yet?' he asked, getting up from his seat.

'Not yet. Do you think she'll be surprised? She asked.

'Honestly? No. Bess seems to know everything. If she hasn't already suspected, I'd be worried, wouldn't you?' He opened the door for her.

'I think you're right there,' replied Nell who turned back and said goodbye to Vera.

After she walked Francis to the railway station at the end of the road, she met up with Bess who was already waiting on the corner of the street so they could walk into work together.

'Where have you been?' she asked, offering her a cigarette from a pack.

'I went for a cup of tea with Francis,' she said and took a cigarette.

Nell lit the cigarette and handed the matches back to Bess. She wanted to tell her about Francis but she knew it would mean the whole street would know by tea time. Yet she couldn't keep it to herself for much longer. If she didn't tell her now, she'd burst.

'You'll never guess what happened yesterday evening?' she asked coyly, as they began their slow walk into work.

Bessie raised a brow and lowered her new sunglasses.

'No idea but do tell.'

'You know how I said me and Francis would never work?'

Bessie's eyes were scrutinizing her.

'Yes, I remember,' she said, her smile widening as if she knew what was to come.

'We decided to give it a go, begin a relationship.'

'That's wonderful,' she blurted, squeezing Nell's shoulders. 'I'm so happy for you both. It's been a long time coming, but at least you've done the hard part now and admitted your feelings for each other.'

Nell laughed. There was nothing Bess liked more than a soppy love story. 'I guess we'll have to see how it goes, what with him leaving for the Merchant Navy soon.'

'Well if you've waited all this time, it'll be worth it. So are you ready for your performance later at the fundraiser?'

Nell gave a cluck of annoyance. 'Yes, I'm ready and I'll have to have a think about forgiving you for putting me on the spot like that,' she smiled as she cast her eyes along the Tawe river. Two Navy vessels were coming into port for repairs. In the hazy sunshine, they looked like two ghost ships on the horizon. It reminded Nell about the letter she'd received from Edward telling her that everything was fine and he didn't want her worrying about him, but she couldn't help it. They were in her thoughts every day.

'But you have something to be joyful about today, Nell. So singing should come easy for you.'

'You have an answer for everything, don't you, Bess.'

Bess flashed a cheeky smile.

'Of course I do, what do you take me for?'

Hands poised above the keys, Nell looked up as the office door swung open. It was barely nine o' clock and she had already been typing for the past hour, wondering where Sarah had got to. It wasn't like her to be late. Sarah came in, rushed to her desk sniffing back tears. She flopped into her chair and cried hard into the palms of her hands.

Concerned, Nell rose from her chair, wincing as her new shoes constricted against her sweaty skin.

'Are you alright?' She asked, resting a comforting hand on her shoulder.

'It's my Howard.' Her shoulders shook.

Nell didn't like the sound of what was coming next.

'He's had his papers, Nell.'

'Oh Sarah, I'm really sorry, honey. Is he in the Army?'

She nodded.

Nell knew how she felt having said goodbye to three brothers. She took a clean handkerchief that hung out of the pocket of Sarah's bag on the desk and handed it to her. 'We're all in the same boat, doll. I know how you feel, I really do.'

Sarah blew her nose and nodded.

'I saw him off just now, Nell, that's why I'm late. Oh, Nell, I miss him terribly already.'

'Come on, let's go down the canteen for a cup of tea, it may not solve our problems but a bit of a banter with the girls is what you need right now, trust me. In times like these, you need good people around you.'

It's what Nell needed too. In a few days, she was also going to say goodbye to Francis and knew she had to heed her own advice when the time came. Her mother's words of wisdom at breakfast the other morning was to keep herself busy. It also reminded her she needed to find something to fill the empty space when she wasn't at work.

'Thanks, Nell. I really appreciate it,' Sarah said as they left the office.

'My Francis is leaving this week, too. He's off to the Merchant Navy so you're not alone.'

'Is he? It's going to be tough for us all. Maybe we should get together once in a while even if it's just for a cup of tea and a chat?'

'Good idea.'

She pushed open the canteen doors, bumping into Judith, a woman who thought she was above everyone who worked there. Not even Bess could stand her and she had to work with her on the cosmetics aisle.

'What's the matter with her?' she asked with a nod to Sarah who was wiping her tear-stained cheeks.

'Her man is leaving for the war,' Nell said, annoyed at Judith's insensitivity. 'Have some compassion, will you.'

'Well, mine has already gone, love. You've got to get used to it. Here…' She slapped a copy of the paper against Nell's chest. 'Have it. I've read the thing inside out.' She then left the canteen.

'Ignore her. Come on, take a seat here and I'll get the tea.'

'It's on me, Nell. Here,' said Sarah twisting the clasps on her purse. She handed her some change.

Once she brought the tea over, Sarah was busy powdering her nose from a silver compact.

'Staff discounts,' she winked when she saw Nell looking at it.

'That's handy. I'm almost out of red lipstick so I may get some when I get paid.'

They had a lengthy chat about cosmetics and films and after a while, Sarah seemed more like her old self and she thanked Nell, saying she had to get back to work. Nell drained the rest of her tea and flipped open the paper to an advert for the ARP.

'Thinking about joining are you?' said Bess, taking a seat opposite her.

'Huh?' She looked up, wondering where she sprang from.

'She pointed to the advert, of a picture of a woman smiling. 'That. I said are you thinking of joining? Didn't Greenwald say he was short of people?'

'Oh, I reckon I could do, Bess. What a brilliant idea. I was actually thinking of doing something that would help the war effort.' She paused for a moment, assessing Bessie's face. She was pale and sickly looking, which was unusual as Bess would normally over-do her make-up and look presentable wherever she went, even to the local shop. 'You look really poorly if you don't mind me saying. Are you alright?'

'Not particularly. I think I may have eaten something I shouldn't have.' She rubbed her belly.

'Maybe you should ask for the rest of the afternoon off?'

Bess scooped a heap of sugar into her cup.

'No, I can't afford to, Nell. I'll be alright. I've only another two hours 'til I get off anyway and besides I want to hear you sing in front of the customers. It's going to be the highlight the week.'

Nell couldn't help but smile.

'Well take it easy. I'm not on for another hour at least.'

At that moment, Bess covered her mouth and rushed out of the canteen. Nell sprang to her feet and was going after her when her boss Mr. Thomas came out of his office obstructing her path.

'Nell, just the person I wanted to see,' he said, pushing his glasses up the bridge of his nose.

'Oh?' She stopped in her tracks, catching sight of Bess rounding the corner to the female toilets.

'There's nothing wrong, Miss Adams. I've left you some work on your desk, would you be kind enough to get it done before you take off for this fundraiser? It's rather urgent.' He checked his watch. 'Well that'll be all, hope you've settled in well here?'

Torn between going to check on her friend and keeping the boss happy, she nodded.

'Yes, sir and not a problem, consider it already done.' She crossed her fingers behind her back, hoping she'd get it finished in time, but first, she needed to check on Bess.

'Thank you, I do appreciate it.'

Once he was out of sight, she ran down the corridor and pushed open the toilet door but all the cubicles were empty. Thinking that Bess had already gone back to work, she made a mental note to check on her later and headed back to the office.

When it was time to go downstairs, Nell made a beeline for Bessie's counter and was pleased to see her with a bit of colour on her cheeks while serving a customer.

'Are you alright, now?' she asked.

'Yes, Nell. Must've been that sandwich I had this morning on break. Hey, the party at the

Naval is tomorrow, isn't it? Do you have anything to wear?'

'Only that dress Alf got me.'

'Meet me tomorrow morning and we'll go shopping. I'm so happy it's payday today.'

'Feeling rich, are you?'

'Why not, there's a war on, so I may as well enjoy myself while I can.'

'I don't blame you either. If I could do that, I would but I need to help Mam with the rent, too.'

Bess glanced over Nell's shoulder. 'It looks like it's getting busy in here,' she said with a nod to the shop floor.

Nell turned around and saw that a rather large crowd was walking around the store. They were being directed to the stage by Crawford who was walking around with a metal bucket to collect change. Nell felt her stomach flip with nerves. Just then, a young boy appeared out of the crowd and was heading towards her. It was Jim, the lad they were raising money for.

'It's Nell, isn't it?' he asked, quite shyly. 'Thank you for doing this, I really appreciate it and so does my mother,' he said with a glance to the frail woman with blonde curly hair talking to Crawford.

'It's nothing, Jim. It's you I should be thanking for going out there, protecting our country.' She thought she was about to cry and pulled him in for a hug.

The boy blushed and walked away awkwardly to the small crowd of customers who had gathered around the wooden stage set in front of the checkouts.

Bessie patted her arm. 'There's Henry Wilder,' she whispered in her ear. 'Don't make it obvious, but he's the one with the mustache and brown hat browsing the shelf over there. He owns the Empire Theatre and is always looking for new acts. In fact, he loaned us the piano. You never know, Nell, it could be your lucky break.'

This information didn't sit too well for her and made her more nervous about singing in front of everyone. It had been her dream to sing on a stage one day and to earn a living from it, but that's all it was; a dream.

Crawford bellowed. 'We have raffle tickets, come and buy your raffle tickets...'

Staff went outside enticing yet more people into the store and it didn't take long for the shop floor to become packed. Nell could hardly move to get to the stage.

'Excuse me,' she said, pushing her way through a tight throng of people. She had to hitch her skirt up a touch so she could get a leg up on the stage, not a bit nervous like she thought she'd be and introduced herself to the crowd. The last time she had sung in public was at the local pub just before Christmas. The landlord had offered her a weekly spot for a few bob, but college exams had got in the way. She regretted not asking if the offer was still available.

She cleared her throat and the audience fell silent.

'I'd like to thank you all for your kind donations. Every penny is going to help our Jim and his family. Here's a song I think you'll love as much as I do.'

When she sang, she was surprised at how her voice, spilling out onto the shop floor was affecting people. Many sang along, some had tears in their eyes, but most of all she had them captivated and entranced. It made her feel alive.

After she had finished singing and stepped down from the stage, crowds of people gathered around her, praising her wonderful voice, but then as she was about to excuse herself to get a glass of water, she felt someone tap her on the arm then pull her away from the crowd.

'Miss Adams, is it?' A man with a cockney accent asked.

She turned around. It was the man Bess had told her about, the one who owned the Empire Theatre.

'Yes, that's right.' She gave a look of disapproval to his hand holding her arm and the man blushed and removed it.

'Oh, I'm so sorry. It's nice to meet you,' he proffered the offending hand. 'I'm Henry Wilder, owner and promoter of the Empire Theatre. I was just passing and saw they had a talent show or something…'

'Fundraiser,' Nell corrected.

'Well, I must say, you have the sweetest voice I've heard in a long time if you don't mind my saying…'

'Oh thank you very much.'

Nell shook his hand. He had a very firm handshake. 'Could we have a chat somewhere a bit less rowdy?' he asked and guided her towards the stairs leading up to the second floor.

'It's my job to seek out new talent, you see, and I'd love to have you on my books. I'd promote you and get you shows. What do you say?'

Nell couldn't believe this was happening to her and came over all a fluster. 'Oh, wow this is really unexpected, Mr. Wilder…'

'Henry, please. I'm putting on a new show and I think you have what it takes to play the part I have in mind for you, so how about it? Would you be interested in coming along one day?' He reached into his jacket pocket and produced a business card. 'This is my address and number. When you've had time to mull it over, I'd love to meet up for dinner and discuss what I could do for your career.'

This is the dream; Nell thought, but came over worrisome when she thought of her responsibilities at home. She took the card. 'I will give it some thought, thank you…'

Henry Wilder had a look of confusion on his face.

'You don't seem so sure.'

'It's not that, sir, it's just that I have a lot of things going on right now. I'd like time to think it over if that's okay?'

If that's your decision I respect it, but I don't like to see talent go to waste, so please have a serious think about it. The offer won't expire, so if you ever change your mind…'

'Thank you, thank you very much,' she blushed as he nodded a goodbye and left.

'Well?' said Bess. 'What did he want then?' she asked, sidling up to her.

Nell stared at the card, hardly believing that someone as influential as him would be interested in little old her.

'He asked if I'd be interested in singing for him at the Empire.'

'Are you kidding? Well, I can't say I'm surprised, Nell. This could be the start of a new life for you.'

Nell stood, wide-eyed at the card she held and then tucked it into her pocket.

'Maybe.'

Truth was, she had more pressing responsibilities now and remembered her ARP meeting later on that evening. There was no way she could let anyone down in times like these. She cursed the damn war for bringing her back to reality and made a promise to herself that when the time was right, she'd make that call.

'You can't be serious? Are you seriously turning him down?'

'It's not the right time, Bess, too much to do and so little time. How can I sing in a show, and work here? There are only twenty-four hours in the day. And besides, Mam and Dad need all the help they can get.'

At six o' clock prompt that evening, she pulled on her only cardigan that didn't have a hole in it and went downstairs.

'Mam, I'm just popping over Greenwald's. I've decided to help out with his ARP work,' she shouted from the bottom of the stairs.

Mary looked up from scrubbing the kitchen floor. Her face was red and glistening with sweat.

'You're going where? Did he talk you into it or what, love? If he did, your Dad will go over and have a bloody word with him.'

'No, I saw an advert in the paper and I figured I'd be more useful to the war effort this way than sitting in a cramped office…'

'Well good on you, Nell…' David said, emerging from the front room with a newspaper tucked under his arm. 'I might have work over the docks, this time working on ships that need repairing…'

'That's brilliant, Dad…look, I have to go, I'm late as it is,' she said, checking the clock on the wall. She left the house and walked down the street to Greenwald's house at the bottom of the road, opposite the school. During the first year after his wife had left him, the women in the street took pity on him and took it in turns to cook him a meal. It's how her father became good friends with him. Nell had just crossed the road when she saw a tall man dressed in black walking into the house. She squinted in the sunlight, wondering who he was as he wasn't anyone she knew from the area. She walked up the steps and rapped on the door. The paintwork was chipping and the garden overflowed with weeds that reached the window ledge of the bay window that had a lightning bolt crack across the glass.

'Come in, Nell.' She heard Greenwald say and walked on through. She had never been in his home before and was very glad she hadn't. In the hallway, stacks of rubbish he had found at the local tip, was piled high against the wall, leading through to the back room. She inched her way through to the front room where the meeting was taking place, into a fug of smoke and the smell of stale beer.

'Glad you could make it,' said Greenwald sitting on a sofa that he'd probably found at the tip.

Her eyes were drawn to the pictures of Greenwald and his ex-wife atop the mantel. The frames looked as though they'd been polished to within an inch of their life, but the rest of the house made Nell feel grubby. She was already thinking about taking a bath when she got home. The sound of Greenwald's sneeze broke her out of her thoughts to the people in the room.

'I think I need to dust someday,' Greenwald said, wiping his nose with a tissue.

Four men and an older woman sat around the room on mismatching chairs and broken sofas. They all greeted her with a smile and introduced themselves, but it was the tall man she had seen coming in the house that got up from his seat for her to sit down.

'I'm Edward, glad you could join us.'

'Edward was a fireman like me, Nell,' Greenwald said as he picked up the teapot from the rickety coffee table in front of him. He poured himself tea and offered one to Nell but she politely declined when she saw a speck of dirt on the mug.

'I've already had tea, thank you and it's nice to meet you,' she replied, sitting down on the hard-backed chair. She felt ever so uncomfortable.

The woman introduced herself as Mabel. Nell didn't recognize her but it soon became apparent that Mabel had moved to Port Tennant from Bridgend to live with her aunt and uncle on Grafog Street. She fiddled with the frayed ends of her cardigan and looked too timid to tackle this kind of work.

Greenwald handed everyone a copy of the ARP handbook and a black armband that was to be worn at all times on duty. He then went on to explain to them that their duties at the moment were to enforce the blackout and to issue fines to anyone who wasn't taking it seriously.

'We're going to be the most hated people in the community,' Mabel said which made everyone laugh.

'Then so be it,' said Greenwald, now very serious. 'We mustn't give those German bastards any advantage whatsoever. So, if that means fining family, friends and neighbours, even the bloody vicar if it comes to that then do it.'

Everyone agreed.

'I think I'd better get my aunt some of that ARP paper for her windows,' said Mabel, dunking a biscuit in her tea. 'The sheet she's using has moth holes in it. I'm surprised nobody has noticed.'

Nell instantly liked Mabel, so when it was time to go home, she said she'd walk her up to the top of the road.

'Phew, I'm glad to get out of there,' said Mabel when they left the house. 'It stinks terribly of wet dog and stale smoke.'

'Yes, it certainly could do with a woman's touch. So why did you want to join the ARP anyhow?'

'My uncle suggested it, said I needed to get out of the house more,' she shrugged. 'What about you?'

'I wanted to feel like I was doing my bit. Three of my brothers are fighting and all I do in the day is sort accounts out at Woolworths. Hardly making a difference there, am I?'

'Mabel, come on your aunt has your supper ready,' shouted a man at the top of the road.

'Is that your uncle?' asked Nell with concern.

Mabel nodded. 'Yes, he's loud, isn't he? Well nice meeting you, Nell. I'll see you tomorrow.'

'Yes, see you tomorrow.'

Chapter Five

'I won't be long, I'm meeting Bess,' Nell hollered and closed the front door. She checked in her purse for loose change then ran down the street to the bus stop at the end of the road. She glanced over her shoulder, saw it coming round the corner, and waved at the driver to stop. The red double-decker came to a grinding halt beside the curb. The bus conductor, a young man with wisps of dark hair poking out of his cap, held out his hand to help her on.

'Thank you for stopping,' she said to him as she climbed on. He flashed a crooked smile at her, and she embarrassingly turned away, looking for an empty seat.

She spotted one at the front, and inwardly groaned when she noticed Brenda, a friend of the family who lived in the row behind with her son, Alan, who was Nell's age and, like Alfred was in the RAF, sitting next to an empty space in the row behind it. The woman smiled at her and moved up for her to sit down. Oh no, Nell thought as she flashed a pleasant smile in her direction. She hoped to avoid sitting next to her and quickly broke eye contact.

'There's space here, Nell!' She patted the seat for her to sit down.

Her stomach churned. Brenda read the tea leaves and had the innate ability to know things beyond the scope of human understanding. In fact, she gave her the creeps and the last thing she wanted was to hear anything bad today.

'Thank you,' she pulled in the flaps of her cardigan and sat down, hoping that Brenda would talk about the rather hot weather they'd been having.

'Terrible, isn't it?'

'What is?' Nell turned to her sharply, her heart racing.

'The war,' she gave Nell a funny look. 'You have heard about it, haven't you?'

Nell relaxed. 'Yes, it's awful,' she replied, looking out of the opposite window, wondering how long she'd have to endure her company. Just when she thought she was free of the woman, she felt a pat on her arm.

'If you beg my pardon, Nell, can I tell you something?'

Oh God, this is it, she thought, waiting for one of her famous predictions.

'If you must,' she smiled weakly.

'When the time comes, you'll do what is right.'

Nell didn't like the sound of it and stared at her, grossed out by her one cataract eye. 'Not being funny, but what is that supposed to mean, Brenda?'

'I'm not really sure,' she shook her head and furrowed her brow as though she was trying to squeeze more information from the ether, or wherever her information came from. 'I don't see anything, I was just given these words to tell you, that's all,' she smiled, and then opened her handbag. 'Want a sweet,' she held out a white paper bag in front of her as if nothing had happened.

Nell felt unsettled and glanced over her shoulder hoping to find someone else to talk to, but the back of the bus was occupied by old women she didn't know and young mothers busy with their children.

'It's alright, Nell, I'm getting off in a bit,' she said, shaking the bag. She picked out a piece of licorice and popped it in her mouth.

Nell edged slightly away from her. Even though the woman was her mother's friend and was usually quite nice when she wasn't giving messages from beyond, she didn't half scare Nell.

'Yes, thank you,' she took a sweet from the bag, hoping that Brenda would now shut-up.

For the duration of the journey, Brenda sat quietly munching on her sweets, but Nell couldn't help thinking about what she said and what it could mean for her. She wanted to ask her again, but every time she opened her mouth she lost her nerve. Finally, after several minutes, the bus came to a stop at the bottom of Wind Street, under the railway bridge, and Brenda got up from her seat.

'Bye, Nell.'

'Yes, see you again, Brenda.'

Once she stepped off the bus, Nell took a deep breath. 'Thank God, for that,' she muttered as the bus carried on, heading towards St Mary's Cathedral. She wondered how someone as nice as Alan ended up with a mother like her.

Bess was already waiting for her under a cherry blossom tree.

'You'll never guess who was on the bus? Bloody Brenda and do you know what she said?'

'If I knew that Nell, I'd be as creepy as her,' she laughed. 'So what did she say? You'll become famous one day, or what?'

'As if, Bess. She said, and I quote. "You'll do what it is right when the time comes." Talk about being cryptic, I think she makes it up half the time.'

Bessie laughed. 'Fancy you getting stuck with her. Come on, let's forget about the war and silly Brenda for a bit and get our dresses. I'm so excited.'

'Yes, let's get going so I can forget about her too.' She shivered.

After browsing in a few shops, Nell finally settled on a second-hand red number that was marked down in price. 'I'll pay you back,' she said as she took it to the counter.

'It's okay, I know where you live,' Bess joked.

A few days later,

Nell and Bessie pushed open the door of the Naval and the rush of hearty conversations over Mr. Greenwald's piano playing spilled out. Despite being at war, the entire community had turned out and put on a huge spread that filled two trestle tables at the back of the room. She surveyed the room for a table and spotted her mother, Winnie and Francis's mother, Edna, deep in conversation over glasses of sherry. Behind them was the U shaped bar and standing at the far corner sipping on beers was Francis and a fellow she didn't recognize wearing a sailor uniform.

'I'll get the drinks in,' said Bess and she went off to the bar.

'...the boys will be just fine, let's have no more of this talk, eh, Mary,' slurred Edna, who'd already had one too many glasses.

'Is there any room for two more?' Nell pulled out a chair, sneaking another glance at Francis. She waved hoping to catch his attention but the dark-haired, handsome sailor had noticed her and smiled instead. She quickly looked away wondering why Francis hadn't acknowledged her after promising he'd meet her here.

'There you are, Nell,' said Edna. 'You're looking lovely. I'm sure Francis will agree,' she said with a nod towards him.

'Aw, thanks, well he might agree if he came and offered me a dance like he said he would.'

'Oh, he will, give him time.'

The conversation turned to the Great War and the shortages of food. 'I've started putting cans away,' Winnie said, looking thoughtful as if she was reliving those times again.

'Good idea,' said Mary. 'The country was starved and I'll be damned if I ever go through that again.'

David approached the table and having heard their conversation he said he'd start growing vegetables in the plot beside the shelter. This had grabbed the attention of a few other people, who agreed they'd do the same thing and that they would share what they had.

'Here you go, doll.' Bessie put down a glass of gin on the table.

'Cheers, Bess. Hey, do you know those boys with Francis?'

'They came off that ship that docked last night. It's in for repairs or something. Why? Thinking of signing up for the WRNS?' she nudged her arm, knowing that Nell would if she was given half the chance.

Nell looked over again, and this time Francis waved at her, but it came across as being cold, which wasn't like him. She dragged her eyes away from them and took a sip of her drink. 'No, I've already joined the ARP. I'm supposed to report to Greenwald later on this evening for some basic training.'

Bessie, who was surprised to hear this, put down her glass on the table and picked up her packet of cigarettes. 'I know you said you wanted to do something but I didn't think you actually would, Nell,' she exclaimed then sighed thoughtfully. 'You're putting me to shame here. I think I should sign up for something too, but I heard there may be jobs going in the munitions factory.'

'What's wrong with the job you have now?'

'Well, keep it close to your chest but I heard through the grapevine that some of us will be losing our jobs. There'll be staff cuts or something.'

'I hope I won't lose my job, I'm just getting used to having my own money.'

'If it comes to the worst and I'm not saying it will, come with me to the munitions factory. I'll get more an hour there than at Woolies.'

A jaunty tune began on the piano, which was quickly followed by the scraping of chairs across the wooden floor as people got up to dance.

Before she had a chance to express her thoughts on the matter of finding a new job when she had only recently started one, she was pulled to her feet.

'Francis....' She looked up excitedly but then her face dropped. The smiling face of the handsome sailor beamed back at her.

'I'm not Francis but will I do? Do you mind?' The smooth-talking stranger asked as he whisked her around to the dance floor. Nell had no option but to follow.

'I don't mind if my boyfriend says it's okay,' she nodded towards Francis who didn't look bothered as he talked to an attractive blonde haired woman who was sitting on the stool the sailor had vacated.

'Boyfriend?' he repeated with a cheeky smile.

'Yes, the one you were talking to when I came in.'

'Well, I'm Robert, anyway. What's yours?' he asked, avoiding Nell's response.

'Nell. Why do you want to know?'

'I wanted to put a name to such a pretty face.'

Nell felt flattered and also a little guilty to receive such compliments when Francis was only a few yards away, but when she looked over Robert's shoulder, Francis was no longer by the bar. Her eyes darted around the room, across the sea of faces, but he had gone.

'Sorry, you'll have to excuse me a moment,' she said to Robert, but the singing had got louder, the music had become more upbeat, and he twirled her around so fast he couldn't hear. When the music finally ended, she pulled his hands away from her waist and ran across the dance floor to the exit, bumping into Greenwald standing in the doorway smoking a cigarette.

'Slow down, woman. What's got into you?'

'Did you see Francis leave just now?' she asked, slightly out of puff.

He took the cigarette out of his mouth and thought for a moment.

'Yeah, I did while I was playing the piano as it happens. He seemed like he was in a rush or had ants in his bloody pants the way he bolted out that door.'

'I wonder where he went.'

'I'm sure he'll be back soon enough, love. Anyway, I hope you're quick on your feet like that later for training. I think you're going to be a valuable member of the ARP team, Nell.' He patted her on the arm and went back to the pub.

There was nothing she could do now and so she headed straight for the crowded bar, pushed her way between two women and called over to the barman.

'Hey,' she waved. 'I want a small gin, thanks.'

Robert, the handsome sailor she had been dancing with pushed his way between her and another man.

'You took off pretty quickly. I wasn't that bad a dancer. Was I?'

She exhaled deeply, hoping she had got rid of him. Couldn't he take a hint? 'Let's say I pity any other woman who dances with you tonight. You've worn me out the way you dragged me around that dance floor.'

'Here you go, Nell.' Jack put her drink on the bar which she snatched up and drank in one go.

Robert laughed and paid for her drink. 'Compliment received,' he winked, taking out a note from his wallet.

'I would appreciate a warning next time, not that there'll ever likely be one.'

'Oh, someone is little touchy this evening. Is it your boyfriend?'

'Yes. He took off and I don't know where he's gone.' She replied, testily.

'Look, I'm sorry. Let me buy you another.' He put another bill on the bar and pointed to the barman for another refill. 'Francis was his name, yeah?' he asked, now with more concern.

'That's right.'

'I've only just met him, so I can't say much about his character. But I do know he was waiting for someone when I arrived and if that wasn't you, then I'm sorry lady. You deserve better than that.'

'What do you mean he was waiting for someone?'

Just as he was about to answer her she felt a hand clamp down on her shoulder. She turned sharply at the leathery, calloused hand and looked up.

'Bess needs you,' said David. 'She's in the toilets apparently. More than likely she needs to borrow that lipstick of yours,' he rolled his eyes and ordered another drink.

'Okay, Dad.' She turned to Robert. 'So did he say who he was waiting for?'

'It was something about receiving a message from an old flame. I'd go easy on him. The man looked worried about something...'

She thanked Robert for the drink, excused herself and dashed to the toilets by the main entrance. Her mind was all over the place.

'Bess, where are you?' she tapped on the cubicle doors, reeling from what Robert had said.

She heard Bess groan and wondered what was wrong.

'In here, Nell,' came the reply from the last cubicle.

The door unlocked, and Nell pushed it open to see Bess leaning over the toilet with her hands wrapped around her belly. She turned to Nell; her face was clammy and pale.

'What's wrong with you? Have you still got that bug that was going around?'

Bess took a piece of toilet tissue, wiped her mouth then looked up at Nell.

'No, Nell. I think I'm pregnant.'

Chapter Six

Nell stooped down to pick up the wet sheet and flung it over the washing line, securing it with a wooden peg. She felt the prick of raindrops on her forehead and looked up at the sky. Dark clouds were scudding towards her but she didn't feel like removing all the washing she had spent scrubbing and soaking since six a.m. this morning. Hoping it would pass over, she was about to head indoors when she heard the faint sound of snoring coming from the Anderson shelter at the bottom of the garden. She stopped and turned sharply towards it.

'Who the bloody heck is in there?' She marched to the arched, corrugated contraption buried halfway in the earth. At least Dad made use of the roof and planted flowers, except now there were only weeds sticking out like it needed a decent haircut. She pushed open the coal sack flap, surprised to find her Gran sound asleep on the chair. Nell laughed when she saw her holey slippers, but what was she doing with a packed suitcase by her feet?

'Gran,' she poked her on the arm. 'Wake-up, Gran, it's freezing in here.'

Gran woke with a start.

'What? Wait. The bombs,' she jumped up from the chair not knowing where she was.

'What are you doing in here? Mam's going to be furious when she finds out you've been here all night.'

Gran was now visibly shaking with her hands covering her face. 'I don't know. I was in bed, Nell and then somehow I ended up here.'

'There were no bombs last night, so you must've had a bad dream. Come on, Gran let's get you indoors for a warm, strong cup of tea, is it?' Nell wrapped her arms around her and helped her up from the chair. She guided her to the step and across the garden. 'Mam,' she yelled, wondering how nobody had noticed her missing.

'Hang on, Nell. I forgot my suitcase.' Gran went back inside to retrieve it.

'What have you got in there?'

'It's all my old letters and jewels, Nell. I'm not letting the bloody Germans have the little possessions I own.'

She couldn't believe what she was hearing. The most the woman owned were a few pieces of costume jewellery her late husband bought her at the local market. They weren't worth a tuppence.

'What is it, Nell?' Mary looked out of the kitchen window and when she saw her mother-in-law limping her way to the house, she bolted out the door.

'Gran, what are you doing out here? I thought you were still in bed.' Mary took Gran's other arm and helped up the back doorstep. 'Nell, put the kettle on for me, please.'

'She slept in the shelter last night. Said she thought we were being bombed.'

'You thought we were being bombed?' she snapped, but then saw the funny side of it. While her mam took Gran into the living room, Nell filled up the kettle with water and then lit the gas stove. The smell of damp in the air soon became apparent and she remembered the clothes on the washing line; she turned back to the door as the rain pelted down ruining all of her hard work.

'Mam, the clothes are soaking wet.'

'Don't worry about the clothes for now, leave them out.' Mary came back out the kitchen, pulled out a chair and then picked up her knitting resting on top of the fruit bowl, except there was no fruit in it.

Nell scooped two teaspoons of tea leaves into the pot and then poured in the hot water.

'So what have you got planned for the day?'

'I'm supposed to be meeting Francis later. Bessie said that he wanted to meet after work for a drink. Did you know he's signed up for the Merchant Navy?'

'His mam told me yesterday. How do you feel about that?'

'The same as I feel about every other young man leaving to fight a senseless war.'

Mary sighed deeply. Nell handed her a cup of tea.

'What are you making?' she asked with a nod towards the ball of red wool.

'It's a scarf for our boys abroad. I hope to get them done so I can send them in time for Christmas. Actually, did I tell you that Edna got me roped into doing more WVS work? It all helps, I suppose.' She looked up from her knitting. 'She also said they're having a little leaving tea party this weekend for Francis. Do you know anything about that?'

'No, I don't know anything, should I?' she replied, coldly.

'I don't know, love, that's why I'm asking you. You're supposed to be his girlfriend.'

Feeling a little upset as she hadn't seen him since the party at the Naval, she picked up Gran's cup of tea and went into the living room.

'Here you are, Gran, get that down you.'

The letter slot rattled and the dull thud of mail hit the welcome mat. She rushed to the door, scooping up a bundle of assorted envelopes. It had been a few weeks since Alfred left, and she was excited to hear from him, or anyone right now to take her mind off Francis. She flipped through the letters and noticed her brother's handwriting.

'We got mail, Mam. It's from the boys.'

She ran into the living room. Her dad got up from his chair, and her mother threw down her knitting needles into the fruit bowl and came from the kitchen.

'Here, let me read it to you,' she said, standing in the front room.

'I hope they're keeping well, I've been so worried about them.' Mam said, pressing a hand to her heart.

Nell unfolded the one sheet of paper and looked up to check if all the family were ready before she read it out. She took a breath and calmly focused on the black cursive writing.

Dear Nell,

Edward and I got on our ships a few days ago and are due to sail soon, so when you get this we shall be on our way. We completed our training with flying colours, I'm proud to say. Best day of my life! Feel like I've actually achieved something. I'm missing home and everyone so badly but I know I'm here to do my part. I hope Mam and Dad are okay and that Gran hasn't gone hiding again. She can be so funny but now there is a war on I do hope you will all be safe. Sorry if this is such a short letter, but we have run out of food and as the assistant cook it's my duty to salvage something from nothing. I can assure you it will be the most difficult thing I'll be expected to do. I'm missing you all so much.

Love,

Sidney

'*A cook?*' David scoffed. 'The boy didn't know one end of a knife from the other living at home.'

'It's making a man out of him, David,' Gran butted in, 'and how nice of him to give his old Gran a mention,' she smiled happily and took a sip of her tea.

Dad shook his head in amusement at her and began to fill his pipe.

Nell's shoulders slumped, as though a few lingering burdens that had taken residence had been washed away. She turned to her Mam and handed her the letter.

'I must get to work, Mam. Don't worry if I'm a bit late home this evening.' She half expected her Dad to say something about her drinking but he didn't. Mam slipped the envelope into the pocket of her apron and looked up at Nell.

'Don't worry, love. Go and have a nice time. Just be home before dark, okay, and make sure that Francis walks you home.'

'I will Mam. See you later.' She pecked her on the cheek.

Knowing her brothers were safe freed up mental space for tonight, putting her in a happier mood than when she woke up. About to close the door, the clash of metal on metal made her jump. A truck had parked halfway down the street, and three men were ripping up Mr. Morgan's garden railings. She called for her Dad who came rushing out the door.

'What are they doing?' she asked.

'Ah,' he replied, looking down the street. 'I was told about this. They're requisitioning the railings for ammunition, Nell. That's the way it is, I suppose. Any little thing we can do or give up helps the war effort.'

A wave of sadness enveloped her. If the war wasn't content with taking their men, it was now tearing up their homes. Whatever next?

'It's really sad.' She thoughtfully looked in the direction of the docks. Things were changing far too much, and in a short space of time, too. All she wanted was for it to stop so life could get back to normal.

Where could he have got to? She stood under the awning of a bakery shop. A cold sharp wind blew, catching her bare legs. She shivered, tugged her skirt down a touch and stepped back against the building to take shelter. The sky was now the colour of gunmetal and within seconds a rumble of thunder unleashed and a torrent of rain came down drenching the entire area. She watched as passing men pulled up the collars of their overcoats and held newspapers above their heads in a feeble attempt to stay dry. Yet there was still no Francis. The cathedral bells pealed drawing her attention when a young couple stood in the doorway having just got married. She watched them as they ran up the path towards the waiting car when there was a tap on her arm. She turned, struck to see Francis's Mediterranean blue eyes looking down at her.

'Sorry I'm late. I had something to sort out.' He smiled and placed a kiss on her cheek.

She thought there was something different about him and stepped away. Despite his hair being sopping wet, she could see it had been cut and parted to the side. She cast her eyes downwards at his long black overcoat that was partly open revealing a well-cut suit. He waited for her response.

'So what do you think? It's far more grown up than I thought but...'

She searched his face sensing he held something back, something important he'd forgotten to mention, like why he left early at the Naval and why she hadn't seen him since, but she smiled anyway. She didn't want to cause a scene outside in public, it wasn't her style and not very lady-like.

'You look marvelous Francis,' she finally said, caressing his cool cheek. 'I got worried for a moment. I thought you may have forgotten about me,' she added, deciding to give him the benefit of the doubt.

He cupped her face and kissed her on the forehead.

'Nell, I could hardly forget about you. You're the most beautiful woman I have ever seen.'
She blushed.

'That's a nice thing to say,' she replied, still convinced there was something more going on. 'So let's go dancing. Make a night of it, what do you say?'

'Ah...'

'Is there something wrong Francis?' she asked, thinking how disappointed he looked.

'If that's what you want, Nell,' he held out a hand for her to take.

'Definitely,' she slipped her hand in his and skipped in the rain, laughing until her belly ached.

'You're happy today,' he said as he lifted her up and twirled her around.

'It's wartime, Francis, I think we need to make the most of our days, don't you?' She took his hand and ran up the pavement, pulling him along, loving the feeling of the rain splashing on her face. She stopped outside a pub called The Three Lamps and looked at him for approval. Even in the pouring rain, two men were standing in front of the lattice window, sipping on their pints. By the scuffs of dirt on their faces, hands, and clothes Nell knew they must've finished a shift at the docks. They reminded her of how her Dad would normally look when he came home from working there. When they saw Nell looking, they raised their glasses. She said hello and urged Francis inside out of the rain.

'Come on, Dad used to come here after work, he said it's a nice little place.'

'Nell, I was hoping to take you somewhere a little classier.' He said; lowering his voice, but gave into her when she gave him a mocking pout. He sighed. 'Okay, if you insist.' He pushed open the door for her and loud raucous laughter could be heard from the corner where men were playing a game of darts.

'We'll go somewhere else afterwards, I promise,' she said, noticing the barman wiping glasses behind the bar. She politely said hello and he acknowledged her with a smile. He told them if they wanted some peace and quiet there was room at the back of the pub.

Nell thanked him and was looking around for a seat when she felt Francis' arm sweep under hers. He led her to a table at the end, near the back doors and pulled her out a chair.

'That'll do,' he said removing his coat. He slung it over the back of an empty chair. 'What can I get you to drink?'

'Just a small sherry, thank you,' she replied, sweeping her sopping wet hair back. A minute later, he returned and sat down. Nell took a generous sip of her drink, watching him as he stared into his glass.

'What is it, Francis? You've looked like you've been carrying the weight of the world on your shoulders ever since I met you earlier,' she said, swilling the liquid around in her glass.

'Nell,' he took a sip of his pint and placed it back on the table. 'I wanted to ask you something.' He looked her in the eyes now and held her hand.

'Oh? Is there anything wrong?'

'No, of course, there isn't, you're such a worrier, you know that?'

Her heart pounded and her hands felt clammy. She drank the remainder of her drink to dampen down her nerves, wishing he would hurry up; she couldn't take the suspense any longer.

'It's like this, Nell...'

'Get on with it.'

'You know I'm leaving soon, and well, the future is uncertain whether we like to admit it or not.' His brow glistened with sweat. Nervously, he picked up his drink, took a sip and put it back down again.

'Look, you're scaring me silly here. Just come out with it...'

The sweat poured down his face, or was it splashes of rain, she couldn't be sure. Whatever it was, he was nervous and she had never seen him in a state like this before. She noticed he started fiddling with the sleeves of his jacket. Unable to stand the shiny face any longer, she reached into her handbag for a tissue to give to him. 'Where's that bloody tissue I had...'

'Okay, Nell here goes.' He took a handkerchief from his inside jacket pocket and wiped his forehead.

'You know I'm leaving soon, well, I wanted to ask you something before I went.'

She watched him with curiosity as he rifled through his coat pockets for something. She was becoming increasingly concerned and thought she would put him out of his misery and say she suspected he went off with the woman she saw at the Naval. As she was about to open her mouth he presented her with a red velvet box.

'This is for you,' his fingers fumbled with the lid. He laughed nervously as he tried to pull it open.

'Oh my God, are you serious?' she said, covering her mouth with her hand. This was the last thing she expected to happen tonight.

He opened the box and inside was a garnet ring set in gold.

'It was my grandmother's and now I want you to have it,' he took it out of the box, got up from his chair and knelt on the sticky floor beside her on one knee.

Nell couldn't think of anything to say, let alone formulate any words into speech.

'Nell Adams, you're my best friend and love of my life. Will you do me the honour and be my wife?'

She looked down at him, and for the first time in a long time, she saw the wide toothy smile that melted her heart at the beach and knew he was the man for her.

'Say yes.'

'Yes,' she cried, wiping her tears with the sleeve of her damp cardigan.

He slipped the ring on her finger and kissed it.

'You've made me the happiest person alive tonight, Nell.'

He sat back down, taking a deep breath. 'I haven't the foggiest what you thought all this was about but I hope I've made you happy.'

Nell stared at the ring glistening from the overhead lights. All her worries about him cheating at the Naval were long gone. Maybe it was a misunderstanding.

'I've never been so happy. Do you think we should tell everyone straight away?'

'With the size of that rock on your finger, I doubt it will go unnoticed.'

Nell smiled and held out her hand. 'Come on, come and have a dance with me before we go home.'

Not even the rain felt like a hindrance as they walked home arm in arm through the darkening streets. She occasionally glanced down at the ring on her finger, hardly believing what had happened this evening. But once they began walking up Jersey Terrace, her joy was interrupted by the sight of the neighbours chatting to her mother on the doorstep. Knowing this only meant that something was wrong around here, she ran up the street. Francis followed behind.

'What's happened?' she asked breathlessly as she reached the bottom of the steps.

'It's Gran. She's gone missing again.'

'Not again,' she sighed, dashing up the steps. The neighbours parted a way to the front door. Her mother, now used to her mother-in-laws shenanigans, just shook her head and threw her hands up in defeat.

'I give up Nell, I've searched everywhere and I've got the local kids looking.'

Now she had to give her the good news later on and went through the house. 'How long has she been missing, Mam?' She called, changing her damp shoes and coat.

'Since half four, Nell,' she shouted back. 'She must be back before the ARP come around.'

Nell put on her camel coloured coat she'd bought at the second-hand market and rushed back out the door. 'I'll go and have a look Mam, but I think it'd be best if you called the police, too, just incase.'

'I will do, but after the last time they told me to keep a tighter rein on her.'

'A tighter rein?' she muttered. 'She's old not a bloody baby, Mam.'

'I'll help you look for her Nell, let's go,' said Francis, anxious to leave.

'So, you managed to meet up then?' asked Mam, looking at both of them curiously.

'Yes, Mam,' she said with a glare at Francis not to say anything. 'Come on, you can help me look around the back lanes.'

Nell pulled up the collar of her coat as a shield against the biting cold, wondering where to start. She searched through the back lanes, but nothing. She headed towards the back door and as she walked past the Anderson shelter she heard sniffles.

'What the hell...' she turned around, and opened the flap of the shelter and saw the old lady sitting on a chair with a garden fork in one hand, and a mug of tea in the other. 'Gran, what are you doing here?' She knelt down beside the woman checking to see if she was okay.

'Bombs. Don't you hear them, Nell?'

'No, Gran, we haven't had any bombs. Come on, let's get you inside, Mam is worried.' She helped the woman up from her seat and removed the garden fork from her iron tight grasp. 'That's it,' she exhaled and helped her out of the shelter. 'Mam,' she shouted. 'I've found her.'

Cries of relief could be heard from the street. Mary came running out the back and took Gran's hand. 'You've had us worried, Mam. We almost had the police here.' She looked at Nell. 'Where did you find her?'

'In there,' she pointed to the shelter wondering if this was the right time to tell her about her engagement. She sighed and walked into the house lit with a few lamps and poured herself a cup of tea from the green pot. Now with everyone going or gone, she knew she had to busy herself even more.

'I should've bloody guessed,' she said, shaking her head in disbelief.

'What's that?' Nell heard her dad say as she scraped dripping across a piece of two-day-old bread.

'It's a snack, dad. I'm feeling peckish. Do you want one?' she asked, offering him her slice.

Her father's face melded into a smile. She saw him look curiously at her hand and she blushed with embarrassment.

'I meant that bloody great rock on your finger. Do you think your old man is daft enough not to notice?'

Mary walked back into the kitchen having caught the end of the conversation.

'What's on her finger?' She asked, looking at Nell's hand. 'Oh my God; is this what I think it is?' cried, Mary.

Francis backed away slightly towards the open door. David pointed a finger at him.

'I'm sorry, Mr. Adams, I...I, I know I should've asked your permission first,' he said, hands held up in the air. He then saw that he was smiling and he too, relaxed and laughed. David pulled Francis in for a hug.

'You're a daft bugger. How long have we known you, boy?' He affectionately slapped his face. 'I'm happy for both of you. She couldn't have picked anyone better in my honest opinion.'

Nell put down the plate and took both of her parents' hands. 'I was going to tell you earlier but...well, yes, Francis has asked me to marry him and I said yes.'

She watched her mother's expression change from shock to joy. 'Oh Nell, that's wonderful news,' she shrieked, pulling her in for a hug. 'I can't wait to tell everyone. Hey, what about an engagement party, Francis?'

'We could have a little tea,' said Gran walking into the kitchen. 'No time like the present, is it, Mary?'

'Gran is right. I'll tell you what, let's have a few drinks now. I'm sure my mother wouldn't mind. In fact, I'd better go and tell her the news,' he said, putting an arm around Nell.

With that, they heard the front door opening and Winnie came rushing down the hallway.

'Mary, you'll never guess what's happened?'

Alarmed, Mary rushed into the living room, and Nell followed behind thinking something bad had happened. But by the way her smile lit up her face; Nell knew Bess had told her the news about the baby.

'I'm going to be a grandmother.' She pressed a hand to her heart and burst out crying.

For once there was joy all around, and when Mary exchanged news about Nell, David went to his cabinet beside the sofa and pulled out a bottle of Scotch he had been keeping for special occasions.

'Get the glasses, it's time for a celebration,' he said joyously.

'Hang about, Dad, let me get Bess and Edna,' said Nell.

She ran out the front door into the dark street, feeling uplifted and happier than she had been for a while. She pushed open Edna's door and hollered for the woman to come out.

'Edna, come over the house, we've got some good news to share.'

Bess opened the bedroom window.

'What's happening; Nell?' she shouted. 'Oh don't tell me. Mam has been telling everyone about the baby, am I right? She's going to bore everyone until this baby arrives, you know.'

'Yes, she has said and we're having a celebration because I've also got some good news to share, too. I've just got engaged.' She flashed her ring.

'You're celebrating what?' Bess said incredulously. 'Sorry, say it again, Nell, who is engaged and to whom?'

'Who do you think?' Nell laughed, realising that she was joking. 'Come over before Dad drinks all the Scotch.'

'Nell,' said Edna standing on her front step. 'You almost gave me a bloody heart attack. What's all this shouting, what's going on?'

Bess rushed out of the house and closed the front door. 'She's engaged, Edna. Come on, we're having a drink at the Adams' to celebrate.'

'Not you, my lovey,' Edna barked. 'You're having a baby. Hang on; did you say you and Francis are engaged?' she looked at Nell.

Nell laughed and took Edna's hand to help her down the steps. 'Yes, we are. He asked me this evening and I said yes.'

'Oh my giddy aunt,' she chuckled, pulling Nell in for a hug. 'I thought it'd never happen.'

After a couple of stress-free days, the day she wasn't looking forward to finally arrived. She thought she'd be used to saying goodbye to everyone she loved by now, but still, it never got any easier. She finished her breakfast, said goodbye to Gran and left the house before it was eight o'clock. Winnie, who was sitting on the front porch smoking a cigarette, shouted over that Bess had a bout of morning sickness and she would be in later this afternoon.

'No bother, tell her I hope she feels better soon,' she said, now dreading the long, lonely walk into work. She'd hoped Bess would be by her side to distract her from thoughts about the impending goodbye she had to endure later on.

Sarah looked up at her from her desk.

'You've been looking at that clock all morning, Nell.'

Nell drew her attention back to the typewriter. 'I'm leaving an hour early today. Francis is leaving for Newcastle to get his ship.'

'Sorry to hear that, doll. I know how you feel. If you want to pop off and get ready now, I don't mind finishing that up for you.'

'Are you sure?'

'Yes, give it here.'

'You're fantastic, thank you.' Nell picked up her bag and coat and hurried to the bathroom to fix her hair and make-up. On her way out, she was accosted by two elderly women on the shop floor who had spotted her name tag.

'Excuse me, love. I'm looking for the new dinnerware set you've got in. Could you show me where it is?'

Aware the time was getting on, Nell smiled pleasantly and looked around the shop floor for a Sales Assistant but they were all busy.

'If you follow me, I'll take you.' She didn't have a clue where it was, and since there was a queue formed on the cosmetics aisle she couldn't interrupt the girls to ask. She took the women to the homeware department and began searching the shelves.

'Do you know what colour it is?' she asked, trying not to sound irritated.

The woman was busy searching in her handbag. Nell's patience was wearing thin. The other woman poked her friend on the arm.

'Dear, the lady would like to know what colour the dinner set is.'

'Oh, sorry,' she looked up at Nell. 'I think it was blue.'

Nell rummaged through the shelf again but there was no blue dinner set. 'I'm afraid we don't have any blue ones.'

The woman looked disappointed.

'Could you check if you have any in stock?'

'Well, it's not my department, I'm afraid. I'll have to fetch a manager, just give me two minutes.'

She took a deep breath and looked up at the clock. Walking out of the stock room was Mr. Thomas. 'Sir,' she yelled, rushing towards him.

'Nell, aren't you supposed to be seeing your fiancé off today?' he asked, looking at her over the rim of his half-moon glasses.

'Yes, but there are two old ladies at the home ware department and they're looking for a blue dinner set. Could you help them?' she pleaded.

'Of course, Nell, you'd better hurry,' he checked his watch. 'His train should be leaving in twenty minutes.'

'Twenty minutes?' she said, horrified that she may have missed him by the time she got there.

Dashing across the shop floor towards the doors, people stepped aside, wondering what was going on. A woman, who had just opened the door, saw Nell bolting towards it and backed up against the frame as not to get bowled over by her. She shouted thanks, but there was no time to look back as she made a run for it up the busy High Street. She made it as far as the Adam and Eve public-house but started to slow down as the muscles at the back of her legs began to ache. Taking a few deep breaths, she began to think she wouldn't make it but there were only yards separating them now and she'd be damned if she'd miss him for the sake of a few bloody yards. She sprinted to the end of the road where the grand, curved building of Swansea Station stood. There was a crowd of khaki and the distinctive blue of the RAF and Navy surrounded by families waiting to say goodbye to their men. Tapping her handbag as her impatience grew, she watched the taxi cabs whizz by until they stilled giving her the chance to run between them to the other side of the crossing. As she made her way to the entrance, her eyes darted around the building looking for him in the sea of faces, but it was hopeless. She pushed her way through a tight, rowdy crowd into the foyer when it was announced over the tannoy that the train to Newcastle would soon be boarding.

'Excuse me,' she said breathlessly to the guard standing beside the pillar. 'Has the 1. 15 p.m. train to Newcastle left yet?'

He checked his watch.

'No, love, it's due out in another ten minutes. There's been a slight delay.'

'Great.' She relaxed until an arm slipped around her waist. She turned around with her handbag raised ready to hit whoever it was, only to find Francis beaming in front of her. Without hesitation, she flung her arms around him and buried her face into his chest.

'I thought I'd missed you.' She whispered in his ear.

'I knew you'd make it, Nell. You've never ever let me down,' he said, squeezing her tight.

Through tear filled eyes she saw Edna and her mam approach looking smart in their coats and matching coloured hats.

'Oh there you are, Nell, we've been outside looking for you,' Edna said a look of relief etched across her face.

'I had customers come on to me in the shop, but I'm here now.'

Francis took her shaking, clammy hand, brought it to his lips and pressed a kiss on her knuckles.

'Well ladies, this is the end of the road,' he bent down to pick up his kit bag with his free hand and slung it over his shoulder. In the other, he kept hold of Nell.

Edna cried and Mary reached up on tip-toe to give him a hug. 'Take care, and write to us won't you?'

'I will, Mary.'

Edna was sobbing into her handkerchief and Mary pulled her in close to comfort her. 'Come on, love. He'll be back, they all will,' Mary tried to reassure her.

When Francis turned to Nell, he seemed to have a desperate, almost pleading look in his eyes that he needed to be reassured that everything would be okay.

Hoping she wouldn't leave Francis with the memory of her red, swollen eyes and blotchy face, she wrapped her arms around him. 'I'll be waiting for you and don't you worry about your mum. You know we'll keep an eye on her.'

'I know, and I'm very grateful to you both.' He delicately brushed a strand of her hair over her ear. 'When I come back on leave, I was thinking we could get married?'

Nell didn't want to think when that would be. 'I'd love that very much. I'm proud of you.'

The train whistled, and puffs of steam billowed from its funnel. The guard shouted to let everyone know that it was ready to board. Nell felt a jolt in her stomach knowing that this was it, the final goodbye until who knew when. She planted one last lingering kiss on his lips that tasted of his salty tears and he turned to leave shouting that he loved them. She watched him through misty eyes as he joined the flow of the crowd onto the platform until she lost sight of him.

'Come on, Nell,' she heard her mother call after her. The noise in the station gradually whittled down as everyone began leaving. Forcefully, she pulled herself together and went to join her mother and Edna now standing outside the entrance.

'Shall we go to the café for a cuppa before we head home?' said Mary. 'Today has been the worst. It brought up those horrible feelings I had when my boys left.'

Nell put an arm around her mother and they all headed across the road.

Chapter Seven

It had been a hard few months since the boys had left, but Nell was determined the family would celebrate Christmas despite her mother's objections. It took a lot of persuasion on her part, but she managed to get her dad to cut a small tree down from the hill, a tradition that usually involved all the men of the family. And as today was her last day at work before the office closed until the New Year, she was looking forward to her little shopping trip to town this afternoon with Bessie. She twitched aside her thick, red bedroom curtains, and rubbed the condensation with the edge of her hand. In the early morning light, the snow that had settled overnight gleamed bright and made everything, even the shelter at the farthest end of the garden look prettier. She shivered and tightened her woolen dressing gown and put her slippers on. Bending to find an extra pair of stockings in the drawer of her dresser, she caught sight of the tin in which she kept all of her letters and sat down on the edge of her bed.

She picked out Alfred's last letter, despite having read it many times.

Dear Nell,

All is fine here at the barracks. I did a few test flights this morning – seems like I haven't lost my touch.

The reason I'm writing, Nell, is because I know Christmas is coming and you know how Mam likes to have all of us around for the holidays, so I can imagine how devastated she must be feeling now all she has is you. So please, do me a great big favour and make sure she celebrates. I'd really like that. I've sent you some money to buy a few little things, also. Congratulations on your engagement, too. I'm so happy for you Nell. Hope I get to be at the wedding.

Love,

Alf

Her heart swelled at the words. For such a short letter, it meant the whole world to her. Perhaps Christmas was really needed this year, she wondered, tucking the envelope back in the tin. The only person she now had to convince was her mother. She carefully placed the lid back on the tin and proceeded to get dressed. To her surprise, she could smell the hint of a cake baking in the oven.

'Mam,' she shouted as she ran down the stairs. 'I'm off to work now. Is there anything you need at the market?'

'Eggs, please Nell. Thank you. I thought I'd make the cakes you like. Tom said he could get me a few ingredients from that farm he's working closely with, but I've been told to keep it under wraps if you get me. It's only for the locals. We don't want outsiders getting wind of anything.'

Nell knew what she meant. The past few weeks Tom the grocer had been dealing with a farmer friend of his to supply him with extra products.

'I will do Mam.'

At the office, Sarah and Nell sat at their desks, tipsy on a bottle of scotch Mr. Thomas, the manager, had given them for Christmas. Sarah burped, covered her mouth and began laughing at nothing in particular. Nell, who wasn't used to large amounts of alcohol, was enjoying herself immensely.

'It was good of him to let us have a sip during work hours, wasn't it?' Nell raised her half-finished glass for another refill. 'But I suspect we're going to pay for this later on.' She rubbed her head, feeling a headache coming on.

Sarah rose to her feet, staggered, and then regained her composure as she reached over her desk for the bottle. She kept swaying as she poured. It sloshed into the glass with most of it ending up on a brown file sitting on the edge of her desk.

'We can hardly call this a sip, can we?' Sarah found it amusing, falling back into her chair laughing again. She passed the glass to Nell who quickly got up from her chair to salvage the dripping wet file.

'Oh no,' Nell lifted the file feeling guilty. 'What is this anyway?' She asked aware her words were slurring.

'No idea. All the files had been cleared and put away earlier. No more work until 1940 now,' Sarah beamed, refilling her glass.

Curious, Nell flipped through the wet pages and gasped at what she read. 'Sarah, you need to look at this.' She held out the file for her to take and stood with a hand pressed to her forehead. Sarah hushed up and put down her glass. 'What is it?' she asked, now serious as she took the file from Nell.

There was a couple of moments silence and then her mouth gaped open in shock.

'Oh bloody hell. I don't think we were meant to see this.'

'He has to cut office staff. That means...'

As if on cue, the door to the office opened and both girls swerved around to see Mr. Thomas. He took his handkerchief and patted away a slick of sweat across his forehead.

'Do you have a minute, girls? I couldn't help but overhear the last bit of your conversation...'

Nell threw a concerned look at Sarah who then stood up and walked around her desk.

'Is this true, Mr. Thomas that Nell is losing her job?' she held up the file for him to see.

He nodded. 'You weren't meant to see that, I was hoping to talk to you after work but I think now seems like the best time.' He pushed up his black-rimmed glasses and sat down at the edge of Sarah's desk.

'I'm losing my job?' Nell said quietly.

'I'm afraid you are, Nell. I simply can't afford to keep you both on.'

Nell felt heartbroken. She loved her job and hoped she'd have a long career with the firm. 'It's not your fault, Mr. T. There's a lot worse going on in the world today. I'm sure I'll find something else very soon.' She smiled tight-lipped with her fingers crossed behind her back.

Sarah chimed in. 'You're right, Nell, it's bad timing but not something that could be helped, I suppose. I heard there'll be more opportunities for women now, what with the war...'

'I did all I could, believe me. You're a good worker, Nell, and I will write you a glowing reference.' He stood up and proffered his hand.

Nell stood up and straightened down her skirt. She shook his hand. 'I'm going to miss this place,' she said and dabbed away her tears.

'I have given you a little bonus in your pay packet,' he said, reaching into his jacket pocket and handing them both a brown envelope each. 'Again, I'm so sorry, Nell. It's such terrible timing.'

Once he had left, Nell slumped down in her chair, staring at her wage packet. She loved working with Sarah and the thought of finding a new job filled her with dread.

'Oh, Nell,' Sarah came over and gave her a hug.

'That news sobered me up pretty quickly anyhow.'

'I'll tell you a little secret. I've decided to join the Land Army, so there may just be an opening come the New Year.'

'Have you really? How did you come to that decision?'

'My sister is joining. She's my only family here now that Howard has gone. No sense in being on my own, is there?'

Nell knew she would miss Sarah a lot and promised her that they'd keep in touch. They exchanged small gifts and their addresses and said their goodbyes.

Nell thought she may as well laugh about the job as there was nothing she could do about it. Besides, she had done enough crying since the war began. She got up from her seat, put on her coat then cleared her things away from her desk. When she went onto the shop floor that was busy with last-minute shoppers before it closed for the holidays, she checked her pay packet and thought she'd buy an extra few gifts. She picked up a box of talc for her mother and Gran and a tub of Cocoa for her dad. Bess was on the till when she approached, and she could see how stressed she looked, even with the wide, red-lipstick smile she painted on her face.

'I'll be glad to get out of here. It's been crazy, Nell,' she said, ringing up the total.

'It was upstairs, too. I've been laid off, no work for me in January.'

Bess looked incredulous.

'Really? Oh, I'm sorry, Nell. I had no idea they were laying people off so soon. I expect I'll be next.'

She shrugged. 'No problem, I'll find another. So, do you want to come and spend the rest of my bonus with me? We have a while before the shops close.'

'Give me ten minutes. I need to pop into the market for a few things for Mam.'

The last call for shoppers went out and once the final customer left, Mr. Thomas went to lock the doors. Bess went upstairs to get her things whilst Nell browsed the near-empty shelves.

'Merry Christmas, girls, thanks for all your hard work,' Mr. Thomas said while unlocking the main shop door to let the staff out.

'Yes, same to you, and a Happy New Year,' Nell waved and turned to cross over the road, shuffling her way through a few inches of snow. A gust of freezing wind blew up the street knocking Nell sideways into Bessie.

'Watch it, Nell,' Bessie caught her arm as she almost tumbled backward off the pavement. They both giggled and set off to the market on Oxford Street.

'I had a letter, well several of them because the post got held up.'

Nell turned sharply, wondering why she hadn't mentioned it earlier.

'Were they from William? Is everything okay?'

'He said his ship had a close call on the Pacific, a German U boat just missed them and sunk another. He described it all in such incredible detail I swore I was there watching it with him.'

So that explained her mood, Nell thought, and put her arm around her. 'At least he's alive, Bess, we can't sit and dwell anymore, can we? We have to keep going for the boys.'

'You're so right, Nell.'

The indoor and fully enclosed Swansea market was awash with shoppers hovering around the stalls, hoping to grab a last minute bargain.

'Hey, I think we'd better hurry, it looks as though they're packing up for the day,' Bess pointing towards the man selling vegetables.

'Mam wants a few things for Christmas dinner. It took a lot of effort to get her on side, so now she's insisting that Christmas will go on no matter what,' Nell said picking up a handful of potatoes and placing them on the weighing scale.

'11d.' said the old man wearing a flat cap.

Bessie picked up a few apples.

'I'll make us a pie for Christmas Day,' she chimed in as Nell opened her brown leather purse. 'Could you put them in a paper bag, please?' she asked, handing over the note.

'Mam said we'll have Christmas dinner together this year, so your mam doesn't feel lonely now there's a war on.'

'Yes, I know,' Nell replied, wondering how her brothers would spend their first Christmas.

'Chin up, Nell, the war could be over by New Year's.'

Nell wasn't convinced but smiled tight-lipped, scooping her arm in Bessie's as they walked around stalls to the exit.

Outside, tiny flurries of snow began to fall again, quickly topping up the black patches of sludge across the pavement. Huddled for warmth, they walked along Caer Street, turning the corner into Wind Street. A chorus of voices singing *We Wish You a Merry Christmas* filled the bitterly cold air.

'Penny for the Salvation Army, miss,' asked an elderly gentleman in a green trench coat standing around a brazier.

Nell immediately felt sorry for the man. He looked frozen. She reached into her bag for her purse.

'Here, it's all I have left, I'm afraid,' said Bessie as she dropped a few coins in his bucket and noticed a bar of medals across his left breast pocket.

'First World War, lovely,' he patted his pocket. 'I didn't think I'd survive that one let alone see another.' He held out his bucket to Nell who also dropped a few pennies she could spare.

'My Dad said the same thing,' Nell replied noting another old man sitting in a wheelchair behind him.

'Nothing can last forever though,' he forced a smile and doffed his hat as the girls bade a nod farewell. They went on their way, the last chorus of the song ringing out as they crossed over the road to head on home.

Nell was happy to close the front door out of the biting cold, knowing she didn't have ARP duty for the next two days, thanks to Greenwald. The sound of laughter filled the otherwise empty house, despite it being the first Christmas of the war. She could already smell the aroma of the pine tree and felt the pang of excitement that Christmas brought along with it.

'I'm home,' she intoned and pulled off her gloves and coat. She hung the coat on the balustrade and went down the hall to the front room where Winnie and Edna were sitting on the sofa wearing the smart frocks they only kept for big occasions. David was passing around a tray of gin he'd saved.

'You'll never guess what, Nell?' David handed her a glass. 'Sidney phoned across the road to say he'd be home for the holidays. His leave coincided with Christmas. Your Mam is ecstatic.'

'That's brilliant news!' She beamed and took the glass. 'So we're expecting him tonight?'

'I think so. His letter had been delayed and he called to ask why nobody replied.'

'Hello love how was your day?' asked Winnie, slurring on her words.

'Not good, I'm afraid,' she said and went to the kitchen where her mother stood languidly by the stove.

'Work finished for the holidays?' Mam asked.

'Yes, but try for good,' She replied, and dumped her bag on the table.

'What's happened? It seemed like a solid, dependable job.'

She shrugged, sniffing her mother's broth bubbling in the pan. 'Staff cuts. The last one in first one out, I suppose. But, oh well, I'm sure I'll find something else. I have plenty of skills and experience.'

'You will find an even better job with your certificates,' her Mam said and patted her sympathetically on the arm before going back to the soup on the stove.

'Thanks, I'm sure there's another job out there with my name on it. I'll be back down in a bit, Mam. I'm going to get changed.'

The front door knocked and she called out that she'd answer it. Thinking it could be Sidney, she felt a pang of excitement, but when she opened the door a young boy stood on the doorstep holding out an envelope. Nell reached out to take it and looked at the official military stamp.

'Shall I wait for a reply?' he asked.

Nell looked over her shoulder, saw the family enjoying the festivities and looked again at the envelope in her hand. She knew whatever the letter contained would destroy the little happiness her parents had had in a while and decided to keep it to herself until Boxing Day. She ripped it open and read the typed script. Sidney had gone AWOL. Her heart sank. He wasn't dead and while there was still hope, her parent's deserved this Christmas, so until then it was her secret. She'd deal with the consequences when the time came.

'No, no reply,' her voice shook. She jammed the telegram in the envelope, thanked the delivery boy and closed the door.

'Who was that?' David shouted.

'Just a couple of carolers,' she lied, dashing upstairs with the packages she bought and couldn't wait to wrap. She put her bag and the letter on the desk and slipped into her nightgown and robe. She *was* doing the right thing, wasn't she? She ran through everything in her mind again, that she'd tell her parents *after* the holiday and pushed the letter under her book. That's unless Sidney turned up tonight and then she'd have him confess and hand himself over to the military police.

From downstairs, she could hear Christmas tunes playing on the radio which would normally get her into the spirit of things, but the thought of the letter kept bringing her back to reality, there was a war on and her big brother was missing. She pulled her dressing gown tighter around her and leaned back in her chair, carefully wrapping the presents on her lap.

Mary called out that the soup was ready if she wanted some. She piled the presents in her arms and went downstairs. The guilt of hiding information about Sidney was eating away at her. She took a deep breath, went into the front room and placed the presents under the tree.

'You didn't go and buy us anything?' said David.

'It's just something small. I got a bonus from the manager, so I have money left over to help with the rent.'

Her dad wrapped an arm around her shoulder and pressed a kiss to her forehead.

'Don't go worrying about bills tonight but thank you, it's a lovely thought.'

Edna and Winnie broke out into a song that was playing on the radio and Gran sat with a glass of sherry mid-way to her mouth, unimpressed.

'Don't be so grumpy, Mam,' David laughed. He took Nell's hand and danced around the room. She couldn't remember a time when she saw her dad this cheerful, even though he had had his fair share of alcohol which he had been saving weeks prior to the festive season. Once the song ended, Nell slumped down on the sofa next to Gran when the topic of conversation turned to the boys abroad.

'Wherever they are tonight, I hope they're safe and well,' said Mam, sniffing back tears behind her glass.

'Hear, hear. Let's hope this will be the first and bloody last Christmas of the war,' Edna chimed in and raised her glass.

Nell felt guilty.

Sitting around the crackling fire drinking a cup of coffee, and listening to the radio, Nell thought about her gifts and decided to share them with the family this evening. She got up, reached under the Christmas tree, and cleared her throat to get everyone's attention. They all stopped what they were doing and looked in Nell's direction.

'I know the last few months have been hard on everyone, so I'd like you to have these,' she said handing them each a small brown package. 'It's not much as, to be honest stock has been pretty low on everything the last few weeks.'

'Oh Nell,' her mother burst out crying. 'You really shouldn't have done this after losing your job.'

Nell was about to speak when a knock came at the front door. She looked up at the clock on the mantel lit up by the glowing flames of the fire and wondered who would be calling at such a silly hour.

'It's probably one of the neighbours wanting something,' said Mary.

'I'll get it,' said David and he got up from his chair.

'Be careful you don't let any light out,' Mary called after him.

Nell looked at the door, wondering who it could be.

'Mam,' she whispered as she heard a familiar voice. 'Mam, you'd better come quickly,' she said excitedly, pulling the woman to her feet. If this was who she thought it was then her problem was solved.

'Jesus, Mary, get here, it's our Sidney,' David's voice cracked. 'It's our Sidney, home for Christmas.'

Nell couldn't believe that he turned up. Her father closed the door and switched on the light. Standing by the door was indeed, Sidney, smiling with a kit bag by his feet. His blue eyes crinkled under the dim light bulb.

'Sid!' Nell screamed, shaking as she fell into his arms. 'Oh my God, our Sid is home.'

'It's good to see you, Nell,' he said, hugging her.

'You have no idea,' she cried. 'No idea at all.'

Nell moved aside for her mother and then stood with her back against the door with hands covering her mouth. After the letter she'd received earlier this afternoon this was a miracle, she thought, as the weight of the burden lifted away.

He wasn't the young boy he'd been when he left. Sidney seemed taller, older and had lost his boyish good looks even though he'd only been gone a year.

'Let's get you a drink and something to eat,' said Mary walking him out to the kitchen.

Once she had got over the shock of seeing him, Nell managed to pull him aside from everyone for a quiet word.

'Even though it's lovely to see you, I want to talk to you about something that can't wait,' she said, pulling him by the arm to the hallway. 'It's really important and could've almost destroyed Mam if she had got the letter first.'

Standing under the staircase, out of earshot from everyone, Nell produced the letter that arrived earlier and held it up in front of him.

'Aren't you happy to see me?' he asked, refusing to look at it.

'More than you'll ever know. Do you know what this is?' she shook it furiously.

His eyes panned to the envelope and a flash of guilt struck across his face. He turned to look away.

'You're not on leave, are you?' she whispered. 'You ran away.'

'I can't talk about this right now, Nell. So you're not going to tell her?'

'No, it's Christmas and I'm not having her upset this evening. It's bad enough that it's Christmas and there's a war on.'

'I'm tired, Nell, we'll talk again. I promise.'

He went to walk away and she pulled him back. 'The navy will find out where you are soon enough, so make sure Mam knows everything before she gets the shock of her life.'

The arrival of Sidney brought joy to the household on Christmas morning. Nell went to help chop the few carrots and cabbage they had in the kitchen. Sidney walked in and went to sit on the back doorstep lighting a cigarette. She looked at him, thinking he was a bit quiet so offered to make him a drink. He shook his head and blew out a puff of smoke.

'No thanks, Nell. I've been thinking about what you said, but I don't think I can go back, I can't…'

'Why ever not?' she asked delicately. She stopped what she was doing and went to sit down on the step next to him.

'Don't tell Mam, please Nell. I don't want her to worry.'

'Okay, I promise, but you need to tell me everything.'

'Back in September, my ship was gunned down by the *Graf Spee* off the coast of Norway…'

Nell gasped with shock.

'…we were bound for London when I heard this lad screaming across the deck that there was a German ship in the distance. Before I could make a run for it we were being shot at. They kept pounding at us, Nell. I didn't think we'd get out of it alive if I'm honest. Anyway, some lads jumped ship, but I ran across the deck, narrowly missing a bloody bullet that went straight through the metal several inches from my head. If it wasn't for my pal Adam who pulled me inside, I doubt I'd be sitting here now. It was at that point we realised we weren't going to get any further and before they could sink us, a Norwegian torpedo boat, *Storm* towed us to safety.'

He hung his head low and took another drag on his cigarette when the front door slammed closed. She saw how jumpy he was and felt sorry for him.

'It's just the door, silly, calm down.'

He seemed bothered and got to his feet. 'Who is it?' he asked.

'I don't know. Dad, maybe,' she shrugged thinking how it was such an odd thing to ask. She went back to the vegetables and closed the door to stop the heating leaving the house.

'How about we open the presents, Nell?' asked Mary.

Nell looked over her shoulder and saw Sid pacing the garden. She tapped the window urging him to come inside.

Chapter Eight

After his revelation to Nell on Christmas Eve, Sidney had kept himself busy over the last few days and had stayed out of the family's way. When Nell went to hoover in the front room to get it ready for the New Year's celebrations that evening there was a knock at the door. She looked up from what she was doing and saw her father sprint down the hallway to answer it. She didn't like to think who he saw standing behind the glass for him to exert himself. Wondering what was happening she propped the hoover against the door frame and went to see what was going on. A Naval officer and two Military Police Officers stood at the door. The officer removed his cap when he saw Nell.

'Morning, gentlemen, is there something wrong?'

'Are you Mr. Adams, father of Sidney Adams?'

'I am.'

'Mr. Adams, I'm sorry to bother you, but we're here about Sidney. You may or may not know that he absconded from his ship when it docked in Newcastle just before Christmas, and we've reason to believe he has shown up here.'

'He did what?' David said as though the wind had been beaten out of him. He turned to Nell, who had never seen her father looking so shocked.

'He went out this morning,' she said to the officer. 'We had no idea what he did, believe me, but I can tell you he's not been himself after what happened. Please go easy on him, sir. He's a good man…'

'Nell, what's going on?' asked Dad. 'Why would Sidney do something like this?'

'I'll tell you later.' She went to get her coat and then excused herself to the officer to get out the door. The policemen moved aside. 'I'll go and see if I can find him and talk to him. Will you wait?' she turned back to the officer.

'Yes, but you must warn him it's a serious offence.'

'I will do,' she said and did up her coat as she marched up the street. She had a feeling he'd be up on the hill at his favourite spot that overlooked the bay. If he wasn't there, she feared what would happen to him if he didn't show up at the house, or if he showed up without her reaching him first. He'd surely run again.

She took a shortcut through the cemetery and climbed over the wall onto the footpath at the bottom of the hill and followed the uneven, winding path to the top.

Once she had reached the summit, the derelict house they used to play in when they were children appeared from behind the pine trees. There was a billow of smoke rising into the low clouds.

'Sidney? Are you here? If you are, please don't run I must talk to you.'

She heaved herself onto the flattened part of the steep ascent and saw Sidney huddled against the crumbling wall in his trench coat.

'I can't go back, Nell…' he said.

'Oh, Sid, if you don't it'll cause more trouble than what it's worth.'

She tucked her coat under her and sat on a small boulder.

'You didn't see what I did. I can't go back. I won't.'

'Remember how proud you were on the day you passed out? You wanted to serve your country no matter what.'

'I get flashbacks to what happened that day…'

'Then for God sakes, tell them. The military police are there too, Sid, and Dad is a mess. He doesn't know what's happening.'

'They're just going to send me back.'

'You can't know that yet. Please listen to me. There's no point being on the run. They'll catch up with you eventually and it'll make matters worse.'

'I bet Dad is disappointed in me?'

'Poor Dad doesn't know what happened to you yet. Oh come on, Sid, nobody is disappointed. But I do think you'll be doing the right thing, you'll soon see.'

Sidney exhaled deeply.

'I'm doing this for Mam and Dad,' he got up.

'I'm proud of you for this, come on, before it gets darker…'

When they got to the house, Nell walked in first hoping to diffuse any arguments from her parents. Sidney was in a fragile state, and the last thing she wanted was for him to leave again.

Mary came rushing out of the front room, her eyes clearly red from crying.

'Sidney, how could you do this?'

'Mam,' Nell interjected. 'Hear him out first.'

'I hope you didn't know about this young lady, or there'll…'

'She didn't know anything,' Sidney stepped forward. 'Leave her out of it. This is my doing, Mam. What more can I say but I'm very sorry.'

The officer, who was sitting on the sofa drinking a cup of tea, stood up and acknowledged Sidney with a weak smile. He straightened down his jacket and put his cap back on.

'There'll be serious consequences for this…'

'Before anyone says anything, let me tell you that he's sorry for the trouble he's caused but he's not very well, sir,' Nell pleaded with the officer.

'Okay, well, let us be the judge of that.' The officer nodded to the MP who took Sidney's arm. 'He'll have to return to base ASAP and stand trial for desertion. Thank you very much for tea, Mrs. Adams, but we should be getting back.'

Mary gave Sidney a hug and when it came to Nell, he lowered his head. 'I'm sorry for getting you involved in my problems. Thanks for making me see sense.'

'It's alright. I hope everything works out okay for you now.'

'I hope so too. And I'm sorry again that you were the one to take that telegram. In some way, I'm glad you did and you had the sense to keep it from Mam and Dad.'

'It wasn't an easy decision, and I had every intention of telling them. I guess it's just as well you turned up when you did. You had no idea of what was going through my mind for those few hours. It was hell.' She took a deep breath. 'I'm glad you're okay and hopefully, now, you'll get the help you need.'

'Thanks, Nell, I won't forget this.'

'Don't worry, I have a long memory.' She gave him one last hug and they headed out the door, to the car.

That evening, the family decided to welcome in the New Year at Edna's house with cups of tea and sandwiches. Not another word was mentioned of Sidney's mistake, Mary forbade them to talk about it, wanting to put it behind her. At five past midnight, after the not so cheerful rendition of *Auld Lang Syne* around the piano, Nell and Bess quietly slipped out the back door for a bit of fresh air.

'Another year has gone, already,' said Bess sitting down on the back doorstep. 'I think we can forget about a resolution to this bloody war anytime soon then.'

Nell sighed.

'I'm gasping for a fag.'

'Me too,' she replied, looking up at the night sky. 'Shall we break the rules just for one night?'

'What have we got to lose? I can always impose a fine on myself for a bob or two.'

PART TWO
1940

Chapter Nine

After an exhausting night on ARP duty at the town center, Nell strolled home along Tennant Road and tucked her freezing cold hands deep into her trench coat pockets. It was a frosty morning, and not yet light except for a tinge of blue in the sky to the East sneaking behind the roof of the terraced houses. She heard whistling, and came to an abrupt stop, squinting to see who was standing on a step ladder outside the shop window.

'Hello?'

The whistling stopped and there was a clatter of something hitting tin.

'Good morning, you're out early.'

It was Tommy, the local grocer and he stepped down from the ladder.

'Oh, I'm sorry Tom. I didn't realize it was you. It's been a long night, I say.' She yawned into the sleeve of her coat.

'ARP duty is it, Nell?' he asked, taking a rag from the back of his trouser pocket and then wiping his hands.

Nell took a closer look at what he had painted on the window.

'Rationing starts today?' she shrieked, almost waking up the entire neighbourhood. Had she been so busy the last few months since the war had been declared that time seemed to have passed by so quickly?

'Yes, Nell, rather unfortunately, it's upon us. Oh, before you go, tell your mam to get here early,' he winked and bent down to pick up the paint can.

'Okay, I will tell her. Thanks, Tom,' she said, remembering how her mam had been in a fluster last night before she left for work.

'No problem, Nell. I don't have half the stock I normally have. We're in interesting times, Nell.' He returned to his painting. 'Interesting times,' he whispered and mounted the ladder.

Dispirited, and with a twist in her gut, she walked on, wondering what it would be like to go hungry. Even though her family wasn't well off, they'd always managed to put a meal on the table.

Pushing the front door open, she stomped her feet on the rug in the porch and called out for her mam.

'In here, Nell,' came the reply.

She walked into the front room lit with one lamp in the corner and saw her mother kneeling on the threadbare rug beside the wooden cabinet searching through papers.

'What are you looking for?'

Mam sighed and dropped the bunch of envelopes on the floor. 'I've been looking for the bloody ration books, Nell. I put them away a few weeks ago but I'll be damned if I can remember where.'

She took a long breath and got to her feet.

Nell didn't think it was a good idea to tell her what Tom had said about the limited stock at the moment as it would only panic her even more. She put her hands on her hips and glanced around the room.

'Where haven't you looked?' she asked, with a quick look at the clock on the mantel. Oh bugger, she thought, as she heard the clock struck 5.45. Tom's opened at 6.30 for the newspapers.

'Nell, I have looked every bleedin' where.' She threw her hands up in defeat and left the room. Nell followed and saw her mother's black handbag hanging on the back of the chair.

'What about your bag, Mam?' she lifted it off and passed it to her. 'Check, and make sure you check the pockets and I'll go and look in the kitchen.'

'Why now?' she mumbled to herself, finding a piece of paper with a list of food items on thc work surface. 'Here's your shopping list,' she yelled, reading it through.

'Thanks, Nell. You know, Shirley said there'll likely be long queues.'

'You're telling me,' she replied, thinking her mother had been a little optimistic about hcr intended purchases. She put the list in her pocket and opened the cupboard door, pushing aside the jars of dried fruit. 'Do you want a sandwich, Mam, before we go?' she asked when she saw the brown cards she had been looking for tucked to the side. 'Mam, I've got them,' she waved them about. 'So now you can stop stressing.'

Mary came rushing into the kitchen, a look of relief on her face.

'Oh, thanks, Nell. Eh, aren't you tired?' she said and put them safely in her bag that now hung in the crook of her arm.

'Oh I'm alright, Mam,' she lied. The truth was she was freezing cold and wanted a long soak in a hot bath.

'It'll be nice to have a bit of company,' she slipped on hcr glovcs. 'I was talking to Edna last night at the Community, and she also reckons there won't be much left if we don't get there before the shop opens. What if we don't have enough to last us the week?' she fretted and looked into the silver teapot on the counter while she made adjustments to her hat.

After what Tom had told her this morning, Nell understood her mother's fears but thought it was best not to show her that shc was also concerned.

'Well let's go now then, to avoid the rush,' she suggested, turning back to the cupboard and pulling out a pot of jam. She quickly spread some across a slice of bread and took a bite, thinking it was best to heed Tom's advice and arrive early. She glanced up at the clock hanging above the back door and noted they'd be there half an hour before the shop opened. It meant she'd have to stand outside in the freezing cold again.

'Right, shall we go then?' Mam stood up, buttoning up her coat.

'I'll just get my other coat.' Nell ate the last bit of her bread and went to the closet under the stairs.

The stairs creaked above her, and her father appeared down the hallway, grunting a "good morning" as he passed.

'Nell, why did you let the fire go out?' he moaned.

'I haven't long got back from duty, Dad. Bloody hell,' she muttered, pulling on her coat. 'Dad, we're off to the shop, do you need anything?'

He knelt bcside the grate, chucking wood onto the fire. 'Nell, can you try and get us some tobacco. The amount of stress this is causing, I'll need it later.'

Mary shook her head in despair.

'Oh bloody hush, I've spent the entire night working out the shopping list and I don't even think we have enough money for all we need.' She turned to Nell. 'Come on, Nell, it's best to go now. Would you grab my basket under the stairs, please? Bess said her mam is leaving before they open as well, so we'll call in on her on the way.'

'...and a box of matches,' Dad shouted after them as Nell closed the door, stepping out into the cold that struck her bare legs.

Winnie was already on her doorstep clutching her woolen scarf around her neck.

'I was about to knock the door, Mary. Come on you two, let's go so we'll be first in and home, out of this bloody weather,' she said, making her way down the steps.

'Good God, woman, I can't keep up with you,' Mary huffed as Winnie marched down the street. 'Any quicker and they'll be snapping you up for front-line duty.'

Nell looked on in amusement at the pair as they went on their way. She happily followed behind, yawning and hoping for a good kip later before meeting Bess at the café for a natter.

Just as they rounded the corner on to Tennant Road, another group of women was already making their way from the side street. Nell was surprised to see a queue already formed outside Mr. Hill's Grocers.

'Looks like everyone had the same idea.'

'If this is things to come, Nell, I despair.' Mary's lips chattered in the cold.

They joined the back of the queue, next to Emily, a young woman with two small children in tow. Dylan, the eldest clutched his mother's legs tightly, frozen from the harsh winter weather. Nell knew the woman from school.

'I've been here for half an hour,' she said, sounding exhausted. 'I couldn't get anyone to watch the babies for me. Poor mites are cold and hungry.'

'Would you like me to hold him?' Nell offered, holding out her hands to the toddler propped on her hip.

'Would you mind, Nell? He weighs a ton for the little he eats.'

Nell took the child, pulling a funny face at him. He chuckled hard. 'Come here, lovely, so what's the matter, eh?' She bounced him on her hip. 'Have you heard from your brother Albert?' she asked, turning to Emily.

She shook her head.

'Not recently. I know it's hard for them an' all being abroad, fighting for us, but life isn't all rosy for us stuck here either. I was supposed to start a job last week at the munitions factory, you know the one, in Landore?'

'I think I've heard of it,' said Nell.

'Well my mother moved to Haverfordwest to be with her sister, so I had nobody to have these two in the day for me. There's no point asking the kids father,' she replied, bitterly.

'Couldn't you go with your mother? I assume it would be much better than the city for the kids' right now,' asked Nell, hoping she wasn't intruding too much, but Emily seemed happy enough to talk. It was as though she hadn't seen anyone in a long while.

'No, their father wouldn't allow it. He didn't want me to send them to strangers either, even though I thought it'd be good for them.'

Nell exchanged a pleading glance with her mother. She wanted to help her in some way but didn't know how. Emily looked painfully thin, with her cheekbones prominent and black under her tired looking eyes. Nell knew her mam would know what to do.

'Listen, Emily, if you can get another interview at the factory, Edna and I have started helping out at a nursery in St Thomas. I'll chip in for the first week until you sort yourself out.'

For the first time since they started talking, Nell saw the woman's eyes flash with life.

'Oh, Mrs. Adams, would you really do that for me?' her face beamed with happiness. 'I'd be ever so grateful if you could. Oh thank you, I'll make an appointment with them as soon as I can.' Her eyes filled with tears as she reached down to hug the older child hugging her legs for warmth.

'You're too kind, Mam,' Nell said quietly.

'I don't think that girl has ever had a spot of luck, bless her.'

The news had quickly spread down the queue, and heads began to turn at the commotion at the back.

'What's happened,' bellowed Mrs. Crocker lifting her head to see what was going on.

'Mrs. Adams offered to help with child care,' cried Emily. 'Isn't she fabulous everyone?'

There were cheers and claps from the women. Many patted Mary on the back, but she didn't like a fuss made over her and tried to dampen down the praise saying that it was something anyone would do in times like these. Except Nell knew not everyone was as generous as her mother.

Fifteen minutes went by and Nell and Mary had finally joined the queue inside the shop. They cast critical eyes around the store, looking at the wooden shelving and had the shock of their lives. The shelves that were usually brimming with tins, fresh bread and vegetables were now sparse and almost empty.

'Oh dear God, it looks bleak, Nell.'

'I was told that would be the case, Mam.'

When they approached the counter, Mary took out her ration books from her pocket.

'How's it going, Mary?' Tom asked, measuring out white sugar on the scales.

'I'm not sure how to answer that yet,' she said, looking at the amount of sugar he passed her. He took the ration book, stamped it and then gave her a small portion of butter and bacon.

'That's it, I'm afraid.'

'Good gracious and this has to last me a week? I'd use that butter up with one round of toast.'

'Afraid so, Mrs. Adams and I think it's only going to get worse before it gets better.'

Nell inwardly groaned. She feared something like this would happen when they introduced rationing.

'And an ounce of tobacco please, Tom,' she noted her mother's annoyed expression. 'It's okay, I'll get it for him, saves him moaning at us later.'

Nell met with Bessie at Di Marco's ice cream parlour and café on Port Tennant road later that afternoon. They were both in deep conversation over the pitiful rations they'd received when Nell heard a commotion outside. It piqued her interest and she turned to the window to see what was happening. On the opposite side of the road, a man wearing a pair of overalls had a woman by the scruff of her neck and was marching her up the street. Two children were running behind, crying and screaming for their mother.

'Bess, look that's Emily, the woman Mam is helping out. Look at the way that bloke is handling her, I have a right mind to go out there and sort him out.' Furious, she pushed back her chair. Bess grabbed her by the arm.

'Sit your bum down. My Mam said nobody should get involved in the affairs of married couples.'

'But that's no way to treat a woman. Surely you can't stand by and watch it?'

'I never said I could, but look at the size of him compared to you. I don't care if you've had ARP training, you're no match for him.'

Marco sashayed around a table towards them. He was a tall man with dark hair and olive skin. He wore a white apron and spoke with a strong Italian accent despite having lived in Swansea for twenty years.

'Is everything okay, ladies?' he asked, topping up their tea.

Nell sat back down and looked up at Marco. 'Yes, thank you, Marco. The food is always great here.' She slammed her fork down on the table and looked out of the window. She meant the sentiment, but she was full of rage over what was happening outside she didn't realise the affect she had on him.

Confusion flashed across Marco's face, but then he saw what was going on and shook his head in despair at what he was witnessing.

'Oh, I see what you're looking at.' He pointed a finger at Emily. 'I feel so sorry for that poor woman. I don't know why she puts up with such a bully. But one day, you mark my words, he'll get what's coming to him.'

Nell swiveled around in her chair. 'You mean this happens all the time?'

'I'm afraid so, but nobody will stand up to him. Everyone around here is afraid of him.'

'Well, I hope somebody does stand up to him and soon, I really do. Now I understand why she said she wasn't so keen to move from here with her mam. I reckon it's because of that bastard.'

'It's the kids I feel sorry for,' said Bess.

'I still feel like I should go and say something.'

'No,' said Marco, 'you don't want him coming after you. I've heard that he hangs around with a bad sort. Only the other day I was told that he has started stealing from people's homes.'

Nell crossed her arms.

'I'm going to have to tell Mam when I see her. I can't let this go on, not after seeing it with my own two eyes.'

'That's probably the best thing to do, Nell,' said Bess.

Marco nodded in agreement. 'I hope you manage to sort it out, ladies.'

Nell yawned, dangling her legs from the top bunk. She wasn't sure if it was night or day at this point and reached under the pillow for a pile of letters she had spent hours writing. She jumped down from the bunk and winced as she stepped into freezing cold rainwater that seeped in overnight. It was the family's second night in the shelter and on both occasions, they hadn't been comfortable. It had rained almost non-stop for the past week, and the noise on the tin roof was unbearable. She pulled on her coat, yawned again and pushed open the sack flap covering her eyes from the light. Everyone else was indoors now as the all-clear had sounded earlier that morning, but since Nell had two days off from work her mother didn't want to disturb her. As she walked across the muddy garden, the pigeons that were enjoying their little feast of scrap bread flew onto the roof.

'Good morning Gran.' She went into the kitchen and stood next to the boiler that radiated much-needed warmth.

'There's coffee here for you, Nell.'

'Thanks, Gran.'

Once she could feel her hands again, she picked up the mug and sat down beside the table where her gran was busy reading the newspaper.

'Is there anything interesting in the paper today?'

'The usual, love. War, war and pardon my French, but more bloomin' war. So, what are your plans for the day?'

'I haven't got anything planned, Gran. I thought it'd be nice to take time off from the war and just sit and relax, maybe read a book. You don't think that sounds selfish, do you? I mean, what with our boys fighting?'

Gran chuckled. 'Nell, you do quite enough for this community as it is, I don't think they'd begrudge you a day off, love.'

With that, her dad came into the kitchen having overheard the conversation.

'Don't worry, Nell, the war will still be on tomorrow.'

She hoped it wouldn't be. She went into the living room where her mother was folding the black-out blinds and asked if she wanted help.

'It's alright, Nell, I can do it. By the way, we're thinking of putting on a play at the Community, you know, just to get the youngsters doing something. I wondered if you'd like to write it for us.'

'Sure? Well I'd love to, Mam, and oh and by the way I meant to tell you something about Emily yesterday but you were late getting in.'

'What about her?'

'Well, I have reason to believe that she's being abused by her husband. Bess and I saw him manhandling her yesterday outside Di Marco's. Apparently, it happens a lot according to Marco.'

Mary stopped folding the black-out sheets.

'Are you serious, Nell? Oh, bloody hell I don't need this now. I was going to pop up to see her later. One of her kids hasn't been feeling great, poor bugger.'

'Aw, it's not a stomach bug that's going around, is it? I saw the little ones crying and running after her while that pig dragged her up the street. I wouldn't be surprised if the kid is traumatized by what it saw.'

'I don't know. Her house is full of damp which can't be helping. Oh, I do feel sorry for her, but what to do about that man of hers, I don't know. I don't believe in meddling in the affairs of married people.'

'Think of the kids Mam, we have to do something.' Nell smiled tightly. Her mother loved to help people, it was in her nature.

'I'll see what I can do. If she opens up to me I'll help her to take it further. Sergeant Bowman is a family friend so I'll go and ask him for help. I was thinking of asking Florrie next door if she could put them up for a while as she has two spare rooms.'

'That's a good idea. I can't see her refusing, Mam. She's a good woman.'

Later on that afternoon, Nell and Gran were sitting in the living room playing a card game on the dining table when her mother came through the front door. Nell leaned back to get a look to see who else's voice she could hear. Two small children ran up the hallway.

'Hello,' she said to the smallest child who had spotted her cards and was now chucking them around the room. She looked up to her mother and saw Emily standing behind her. Her face was pale and drawn as though she hadn't had a decent night's sleep for months.

'I brought them back with me as Florrie agreed they could stay with her until she sorts herself out. Sergeant Bowman will be paying her old man a visit too. In the mean time nobody can know she is here in case it gets back to *him*.'

'Emily would you like to sit down,' Nell got up from her chair and gestured to the sofa. Timidly, the woman nodded, put down her bags on the floor and sat down.

'Boys, please don't be a nuisance, we're guests,' she told the kids who, despite looking malnourished, were quite excited as they splayed their arms out pretending to be airplanes.

'Aw, they are alright, aren't they Mam?' Nell said, now copying them which only excited them even more. 'So what are your names, again?' she asked.

'This is Dylan and Alex,' Mary said, sounding exhausted already and began removing her coat.

As she was the youngest in the family, Nell never had the opportunity to be around younger children, but already she loved it.

'I'll pop the tea on,' Mary said and went to the kitchen.

Nell stopped spinning as she was getting dizzy and handed the children a biscuit each from the tin that was tucked down the side of the chair by Gran. They eagerly snatched the biscuits from her hand and ran out to the back garden.

'I don't know if Mam told you, but I saw your man marching you up Margaret Street this morning. I couldn't stand back and let it go on, so I hope you're not angry with me for telling her?'

Emily hesitated a moment before she spoke and then shook her head. 'No. If truth be told I rather hoped someone would one day. So thank you, Nell. I really couldn't have left if it wasn't for you.'

Nell leaned forward to give her a hug.

'We are all here for you. So, Emily, how did you get on with getting another interview at the factory?'

The woman's eyes now had a spark of life in them as she spoke. 'I was told I could re-try soon, now your mother offered to help out. Are you going for a job there as well?'

'Oh I might do, I could come along with you and ask if you want?'

David walked into the living room looking frazzled. 'Jesus, those kids are a busy pair. They offered to help dig the garden and ended up making more mess than a German bomb.' He laughed, rubbing the soil off his hands on the back of his trousers. His eyes widened as he looked in Gran's direction. 'Don't touch that,' he hollered to gran who was fiddling with the knobs on his precious radio. 'I thought the little ones were bad, you're just a handful at times, too, aren't you.' He brushed her hand away.

'I want to listen to the news, David. Turn this bloody thing on would you?'

Emily began giggling and covered her mouth with her hand. Nell exchanged a glance with her and they both burst out laughing.

Being out of work and with only her ARP duties to keep her occupied, Nell was becoming increasingly fed up with being at home with nothing to do in the day. When Emily came into the house the following morning with the news that the ammunition factory was taking on more girls, Nell thought it was the only and best chance she had to escape the day-to-day drudgery.

With an induction arranged at midday by the Labour Exchange, Nell met up with Bess outside the house who had also taken an interest in working there.

'Are you sure you're up for work in a factory, Bess? It's going to be a lot different from Woolies.'

'Ready as I'll ever be, I can't sit in the house any longer or I'll go bloomin' mad as your gran says. Besides, the pay's a lot better and I need the money for the wedding, don't forget.'

'Oh gosh, that won't be long now. I'm really looking forward to seeing William again. I miss our laughs. I swear he should've been a comedian.'

'He bloody well is a comedian, Nell.' Bess laughed. 'I can just imagine him spending his free time entertaining the troops.'

Emily was already at the bus stop waiting when they arrived.

'Are you going for the jobs, too, girls?' she asked as the bus arrived.

'Of course, beats sitting in the house, doesn't it?' said Nell as she got on the bus.

Nell sat down next to Emily while Bess took a spare seat behind.

'I'm not being nasty but it's so nice to get a break from the kids,' said Emily, taking her compact from her bag and checking her face in the mirror.

The bus parked outside the tall, metal gates of the factory estate and they got off. A guard was posted outside the metal gates pacing the ground, seemingly bored. He looked up when the girls approached and smiled broadly.

'Job interviews, is it?' He asked, staring longingly at Emily.

Nell cleared her throat. 'Yes, so are you going to let us in?'

'Of course.' He pulled open the gates and stood back to allow them through. 'You need to see Mr. Lovett, he's in the office to the right, but you will need to be searched first…'

Bessie swung around. 'Not by you I bloody hope.'

The boy went red in the face and hurriedly closed the gates. 'Unfortunately, it's not in my job description. You'll need to see her.' He pointed to a fair-headed woman talking to a group of girls by the entrance.

Nell approached her first, and as she did so, the woman allowed the girls through and turned towards Nell.

'Here for the jobs in the filling shed, are you?' she asked, and then checked her clipboard. 'Yes, the three of us,' she thumbed to Bess and Emily.

'I'll just give you a quick pat down to make sure you're not carrying anything you shouldn't't.' She noted Nell's reaction. 'It's alright, we can't be too careful, its wartime. Also, please can you remove hair grips and rings, thank you, girls.'

After they were checked, they took a seat in the waiting area with several other women. They had only just exchanged pleasantries when the door opened and a tall, wiry man with grey hair and mustache came through. He was a cheery fellow with a friendly face.

'Thank you for coming, ladies. I'm Charlie Lovett the safety manager. Would you all come through to the canteen please?'

'Oh we're on the move again,' Bessie quipped. A few girls had overheard and laughed.

Chairs had already been neatly placed in rows and Nell, Emily and Bess took their seats at the front.

'Did he say we're working in the filling shed?' Bessie asked.

'I think so. Why?'

'That means we're actually putting the gunpowder in the shells then. Oh my God.'

Charlie sat on a chair facing them and then cleared his throat to get everyone's attention.

'Welcome and thank you for being here. Now I don't need to remind you the importance of this work, I'm sure you're all very aware.'

There were nods from around the room.

'So I want to start with work safety. If you have rings, hair grips, they must be removed before entering the factory at all times. One small spark could potentially blow us all up, and we don't want that do we?'

There was a ripple of gasps amongst the women. Nell was taken aback by the casual tone of his voice and swallowed hard. Thanks to all her ARP training, she thought she would be better prepared than most. But she couldn't deny that this was a whole different world to the comforts of Woolworths.

'Oh my giddy aunt,' said Bess. 'I'm already missing the cosmetic counter.'

'Too late now,' Nell whispered. 'Just think there'll be more money in your wage packet.'

Charlie then went onto explain their job roles in the filling shed and Bessie, Emily and Nell were then taken outside, to the shed where they were going to fill the shells with gunpowder.

'So,' said Bessie, directing her question to Charlie. 'Before we go inside, have you had many accidents here?'

'No, not that I'm aware of,' he replied confidently. 'You'll be fine girls, absolutely fine. Just follow the rules and you can't go wrong.'

Chapter Ten

Even though large tracts of Europe and many old and famous States have fallen or may fall into the grip of the Gestapo and all the odious apparatus of Nazi rule, we shall not flag or fail. We shall go on to the end. We shall fight in France, we shall fight on the seas and oceans, we shall fight with growing confidence and growing strength in the air, we shall defend our island, whatever the cost may be. We shall fight on the beaches, we shall fight on the landing grounds, we shall fight in the fields and in the streets, we shall fight in the hills; we shall never surrender, and if, which I do not for a moment believe, this island or a large part of it were subjugated and starving, then our Empire beyond the seas, armed and guarded by the British Fleet, would carry on the struggle, until, in God's good time, the New World, with all its power and might, steps forth to the rescue and the liberation of the old.

Summer had finally arrived and Nell woke to the sound of children's voices in the back garden. She went downstairs overhearing on the radio that there had been heavy bombing on Dunkirk by the Germans.

Emily had just come off night duty at the factory and was sitting talking to Mary over a cup of Camp coffee they acquired from Tom's the previous day.

'Fancy coming down Di Marco's for an ice cream in a bit?' she asked Nell. 'I feel like giving the kids a treat.'

'Yeah, I wouldn't mind now that I've got my wages.' She poured herself a cup of coffee, welcoming the warm breeze blowing in through the open back door.

'I feel so guilty I don't spend enough time with them as it is.'

'You spend a lot of time with them. Look,' Nell pointed at the kids out the garden. 'They're happy, aren't they? Anyway, they deserve it, even if they woke me up.' She laughed. 'Did I get any mail, Mam?'

'No, love but there's a few from the boy's there if you want to read them. They're all alright, just missing everyone.'

'Not heard from your fella yet?' Emily asked.

Nell sat down. 'No. He must be busy, I suppose.'

'That's probably it, don't worry.'

Nell noticed how distant Emily was being as they walked along the street. Normally she'd be the first to give the kids a telling off if they weren't behaving in public.

'Boys,' said Nell, thinking it wasn't her place to say but if she didn't tell them to stop jumping off the curb they'd likely get hit by the approaching car. 'Please don't do that.'

She walked in step with Emily who had suddenly snapped out of her daze.

'Look,' she pointed down the street. 'Whatever's going on?'

Nell looked in the direction in which she pointed and could hardly believe what she was seeing. A crowd of angry people was crowded around Di Marco's shop front. It wasn't until they got closer, the muffled chanting soon became clearer, and Nell wasn't happy with what she heard.

'Nazi sympathiser.'

'Scum.'

'Send them back home.'

The angry mob banged at the shop window and door. Nell stood back, trying to get a good look at who would cause such a scene. Her face fell when she realised they were people she had known all her life.

'Vera?'

Nell pulled the arm of the woman's coat.

Vera looked over her shoulder, her eyes cold, full of hatred. Nell hardly recognised her. 'Come to join us have you, Nell?'

'What do you mean? What's happening?'

'They're finally arresting the Italians. Churchill said they must all be detained. Every last one of them is a threat to our freedom.'

Nell was incredulous and stepped back from Vera, aghast at the scene before her. 'We've known the Di Marcos our whole lives, how could you even think they're not on our side.'

With that, the shop door opened and the crowd parted a way to allow the policeman to pass through with Mr. Di Marco and his wife.

'You can't do this,' screamed Nell at the officer who didn't even acknowledge her. Nell pushed and shoved her way to the front of the crowd when another officer put out his hand, urging her to stand back.

Mr. Di Marco's tear-filled eyes met hers and she swore she saw a flicker of fear in them before the police pushed his head forward then down to get into the car.

'This isn't fair,' she screamed. 'They haven't done anything wrong.'

'Nell, come on, let's go.' Emily tugged her arm.

'I can't believe this, can you?' she turned to Emily who looked as shocked as she did.

The crowd began to dissipate as the car pulled away. Nell was furious. 'It's bloody disgusting if you ask me. The Di Marcos weren't a threat to anyone.'

Emily linked her arm. 'I know, Nell. I'm so angry and upset. Let's go home, shall we?'

That evening the family sat around the kitchen table, listening to the news on to the radio. They were tucking into Mary's pitiful vegetable pie when Dad put down his cutlery and shook his head at what Nell had told him about the events on Port Tennant road that afternoon.

'I can't bloody believe what the world is coming to. The poor Di Marcos. That man wouldn't hurt a fly for God's sake.'

'I know, Dad. He was the one who told me about Emily being mistreated. He said nobody would believe him if he said anything.'

There was an uncomfortable silence around the table.

'I liked Churchill's speech on the radio this morning,' Mary said, changing the topic of conversation.

'That Churchill is our man. I like him very much,' David added and then continued eating his dinner.

Nell was surprised as he'd normally witter on when it came to Churchill, but not this evening. He turned to Nell thoughtfully.

'No training tonight, Nell?' he asked, lighting his pipe.

'No, but Greenwald said I'll be having a uniform soon.' She pushed the boiled potatoes around on her plate and excused herself from the table. She hadn't been finishing her meals for days now, and she knew it was because she missed Francis so much. She had written three letters to him the past month and it seemed as though he hadn't had the decency to reply back. At least her brothers always responded. Her mood didn't go unnoticed by her mam either who followed her out to the hallway.

'Nell,' she asked. 'What's wrong? You've been moody since you came in from Bessie's this morning. Have you two had a falling out?'

'No Mam, of course we haven't,' she replied, dropping her gaze to her feet. 'To tell you the truth Mam, I haven't heard from Francis in weeks. Do you think he's forgotten about me already?'

'The way that boy looked at you on the day he left I'd say he's very much in love with you,

Nell. As the saying goes, no news is good news, okay?' She lifted her chin. 'Now finish your dinner, you'll need your strength for patrol tonight.'

'I will do Mam, but...' She sighed.

'What is bothering you, love? Tell me.'

'It seems silly to even mention it now as it was so long ago, but...' She knew she needed to get it off her chest or she'd be in no fit state for ARP duty this evening.

'Remember that party at the Naval for Jack the landlord? Well, he completely ignored me that evening and left without saying a word. I've always wondered what he was up to because Edna told me he never went back home that night.'

'Oh, Nell, don't be daft. I don't think it's in his nature to do anything like what you're thinking.'

'Maybe not...'

'You're engaged now. If it was anything bad I'm sure he would've told you by now.'

Always grateful for her mother's little pep talks, she felt the weight on her shoulders lift a touch and happily returned back to the table to finish her meal, as these days the family couldn't afford to waste anything.

'I thought that was a very good speech on the radio, didn't you?' she asked her dad who sat puffing on his pipe. 'I like how he empowers people and makes us believe that we'll win this war. I'll remember that when I'm on duty later.'

Her father lowered his pipe and she could see in his small, brown misty eyes how proud he was of her.

'You do that, Nell, and yes, very powerful words they were indeed.'

After she had finished her meal; she made her way to her room and got changed for patrol duty. It was only a few hours around the local area tonight, so she didn't have to rush across town to the main office. Once dusk had arrived, she helped her mam with the blackout blinds and left for work.

The night was balmy with clear skies. Standing at the top of her road, she checked her watch and noted she had been walking through the streets for two hours now without having to fine or warn anyone. In front of her, the sky was littered with twinkling stars and the light of the moon reflected on the sea like glass. She thought of her brothers and Francis. She missed them all terribly, and despite what had gone on between her and Francis before he left, he'd always have a piece of her heart. Recalling the memory of the day he'd told her that he loved her she looked up at the stars and smiled.

'We'll see the stars again, Nell,' she whispered, rather hoping the next time she saw a beautiful evening like this, it would be with them all home, safe and unhurt. She turned her attention to the bottom of the street and saw darkness and nothing more where the sea ended and the docks began. It was too quiet, she thought and clutched Alfred's whistle dangling from her neck. Somehow it made her feel protected and she'd vowed she'd never leave the house without it, especially when on duty. She took a long exhale, thinking of everyone and offered up a silent prayer for their safe return.

'Nell?'

'Mr. Greenwald?' She turned in the direction of the voice.

'I've come to take over, Nell. Has everything been alright, yes?' he asked slightly out of puff.

If it wasn't for the whiteness of his teeth, and the luminous flower she gave him from Woolworths she wouldn't have known he was there. It was pitch black.

'There's nothing to report, Mr. Greenwald. Seems like everyone is on their best behavior, tonight, including the Germans.' She chuckled nervously.

'That's a bleedin' first then. Do you know I had to fine three people last night for leaving a gap in their curtains?'

'Awful isn't it? After all the lectures you've given them as well. Anyway, I must bid you goodnight. I really could do with some sleep if I'm honest,' she yawned. She was about to cross the road to go home but felt an unease in her belly. She glanced over her shoulder at Mr. Greenwald. 'It's such a clear night, isn't it? I was thinking moments ago how lovely it was but now I don't think I like it, to be honest, Mr. Greenwald.'

Mr. Greenwald looked up to the sky.

'Why, Nell?'

'A clear night means the Germans have a better advantage, doesn't it?'

'Let's hope you're wrong for once, eh, Nell.'

The house was quiet when she entered. Assuming everyone was asleep, she unfastened her overcoat as she made her way upstairs, hoping to catch a couple of hours sleep before the sun came up and she was expected at work. Creeping across the landing, past her parent's room, she heard her dad snoring. Finding it funny, she concealed a laugh behind her hand as the long-standing joke in the house was that it was loud enough for the Germans to hear, so she ought to fine him according to the guidelines set out by the ARP. Of course, he'd always deny it and blame her mother which made it even funnier. When she removed her coat, she felt the cold chill on her shoulders and quietly closed the bedroom door behind her. Patting her way to the dresser, she found the lamp and switched it on to see a plate of biscuits and a glass of milk left by her mother. She was sure her mother felt sorry for her pacing around the area at all hours, especially now it was winter. Though she didn't mind her duties, she sorely wished the declaration of war had been a bad dream. Sighing heavily, she got undressed, took the glass of milk, picked a book off her shelf and got into bed.

As she lay in bed, staring at the book she held, the words kept blurring and her eyelids felt heavy with sleep. The next thing she saw was darkness. What felt like minutes later her eyelids fluttered open. Unsure how long she had been sleeping, she looked towards the blackout window wondering if she was hearing things. A far off whistling grew nearer and nearer until the sound had her so transfixed she couldn't move. Her heart pounded hard against her chest and then, a deafening explosion ensued, shaking the house like quicksand, jolting her upright. The screams of the family followed, and the thud of running feet along the landing sprung her into action.

'Nell, Nell, come on, get in the shelter,' yelled Mary.

She jumped out of bed, quickly got dressed and grabbed her helmet and coat, and ran out of the room.

'It's okay, Mam; you go down the shelter and stay there until I get back.'

She ran downstairs, threw open the front door and could almost make out Greenwald running up the front steps, holding his helmet on his head.

'Nell,' shouted Mr. Greenwald. 'I need your help love, we've been bloody bombed.'

Someone screamed from their front porch that the Germans were here.

'It's a house on Danygraig Road,' another shouted.

'Get in your fucking shelters,' Greenwald yelled and ran back down the steps. 'This isn't a drill, get to your shelters *now* or I'll fine you all a bob each.'

It seemed too have worked as people ran back indoors, much to Nell's relief as their safety was her first priority. When she looked up the street, she could hardly believe what she saw. Part of her wondered if she was still dreaming. Above the rooftops, a towering, orange flame illuminated the street and from the school, she heard the slow wail of the air-raid siren which sent a shiver down her back. She made her way to the top of the street, heading towards the house that took the direct hit. The residents, like ants, swarmed around the road where she stood. She pushed her way through a crowd of disoriented people who looked as though they were wondering what the hell was going on.

'Excuse me, ARP coming through. And please go to your shelters.'

'Nell, it's number 69, Mrs. Avery and her two kids,' Greenwald shouted above the roar of the fire.

The thought of there being kids in the house made her feel sick. She had to do something, anything, to get them out of there.

'Can I have permission to go in and find them, sir?'

'No you bloody cannot, Nell. It's far too dangerous.'

The fire engines could be heard approaching. Nell surveyed the crowd which now had formed a line, passing buckets of water to put out the flames.

'Let me,' Nell took a pail of water from a young woman who was crying and shaking and headed to the front of the line, throwing it at the flames licking the doorway. She felt her efforts were fruitless and wondered what the family could be going through. She didn't want to think the worst, not yet. 'Hey, there must be a back entrance, supposing the bomb only hit the front room? They could be out the back, sir.'

'Don't do what I think you're thinking, Miss Adams.'

She ignored him, turned, passed the bucket to a man and ran to the terraced house next door. She looked up at the front exterior, noted it was still intact and was about to burst through the front door. She didn't expect the owners to be still standing outside its gates. 'Excuse me! I need to get out to the back garden.' She pushed the man out of the way, ran through the hallway, out to the back kitchen and yanked open the door. The glare of the fire gave her enough light to see her way over the fence into the garden of the stricken house. She kicked open the back door, covered her mouth with her sleeve and ran through as smoke billowed out.

'Is there anyone here?' she coughed, now smothered by the smoke. She felt a tug on her trouser leg and looked down, under the table.

She could barely see, so got to her knees and began patting her way around until a small hand reached out and took hers. Elated, she pulled the child out and pushed the screaming kid towards the door. 'Can you hear me, miss?' she called to the woman lying unconscious. 'Go out the door!' she shouted to the frightened child when a dark figure emerged with a flashlight.

'Come on, lad.' It was Mr. Greenwald's voice.

She found the woman's hand and heaved her out from under the table when a crash, followed by falling debris from the upstairs blocked the doorway into the living area. Now she was surrounded by rubble, she realised she no longer had the woman's hand and began to pick her way through the debris to find her. She heard a small cry and started patting her way to the source, soon finding hair matted with a wet, sticky residue. It was so dark by now, and with the smoke burning her lungs she felt the rising panic and thought she wasn't going to get out of there alive. Fighting her way to breathe she pushed down the overwhelming fear, grabbed hold of her whistle and mustered the last bit of energy she had to let the rescuers know where she was. Seconds later, she felt a strong hand grab her shoulders, pulling her across the kitchen. With a firm grip on the woman's dress, she wrenched her out of the door to safety. She tumbled off the back step, falling hard onto her back. It followed a crushing sensation as the woman's limp body fell on top of her. She groaned in agony when someone, she couldn't see who, lifted the woman off her, and then pulled her to her feet. Coughing and spluttering, she staggered and the world spun around her then blanched to white. Before she hit the ground an arm swooped under her legs and lifted her up over the fence.

'I'm taking you back through next door's house,' the voice said. Too exhausted to argue, the rest of the world passed by in a haze as she was brought outside to waiting paramedics.

The world had asserted itself now and she tried to get back on her feet, arguing she had to get home to check on her family.

'No, you need medical attention first.'

She recognised the voice as Mr. Greenwald's and he wasn't going to take no for an answer. He took hold of her arm and marched her to the back of an ambulance where she sat, watching the firefighters tackle the blaze with their hose. Did this really happen? She wondered, wincing as the medic attended to a cut on her forehead. Once she had been given the all-clear, she leaped from the van and made her way up the street where a small crowd had gathered. She ordered them to their shelters but they didn't comply. Another warden came running towards her, yelling for her to get home.

'Are they okay? You know, the family from that house?' Tears ran down her face coalescing with the dirt and ash on her cheeks. The air smelled acrid, metallic, burnt. She wanted to heave. It was then she put the face to the voice. It was Ashley, Doris's son.

'We're not sure at this point, but the children are safe, Nell, all thanks to you. Greenwald said to get home you've done enough for one night.'

'Are you sure? I'm good to carry on.'

'No,' he replied, firmly. 'We'll check the communal shelters and do a check on everyone.'

'Right, okay. I think I shall,' she said, too tired to stand on her own two feet. 'Let me know how the woman is later.' Exhausted, she walked down her street where the ARP was busy directing everyone back to their homes telling them to get into the shelters as there was nothing more they could do.

'Nell, Nell, is that you?'

Hazily, she looked around for the voice and saw a hand waving her over from the back of a crowd across the street. She sensed the urgency in the voice and shouldered her way through.

'It's Bessie,' Mary's voice shook.

'What is it?' She shouted, a hard edge to her voice. An ambulance had just left the house and was heading down the street. Her heart jumped into her throat. Who could it be? Winnie was standing on the pavement, hands pressed to her face sobbing. 'Winnie, what's happened?'

'Oh, it's you, Nell. Bessie is okay, but…' Her voice cracked. 'She lost the baby. The baby is gone, Nell. Gone.'

Nell's legs gave way under her and she fell to the floor. She reached out for Winnie's arm.

'You need to get rest,' said Winnie passing her to Mary. 'Let's get back to the shelter, for now, there's nothing we can do here.'

Her dad was standing on the porch with Gran, calling them over to get inside the shelter in case any more bombs should fall.

'Jesus, Nell, what possessed you to go into a burning building?' He took her arm, helping her inside the house. He mumbled something to Mary that sounded to Nell that he was going to have a ruddy good word with Greenwald in the morning and led her through the kitchen, into the safety of the shelter. She was cold, and her mother passed her a cup of tea from the pot. It tasted as though it had been made hours ago.

'Get that down you.'

'Thanks, Mam,' she said. 'The bomb hit Mrs. Avery's. You know, the woman whose husband is a major in the army. She and the two kids were in the kitchen when it hit the front of the house. God, they're so damn lucky aren't they? Well, I mean, they were lucky they were in the kitchen when the bomb struck.'

'And you were lucky, but it's thanks to you they're still here to tell the tale,' said David taking a handkerchief from his pocket and then blowing his nose.

Nell looked up at her father who moved slightly out of the candlelight to wipe tears from his eyes.

In her mind's eye, she replayed the events over and over finding it hard to believe that it actually happened. She buried her face in her hands wishing the horrible images and the noise of the bomb would go away. Not one for being affectionate, her father pressed a hand on her knee.

'It looks like the war has started for real then.'

She looked at him between her fingers and felt warm tears splash down her face. She didn't have the energy to comment and so just gave a nod.

It was the following morning, at 6.25 when the all clear sounded, much to Nell's relief. She hadn't slept at all because the events of the night kept unfolding every time she closed her eyes. She climbed down from the top bunk, wrapped the blanket around her and poked her head out of the sack flap. The unexpected attack had left a cold, somber mood over the house, over the community, and Nell wondered how they were going to get through this. War was now as real as it ever could be. Mam and Dad were still asleep, huddled on the bottom bunk, while Gran was sitting half-asleep on her chair clutching the blanket to her chest. Once the all-clear siren had stopped, she left the shelter, recoiling at the stench of burning which lingered in the air. It was then she remembered Bessie and felt as though she had been punched in the stomach.

A half-hour later, the rest of the family made their way indoors, weary and shaken. Nell had made a pot of tea and toast which she had just placed on the table and sat down next to her mam in companionable silence. Moments later, there was a knock at the front door. David went to open it and most of the residents in the street tumbled in with a mixture of fear, shock, and anger across their faces.

'Nell?' Greenwald cried, rushing towards her. He was still dressed in his ARP get-up.

'Mr. Greenwald, I'm sorry for running off like I did, but I just acted on impulse. It won't happen again.'

She'd expected a telling off from him, and it would be no more than she deserved, disobeying orders and running into a burning building. Now she had time to think about what she did, she could hardly believe it herself. She didn't want to think of the "what ifs" right now though and pushed them to the back of her mind.

'Although I thought it was mighty silly of you, I am very proud of you, Nell. You did well getting that family out and you'll be pleased to know that Mrs. Avery is going to be okay.'

'What about children?'

'They're absolutely fine,' he assured her. 'Just a touch of smoke inhalation, but they reckon they will be out of the hospital in about a week's time.'

Winnie and Florrie pulled out a chairs around the table.

'I can't bloody believe it finally happened, can you?' said Winnie. Her hair was tucked in her blue turban. 'And there's poor Bessie, losing her child like that. Edna said she tripped out the back garden when she was rushing to the shelter.'

'Yes, poor girl, and that bloody sound as the bomb landed frightened me so much as well,' cried Florrie. 'I woke up and didn't know if I was still dreaming or not and when I realised what it could be I froze not knowing what to do. I just hope this isn't the sign of things to come.'

'Try not to get worked up,' said David. 'More than ever, as a community, we're going to have to pull together like never before.'

Nell nodded in agreement, but she had heard enough and excused herself as she wanted some time alone before she felt ready to head on over Bessie's. She had no idea what she was going to say to her and so ran upstairs to her room, crying inconsolably into the sleeves of her cardigan. The blackout blind was still up and she didn't feel like removing it. She lit a candle and began to undress. The sound of something falling on the floor got her attention, and she looked down at her feet to see Alf's whistle glinting in the candlelight.

'You must be my lucky charm,' she half-smiled, placing it on her dresser. She sat down on the end of her bed and fell asleep.

'Nell, it's eleven,' shouted her mother. She uncurled herself from under the covers, and for a few blissful seconds, the sweet dream of being whisked away by a tall, handsome stranger whirled around her head until it blurred out to the events of last night. She sat up, cursing the war and got out of bed.

Lunch was a quiet affair and mainly consisted of yesterday's scraps. Nobody felt like eating, but Nell knew she had to keep her strength up so picked up a knife and spread dripping across a slice of bread. Everyone had gone home now, much to her relief.

'Greenwald said you should have tonight off, Nell,' Mary said, as she wrapped the half-loaf of bread in brown paper. She went to put it in the pantry and wiped the table with a cloth.

'Okay, I'll tell him thanks when I see him. Is Bess home?'

As she got up from her chair, everyone looked up at her expectantly.

'Where are you off now?' asked David, chewing on toast.

'I need to see how Bessie is.'

'It was the noise of that bomb that did it, frightened her. Poor dab. She came home not long ago. She's not in a good way.'

'Where's Gran, has anyone seen her?' asked Nell.

There was a clatter of dishes hitting the sink.

'She is refusing to leave the Anderson shelter. Do me a favour love, and take her a cup of tea before you go out.'

'Will do,' she said and took the pot and poured some tea into her gran's china cup. She walked out the back door and lifted the old coal sack. 'Gran, I've brought you tea.'

The old woman had been sleeping on a chair covered with a patchwork blanket. She turned on her oil lamp and squinted up at Nell.

'Oh it's you, have the bombs finished yet?'

'Yes Gran,' she placed the cup on the wooden pallet beside the chair and made for the door.

'That's good, Nell. Scary that was, and so loud.'

She turned to face her. 'It was Gran, very scary.'

When she closed the front door, the neighbours were out on their doorsteps, reeling over what had happened. A few children who hadn't been evacuated were skipping with rope on the road, having fun, oblivious to the news. When she made her way across the road, Edna, who sat on her front step, smoking a cigarette called her over.

'How are you, love?' she asked; her hand shaking with nerves.

Nell shrugged. 'Okay, I think. I haven't heard from Francis for a while. Have you heard anything?'

She shook her head, blowing out a puff of smoke.

'I haven't, but I'm sure he's okay. Our Francis is a tough one, Nell, don't you worry.'

'I'll let you know as soon as I receive a letter, alright, Edna.'

Edna nodded and cast her eyes across the street. The kids were now grouped in a circle singing *Ring of Roses*.

She tapped lightly at Bessie's front door and in the wedge of the doorway, her mam's face appeared.

'How nice of you to come, Nell, come in. She's upstairs in her room.'

'I'm so sorry for your loss.' She hugged her and then started to climb the stairs. She wasn't really sure what she was going to say to her friend.

'Me too, love, me too. I heard what you did last night. I'm very proud of you, as are the family.'

Nell glanced over her shoulder and smiled weakly. 'Thank you, but I was only doing my job, Win. I'll go and see her now.'

'Okay, let me know if she needs anything.'

She took a deep breath and tapped at Bessie's bedroom door before entering. Light shone through the gap in the curtain, marking out Bessie's frame under the covers.

'Hey, Bess,' she whispered walking around her bed. 'I've come to see if there's anything you need?' She sat down at the foot of the bed when Bessie rolled over onto her side and opened her eyes.

'Nell,' her voice broke and the sobs came in gulps. 'Oh, Nell, my baby is gone,' she wailed, clutching at her stomach.

Nell rushed to her side and drew her in for a hug. Her shoulders shook as she cried inconsolably into Nell. There were no words, and Nell sat staring at the beam of sunlight on the wall.

'It was a *he*.' She eventually said and parted from Nell's embrace. She sat herself up and slumped back against the headboard, covering her face with her hands.

'I'm so sorry, Bess. Really I am. It was a wicked thing to happen. Nobody deserves that.'

Bessie brought her hands down and nodded.

'He would've been born about now, Nell. I would've had a son, imagine that. Me: a mammy.'

Nell reached for her hand and squeezed it tight.

'I heard you saved a family last night.'

'Oh that. It was my job,' she shrugged, not really in the mood to talk about it. At least the family was alive and nobody else she knew was hurt.

'I'm proud of you, Nell. You've done so well in the ARP. I hope they know what a treasure they've got.'

'Thanks, but I'm sure anyone would've done it. So do you want me to get you anything, a drink, perhaps?'

'No thanks. Mam gave me soup earlier.'

'Do you think you'll be alright?' she asked.

'Of course, in time, not now but I will be.' She gasped, covering a hand over her mouth. She looked up at Nell. 'Oh God, how am I going to tell William?'

'Just get yourself sorted first and then think about telling him when you're ready.'

'He said that he'd be home on leave soon, but I don't think I can wait to tell him then. I'm going to have to do it as soon as I can, Nell.'

'Okay, if you're up to it.' Nell got up and went to the dresser. She opened the drawer and took out a sheet of paper. 'Do you want to tell me what to write?'

'If you don't mind, I would really love that.'

Chapter Eleven

Please no more bombs, Nell thought as she collapsed, exhausted into the wooden canteen chair. Her head pounded with the lack of sleep and her eyelids began drooping. Having come from a quiet night at ARP duty straight to work, she became aware she still had scuffs of dirt across her cheeks from when she fell in someone's garden. But she doesn't care. All she can hear is the hiss of the tea urn and the loud chatter of the staff as it drowned out her own tired thoughts. Content in a world of her own, she stirred her tea, which she thought had now gone cold and heaped another teaspoon of sugar into the mug. How many is this now? She wondered; too tired to lift the cup to her mouth to find out. There was a poke on her arm and she flinched, dropping the teaspoon into the cup.

'Here, I think you need this.' A plate of sandwiches slid across the table under her nose. She sat up, staring at Bessie smiling and looking more like her old self. She even wore the red lipstick she bought at Woolworths before they finished.

'You look happy,' she said to Bess, and then stifled a yawn.

'There's a war on, I've got to pull myself together.' She pulled out a chair opposite her and sat down, sipping on her tea. But she needn't be brave in front of Nell as she knew she still mourned for her child. 'What happened last night? We heard bombs,' Bessie asked, now scooping a teaspoon of sugar into her own mug.

'Bombs on Jersey Marine, but there were no injuries.' Nell sighed, and then picked up a sandwich. 'So when is William due back?' she asked, wanting to distract her friend from asking more questions she wasn't up to answering. She recoiled at the taste of the national loaf, thinking she'd never get used to it and chewed it anyway surprised at how hungry she was.

The question put a genuine smile on Bessie's face. Nell looked at her curiously, knowing something else had to be going on here what with her getting dolled up to come to work. Bessie took a deep breath and then put down her cup on the saucer.

'Three days, Nell.' She squealed. 'Nell,' she beamed and patted her excitedly on her arms. 'He wants to get married before he has to sail again. Will you be my maid of honour?'

To Nell, the news felt like a break in a storm. Still chewing on her sandwich, she leaped from her chair and threw her arms around her.

'Did I hear right?' asked Joan from further down the table.

'I've got to hand it to you, Joan, you don't half have good hearing,' Bessie chuckled and flashed her ring. 'Yes, it's true girls. I'm going to be Mrs. Evans.' She announced, getting to her feet.

The other girls began cheering and gathered around her offering their congratulations.

'You know I will be your maid of honour. Oh, this is the best news we've had in forever.' Nell burst into tears.

'What's going on over here?' bellowed Mr. Jenkins, the staff supervisor.

Nell swerved around, catching him off guard. The thin, lanky young man stepped back, confusion across his face. 'Oh, Mr. Jenkins, Bessie is getting married isn't that fantastic news?'

His sour face gently relaxed, and he smiled. 'It is ladies, good luck to you, Bessie.' He shook her hand and then stood awkwardly. 'Right then, girls, I'd be very appreciative if you could get back to work.' He coughed and made his way through the crowd who now began to chuckle.

'Silly beggar,' said Patty who stood next to Bessie. 'He's no older than I am and here he is bossing us about,' she laughed. She then turned to Bessie. 'Good luck, Bess, it's exactly the news we needed to hear today.'

After all the girls had gone back to their workstations, Nell tightened the red scarf on her head and also returned to her work. She picked up the watering can and went to fill it with TNT from the barrel. She hated the smell, hated the job knowing what the bombs were going to do. Once the can was full, she returned to her shop and began filling the shell cases and putting them back on the belt. Having read what the piric acid and toluene vapour could do, she tried to be extra careful there were no grains hanging around, remembering one girl sent home from work for nausea.

'Hey,' said Bessie working opposite her. 'Come over for a drink later, we can discuss the wedding.'

'Of course, Bess, I'll be glad to get out of here today for sure.'

'So will I, but hey, where am I going to get a wedding dress on these bloody clothing rations? It didn't occur to me until now.'

'We'll sort it, don't worry,' she said, trying to focus on filling the shell. It was then that the sound of crashing metal could be heard. The girls on the factory floor hushed. Everyone looked up with startled faces as they searched for the source. It was then the piercing screams of a woman echoed around the factory striking fear through Nell. *What poor bugger has been hurt this time?* Amid the hustle and panic, she saw Patty leaning over her workstation covering her face with her bloodied hands.

'Patty, are you alright?' she yelled, unable to tend to her with an open shell full of explosives. She looked over at the office. The door was open ajar and then it flung open wide as the people inside heard the commotion. 'We need help over here,' she yelled to Mr. Lovett as the girls rushed to her aid.

She looked on as Mr. Lovett, the manager raced towards Patty whose hair had been tangled by her machine. Nell saw the blood and looked away, hoping it wasn't as bad as it appeared. The janitor came to Lovett's aid, helping him carefully untangle Patty's hair, but so many had gathered around them that Nell couldn't see her when they rushed her to the office, still screaming.

'Poor woman, I hope she's going to be alright,' she shouted over to Bessie.

Caitlin, who worked to the side of Nell, came back to her station, wiping her brow with her scarf.

'I don't think I've seen that much blood, not even on my monthlies.'

'Do you think she'll be alright to come back to work?'

Caitlin shrugged her shoulders. 'She's going to need a bucket full of stitches. The blood was pissing out of her head.'

Bess made a face as though she was about to be sick.

'Good job you're not ARP, is it, Bess?' Nell said.

'It is, actually. Excuse me a minute, girls. I need a glass of water.'

Caitlin and Nell laughed as they watched her skip over the blood trail leading to the office.

'Just get on with your work, girls. It's all been taking care of,' yelled Mr. Lovett, the suave, handsome manager as he came marching up the aisle, clipboard in hand. 'Geraldine is taking care of her. She'll be fine, I promise you.'

Nell rolled her eyes at him. She didn't like him much. Another girl was telling her he'd often chat up the girls, trying to get them to go on a date with him. One time he'd become nasty when one of them refused.

'How many more will have to go through this, eh?' she said to nobody in particular as she watched the janitor mop up the blood.

'God knows, Nell. If it wasn't for the money, I'd walk out of here.' Caitlin replied.

Lovett looked over Caitlin's shoulder as she filled the shell. Caitlin grimaced, eyes on Nell. 'I can't stand him,' she mouthed.

'I know,' Nell whispered, trying not to laugh when she poked her tongue out at him as he walked over towards Nell.

'You're doing a good job, ladies,' he leaned over Nell's shoulder. His breath stank of cigarettes.

'Oh he's a looker, isn't he Nell?' Bessie laughed, returning to her station. She turned, looking at his backside as he walked down the factory.

'You're so naughty, Bess,' she laughed. 'And no, he's just a prick if you ask me.'

The girls all laughed, leaving a confused looking Bess wondering what had happened.

At the end of the shift, Nell waited in line to get searched before she could change to go home to a well-deserved two days off. The skin on her arm tingled, and needing to scratch it she pulled up her sleeve.

'Are you alright?' asked Caitlin, taking her arm. 'Just as I thought, Nell, it looks like a skin rash due to the chemicals.'

'It's not going to affect my work, is it?'

'We'll see how it goes. I do think you should get it checked out by a doctor though.'

'I can't really afford to lose this job,' she protested even though she hated every minute of it.

'You may not, but even if you do it won't be such a loss. This place stinks, love. You could do better with your qualifications. The likes of us have no chance.'

After an exhausting twenty hours, Nell pushed the front door open to the ghastly smell of fish. Since meat had been rationed, her father had taken up fishing again, using her brothers' rods. She winced and followed the stink into the kitchen, pulling off her coat as she did so. 'Hello?' She tossed her coat on the kitchen unit.

'Everything alright, Nell?' said Mary, plating up boiled potatoes.

David sat at the table tucking into his food and looked up when Nell pulled out a chair. 'You look tired, Nell. No ARP tonight is there?'

'No, thankfully,' she sat down heavily, glad to take the weight off her feet.

'Here you go, love, get this down you. Must be better than that canteen food, I bet,' her mother said, putting a plate in front of her. 'There's plenty of fish for the next few days, thanks to Dad. We won't starve yet.'

She recoiled at the sight of the fish on the plate, picked up the fork, and proceeded to move it away from the potatoes.

'So have you heard the news, Mam?' she asked, surprised her mam hadn't already mentioned it as news traveled fast in the street.

'What's that?'

'Bessie is getting married as soon as William comes home. Didn't you know?'

'She's getting married?' her mum put down her fork and clasped her hands together. 'Is she really? Oh, I do love a wedding. I'll have to call over to Winnie's later, see if she wants a hand with anything.'

'Yeah Mam,' she smiled, trying her best to enjoy her food despite the taste of fish that had come into contact with her boiled potatoes. She was about to mention her rash and that she was thinking of going back into admin work when she thought she heard the drone of a plane. She put down her fork and looked up at the kitchen window. This can't be happening, she thought and then stood up. 'Do you hear that, Mam?' she asked.

'What's that?' asked her dad, his fork mid-way to his mouth.

'I hear it, too,' Mam replied, her voice now shaky.

Nell went to the back door, flung it open and stepped outside looking up at the sky. 'It can't be a raid. The bloody air-raid siren hasn't gone off.'

'Get to the shelter,' shouted David, rushing out of the house.

The family stood by the fence, looking directly at the ocean when a German plane flew unevenly overhead leaving a trail of black clouds swirling like ribbons in the sky across the expanse of the docks. Shaken, Nell pulled her mother in close as two spitfires wildly chased after it. The air-raid signal finally went off, and Nell saw her neighbours dash across their gardens to the safety of their shelters. Yet, Nell couldn't move from where she stood, she had to know what happened, see it with her own eyes no matter how dangerous it was.

'Looks like our boys got it,' yelled Dad, excitedly.

Nell couldn't help but feel sorry for the pilot.

'No matter which way you look at it, Dad, the pilot was still human. Probably has a family back home and now they'll never know where he is.'

'It's just a Jerry, Nell...'

'No,' she said, her voice full of emotion, 'He's just doing a job like our boys are.' She blinked away the tears.

They watched on with terror as the German plane made a nosedive straight into the ocean and the two Spitfires did a sharp turn, glittering like stars in the weak sunshine. She thought about Alf risking his life like this every day and thought she should write him a letter to remind him how much she appreciated and loved him.

'Bloody hell,' her mother pressed a hand to her chest. 'That was so scary, but exciting at the same time. I'm not sure how I'm supposed to feel, to be honest. Eh, David, grab the teapot, love. Best we get in the shelter before Greenwald says anything.'

'Come on, Nell,' her Dad said, tugging at her arm.

'I'm sorry, Dad, I'm just so very tired.'

'I know you are, Nell. You're doing far too much. Sometimes I think you're forgetting you're only human, too.'

Once she got into the shelter, she sat down on the bottom bunk and as soon as her head hit the pillow, she fell into a deep sleep.

After weeks of hearing about the RAF defending the British Isles, and having assurance from her brother that he was safe, Nell walked into Tom's grocers on her way home from the factory to find him and a few others gathered around the radio. About to say hello to everyone, Tom pressed a finger to his lip and then pointed to the radio. She understood it must be important, and so walked towards the counter where three other women stood, wondering what news had them all stony-faced.

It was then she heard the terrible news that London had received heavy bombing overnight. Once the report ended, everyone stood around in stunned silence. It was then an elderly woman standing next to Nell almost collapsed with shock.

Nell and another woman rushed to her aid.

'Are you alright?' Nell asked. Tom came rushing around his counter with a glass of water and handed it to Nell.

Nell pressed it against the woman's lips, and slowly she came around.

'How are you feeling?'

The woman began crying. 'My daughter lives in central London,' her voice shook. 'I hope nothing has happened to her.'

Nell felt choked with emotion. 'I'm sure that won't be the case. Would you like me to walk you home?'

The woman nodded, and Nell helped her to her feet.

'Here are your groceries, Mrs. Tanner,' said Tom. 'Try not to worry yourself now.' He gave Nell a concerned look. 'Take her home, love and I'll get your mam's order ready for you when you come back.'

'Of course I will, Tom.' She picked up the woman's basket and walked her towards the door. 'Where do you live, Mrs. Tanner?' she asked.

'Margaret Street. My son is the local vicar, you know.'

'Oh that's wonderful,' she replied, helping her across the road. The woman was still in shock when she reached her front door.

Nell was about to knock when the door opened.

'Mam, what happened?' When he didn't get a response from his mother, Rev. Tanner looked at Nell for an answer.

'She heard about the bombings in London, Mr. Tanner. She thinks your sister may be... you know.' Nell shrugged as Mrs. Tanner walked into the house.

Rev. Tanner sighed deeply. 'I'm really sorry for the bother she's caused, you see, my sister passed away years ago. She was never in London. Sometimes Mam gets confused.'

'Oh I'm so sorry to hear that. And it's no bother. It's all part of my job,' she pointed to her ARP helmet.

'You're Nell aren't you? Mary's daughter?' he enquired.

'That's right.'

'Wait there one moment,' he went back inside the house. 'I told your mam I had a dress belonging to my mother she no longer wears and she said that you may like it.' He handed her a red gown.

'Oh, Reverend, sir, it's lovely. Are you sure about this?'

'Indeed. Please, take it and enjoy.'

Since Alf had told her she must celebrate Christmas in his absence, when the first specks of snow arrived that November morning she rushed to her desk and pulled out sheets of paper she had been saving and spent the next few hours telling Francis and her brothers everything that had happened and the characters she had met. She ended the letter saying that she hoped the war would be over soon.

PART THREE
1941

Chapter Twelve

The snow fell in droves, and the sharp Arctic cold clung to the air like an iron grip. Nell shivered and pulled the woolen blanket tightly around her shoulders. For the past hour, she'd been sitting at her desk, staring blankly into the flame of the flickering candle. As much as she wanted to write her letter to Sidney, she couldn't articulate her jumbled thoughts into words, hence her several attempts crumpled into balls thrown in her wastebasket. Unsure if she should be angry or happy or maybe both, she picked up Sidney's last letter and choked back the tears. At the time of writing, he had been waiting to board another ship after the one he was sailing on sunk in the Atlantic. The news came as a terrible shock to Nell as she felt as though she'd been reliving her awful nightmares again.

'Silly man,' she huffed, happy he was alive but annoyed he had waited until now to write to her. He'd always been over-protective of her but she didn't need the war wrapped in cotton wool so the blow wouldn't hurt. Did he not realise she was a different Nell from when he had left? Had he not paid enough attention to the letters she had written him? She folded his letter and tucked it back in the envelope, thinking she'd reply another time when her head was clearer. The last thing she needed from her was an angry letter after all he had suffered.

Fed up of feeling the cold, she blew out her candle and made her way downstairs, into the living room so she'd be nearer to the roaring coal fire. As usual, her father was sitting in his armchair that was tucked away in the corner, reading out the war news to anyone who was interested. Nell noticed Gran asleep on the sofa and inwardly groaned at the prospect of another boring evening. She switched on the radio and picked up her novel from the coffee table.

'Don't you have ARP work tonight?' he asked.

'Later on, Dad,' she sat down on the sofa, next to Gran.

'Well, just make sure you get something warm in your belly before you venture out.' He straightened out his paper. 'Almost caught hyperthermia getting wood in for the fire,' he clicked his tongue.

Her father was not the sentimental type, and whenever he made a thoughtful comment she could almost feel his awkwardness. It made her smile, anyway. He began to scan the paper for something to talk about, to change the subject of the conversation.

'I really don't want another evening sitting in that bloody tin out the back,' said Mary, getting up from her chair. 'Anyone for a hot drink?' she asked.

'Please,' Nell said.

'Nell?' Mam hollered from the back kitchen. 'I was thinking how lovely a wedding will be in the snow, what do you think?'

'I think unless she finds a dress in the next couple of days there won't be a wedding.' She picked up the poker and then prodded the wood. She didn't have much faith in Bess finding anything decent in time and since her mother never married, she couldn't have hers.

'Nell,' her mam poked her head around the kitchen door. 'What time do you have to leave tonight?'

Nell looked up at the clock on the mantel that had just struck seven thirty.

'I'll be leaving in another hour. I'm on duty in town tonight.'

'Well, you take care, alright, and wrap up warm. Here,' she opened the drawer in the sideboard behind the sofa and handed her a green woolen scarf. 'I made this for you.' She said proudly.

Nell took the lime green bundle and loosened it. 'It's perfect, Mam, thank you.' She got up from the sofa and gave her mother a kiss.

'I'm going to need this tonight. Anyway, I'll best be getting ready. I'll have my tea before I go.'

It was pitch black when she left the house. She thought she should have left earlier because the snow started to fall again. The pavement felt slick beneath her feet, so she reached for the garden walls to guide her safely down the street. Once her eyes adjusted to the darkness, she felt a little calmer and relished watching the snowflakes fall in the moonlight that illuminated the path ahead of her. She tucked her hands into her jacket pockets and looked up at the clear sky with stars twinkling against the inky backdrop. As she thought back to the first attack on the area, she remembered how the sky was similar to that of this evening. She silently hoped it would be trouble-free and muttered a wish under her breath for protection. When she arrived at the headquarters at the back room of an old shop, a male voice from the shadows called out her name.

'Nice night, isn't it Nell?' It was then Nell could smell cigarette smoke and realized it was Mr. Greenwald.

'Lovely, except for the cold,' she said, and pushed open the door.

When she walked into the small back room, the atmosphere was already electric with activity. Multiple conversations were going on all at once, with directions and orders being given. Edward stood by a chalkboard with a map drawn of the streets. He pointed to the board and said something to a fair-headed woman in an ARP uniform. When he had finished, he turned and saw Nell.

'Evening, Nell,' he said, his brow furrowed.

'Is there something wrong?' she asked, pulling out a chair.

'We think there's a high probability of an attack tonight, so be prepared,' he sighed, picking up the teapot on the desk in front of him. He poured Nell a cup of tea. 'Here, get this in you, you must be cold.'

'Thanks, Edward, I'm bloody freezing.' She took the mug of hot tea and looked up at the board. 'Where are we headed tonight then?'

'We'll patrol around St Mary's and Temple Street, so take the first-aid-kit, would you, Nell? I'll keep you company tonight if that's alright.'

She had walked the same route around town for what seemed like forever, chatting to Edward about the film she saw at the theatre on her day off, not that he was paying much attention. He wasn't the romantic type, preferring the Wild West films he'd frequent on his own. They had just rounded the cathedral wall and were heading towards the Woolworths building when Edward stopped walking, turned abruptly towards Nell and asked her to hush. Instinctively, Nell knew something was amiss and immediately fell silent. The only thing she could hear was her heart pounding madly in her ears and the tree leaves rustling from behind her. It was then what sounded like a swarm of insects heading towards them could be heard. Nell was quick enough to realise it was the low drones of the Luftwaffe and shot a look at Edward who was staring up at the sky. His eyes shone from the moonlight above the silhouette of St Mary's spire. She followed his gaze to where the beams of the searchlights crossed over and saw a horde of German planes gliding across the sky.

'This is it, Nell, be prepared, be vigilant and good luck.' He urged her on towards Wind Street. 'We'll get a better view from up here, so if we're needed we'll know where to go,' he said as a clatter of shells dropped from the sky, hitting the ground like a thousand tin cans.

The ghostly wailings of the alarms sounded as they ran side by side to the top of the road. She felt a jab on her back and swung around. Edward pointed to the sky across the bay. Her mouth slackened, she could hardly believe what she was seeing.

'It's like they've set the sky on fire,' she cried, unable to take her eyes off it. But was it the sky she was looking at? She couldn't tell anymore as fires lit, one by one, across the city's rooftops, melding with the orange of the sky. Edward swung her towards him, cupping her face.

'Snap out of it, Nell. I think we need to get away from here. Try and get to the shelter and remember what you've been taught.'

She nodded, slightly shaking and was about to make a dash for the communal shelter when a piercing whistle of a bomb that got louder, erupted behind them. The earth shook beneath their feet, lifting them off the ground. Nell catapulted in the air, falling face-forward onto the pavement. She felt the hard concrete connect to her head, followed by a pain she had never experienced in her life. For a few seconds, everything went black, then, gradually she roused awake to the smattering of shells and the drones of the aircraft overhead. She clutched her ears, squeezing her eyes shut tight as three more loud explosions ensued. It was then she remembered Edward. She coughed and spat as grit, dirt, and smoke filled her mouth and senses.

'Edward, are you alright?' she screamed. Her head span as she pushed herself from the now cracked pavement, then Edward's voice, though tinny, gave her the reassurance that he was okay.

Nell, though dizzy staggered to her feet and cautiously touched her forehead smeared with blood. She felt as though she was about to vomit, and could feel the burn at the back of her throat.

'How many is that?' Edward shouted.

How many is what? She thought, confused. 'How many what?' There was no reply, which worried her. 'Edward, can you hear me?'

'Bombs. How many came down in that last batch? Can you hear me, Nell?'

'I think I counted five.' She looked up at the roof of the Woolworths building that was ablaze. Edward emerged from a cloud of smoke and limped towards her.

'There should've been six. They come in sixes.' From the smoke, he reached out a hand to her, pulling her in close. He had a trickle of blood running down his face that he wiped away. Nell swayed on her feet. She knew from training that out there somewhere was one unexploded bomb and it was her duty to find it to put it out. Through the confusion, she heard cries and yelling and turned sharply. A man shouted over at them from across the road but she couldn't make out where he was in the shroud of smoke and dirt.

'They're trapped in the cellar of the pub,' he shouted. 'Please, follow me.'

'I'm coming,' she coughed and spluttered again and looked over her shoulder for Edward, but he wasn't there. 'Edward?' She looked down and saw that he had now collapsed. She raced towards him.

'I can't hear,' he murmured, pointing to his bleeding ears.

She knelt down, took hold of his face and looked him in the eyes. 'I need to get you to safety, do you understand?'

He blinked, seemingly confused. She then shouted by his ear. 'I have to go and help some people, so I'm going to lift you to the curb until I can get someone to take a look at you.'

He searched her face for a moment then nodded that he understood. She helped him to his feet and walked him to the curb, where he slumped down in a heap, burying his face in his hands. 'I won't be long, I promise.'

She turned to the man across the cracked surface. 'I'm coming.' She held her tin hat as she bolted across the road.

'Take me to them.'

'It's the cellar of the Adam and Eve,' he said. 'They were all having a pint when the sirens sounded.'

They ran up the street, narrowly missing falling debris that smashed to the ground. She stopped, pulled the man back as bricks continually fell, landing by his feet. The acrid smell engulfed her senses, bringing the feeling of nausea once again.

'It's best if we cross over,' she said, cowering down.

They ran through a street of burning buildings, using the light of the fires to guide their way to a safe path to the pub, but once they had got there, the pub and three other buildings next to it were already ablaze. Despite her fire training, Nell knew this was beyond her and a bucket and shifted her focus to the people trapped inside the cellar.

'The cellar's under here,' the man said, standing next to a pile of rubble.

'Then give me a hand to shift this lot,' she shouted, panic rising. 'They could suffocate in there.' She thought she was about to suffocate too, with the smoke, but got on with it regardless.

'I think this is too much for two people. They haven't got a hope in hell.'

'There's always hope, now come on, dig. We can't give up now.'

Nell frantically picked up stones and bricks, chucking them behind her. In the distance, she heard the sound of emergency vehicles getting closer. Clawing her way through the rubble, she felt the heat intensify on her face and body and thought she was about to pass out. There didn't seem to be an end to the pile of junk in front of her and every second counted for the poor people trapped. She was finding it hard to breathe and briefly stopped, trying to catch her breath, but it was so damn hard with the smoke billowing around her. Sweat, coalesced with blood trickled down her face and, leaning forward over the mound she wiped it away with her aching arm and then returned to the job at hand. She didn't realise that a fire engine had arrived on the scene until a cool spray of water washed over her as they began tackling the blaze. A swarm of wardens, civilians, and firefighters joined them in tossing the rubble.

'What's happening here?' said a man, heaving a brick to the side.

'There are people trapped under here. We need to hurry.'

Soon they had cleared enough to see part of the door. Nell fell to her knees beside it yanking it to open. 'It's jammed.'

Two men raced to help her. Together they heaved it open and stepped back. There were no calls for help, nothing. Nell, still gasping for breath shot a painful, almost pleading look to the firefighter standing next to her. He knelt beside the hole in the ground.

'Is everyone okay?' he shouted.

'Yes, almost…' came the weak reply.

'I hear them, they're okay. It's a bloody miracle.' Nell cried, excitedly. 'How many are you?' she asked.

'Six of us,' said a man. 'Rob hurt his leg though, he can't walk.'

'I'm coming down.'

'No,' said the fireman, pulling her back. 'You've done your bit, let us.'

'Are you sure?'

'Very sure, miss, now step aside.'

Nell stepped back from the scene, exhausted. It was then she remembered Edward and began running back down the road.

'Wait, hold up,' she yelled to another warden about to dash from the scene, having been called to help another. 'I need you to send someone to my friend, he's an ARP and is sitting on the curb opposite the castle. His name is Edward.'

'Don't worry, we'll sort him out if he hasn't been found already.' He assured her. 'Come and give me a hand to put out the bomb on top of Woolworths would you?'

It was daybreak when the all-clear sounded and Nell made her way back to the headquarters eager to see if they had found Edward. That's if the headquarters was still standing. 'Edward, are you here?' she bellowed as she walked into the office.

'I'm here Nell. I can just about hear you, but I'm alright. Are you okay?'

Nell shrugged her shoulders and slumped down on a wooden chair in the office, sipping on a cold cup of tea that had been left. The commotion going on around her asserted itself, and she snapped herself out of thoughts of the things she'd just witnessed.

'Nell, you ought to go home, love,' said Edward limping into the office.

'I'll be fine, Ed…' she said, not really wanting to complain about her aching muscles after everything she had seen tonight. 'Why haven't you gone home?'

He strained to hear her. 'I couldn't leave, Nell. I heard you did good work tonight but you really need some rest. Come back when you've had a kip.'

She nodded. 'I'm not sure if sleep will happen so easily, Ed, but I'll go and check on my family and be back…'

'Go. We know where you live if we need you,' he replied.

As the events of the night continued to unfold in her head, she left the office in silence and stepped out into a cool breeze coming over from the seafront. The horizon was still hazy with smoke and to the right the sun began to rise in the east, reminding her how thankful she was that she had survived another day.

Her thoughts shifted to her family as she walked through the town, but when she looked up there was no town, just an apocalyptic scene before her like she had read in a novel. All that remained of her beloved Swansea was its skeleton. Smoke billowed from corpses of buildings and grey ash spilled everywhere, in the air and on her clothes. She passed a pile of charred rubble lying before her and averted her eyes to the castle. She continued along the path, passing a group of people carrying bundles of belongings. A young child wailed by its mother's legs which she did her best to comfort with an arm gripped tightly around its shoulders. Nell's stomach lurched and she hung her head low as they passed her. Nell figured they had lost their homes in the attack and she wasn't even sure if she had a home to go to, either. Warm tears rolled down her cheeks as she plodded along to the bridge to the other side of town.

'Hey, miss.' A male voice shouted.

She wasn't sure if she actually heard it at first, or whether it was an echo of last night. She looked up and saw an old man sitting on a crumbling wall on the opposite side of the road. His jacket was torn, and he was missing a shoe.

'What is it?' she shouted but thought it was best to check him over.

The man opened his mouth to speak but words failed him. As Nell approached, she saw a bloody gash on his left temple. The blood, now dried, looked like claw marks down his face. There was another fresh cut across his cheek.

'You're hurt,' she cried, rushing to his side. She reached into her jacket pocket for something, anything, to put pressure on the wound. Relieved to find a piece of cloth from the first aid bag she no longer had, she reached to press it against the wound. He shook his head and moved her hand away. 'My wife,' his voice cracked with emotion. 'She's gone, miss.' He looked at the sky, his eyes glassy with tears.

Nell couldn't hold her feelings in any longer and fell to her knees, cupping her hands over her face.

'I suppose she's a lot happier now,' he said and tapped her on the shoulder. 'No need to cry, miss.'

She lifted her head, wiped her tears with her scarf and pulled herself together, 'I'm so very sorry,' she said and got to her feet. 'You need medical attention, sir.' She heard sirens wailing and looked up across the bridge at an ambulance heading her way. She ran out onto the road and flagged them down. 'He needs help,' she cried as they came to an abrupt stop. A man jumped out of the van and rushed over to the old man.

'Good work, miss, we'll take over from here,' he said to Nell.

'No problem,' she replied, exhausted. She gave the man her scarf which he was thankful for, wished him luck and continued on her way across the bridge, giving special thought to her family. As she reached the top of the steep road in Port Tennant, she heard a woman shouting and when she looked around for the source, she saw a young woman standing by the roadside beckoning her over.

'Is everything alright?' Nell panicked thinking there was something wrong with the crying child she had on her hip but was relieved when she got closer and saw it was alright.

'A lad was saying that a Jerry fell out of a plane and landed in a field on the hill,' she cried, bouncing the child up and down to pacify it. 'I'm not so sure myself, you know what kids are like.'

She wasn't sure if she should go on her own or wait and call for Greenwald but seeing how distressed the woman looked, Nell thought she'd go and check it out, it was part of her duty. Besides, there was a good chance it would turn out to be nothing.

'I'll go and see,' Nell said and made her way up the street.

'You take care, miss,' the woman shouted after her.

She hurried to the top of the road, squeezed her way through a gate at the bottom of the hill and walked along the rocky path bordered with trees dusted with frost. So far, she hadn't seen anything unusual and wondered if the recent bombings had everybody in such a panic they were thinking they were seeing German's fall from the sky. It wouldn't be the first time she had heard such nonsense. Kids have wonderful imaginations, as she knew well. It wasn't that many years ago the hill had once been *her* playground. She recounted the long hot summers she spent here having her own adventures along with her brothers. When she came to the end of the path, she looked down the embankment where the trees stretched along the back of the houses. There was nothing. She felt mildly disappointed and was about to head back down the path to go home when she saw something white dangling from a tree. She froze and there was a quickening of her breath as she tried to make a decision on what to do. What if it was a German parachute? And what if there was someone tangled in it? She decided to investigate. The nearer she got, the more the knot in her stomach tightened. It was then she saw the pink coloured flesh of a hand followed by the body of a man swaying behind the bulge of the parachute. She looked back, thinking she really ought to run home and call for help but she had the strangest urge to get a better look at the man she hoped was dead. She reached into her pocket, pulled out her pocket knife and flipped it open. His index finger twitched, startling her. She jumped back, her legs now like jelly. She waved the knife around in front of her and gasped when she saw the German uniform. She quickly stepped further back. Gripping the pocket knife she took a tentative step forward and reached out her other hand to the exposed part of his neck to check his pulse. If he should suddenly move, she felt confident she could plunge the knife into his body. After all, she knew it was her life or his. Tears rolled down her cheeks as she touched his cool skin. Surprised to feel a faint pulse, she moved him around to face her. He was young, barely twenty, with dark blonde hair.

She wasn't sure what to do. He didn't seem like he was in a position to be a threat to her and seeing his face she didn't think she could kill him now either, but she still held the knife firmly above his chest to show, if he did rouse awake, she had the upper hand. She reached on tiptoe and quickly slashed the parachute strings, freeing him to the ground. He fell with a thump, lying face down.

Nell stepped back. Her breath, like a cloud, fanned around her face. Where she ought to have seen his breath, there was nothing. Thoughts swirled around her head. How foolish had she been, coming here on her own? Suddenly, there was a faint wisp of breath melding with the cold morning air.

'Tasche,' he whispered.

She leaned closer, thinking she heard something.

'What did you say?' she replied, her voice trembling as she slowly knelt down beside him. The parachute was now splayed to the side of him. She had no idea what he was trying to say but knew he was in a bad way and she was safe. She rolled him over. His lashes were sprayed with blood from the cut on his head and his eyes flickered open. Bright blue eyes looked straight into hers. He pointed a finger at his torn jacket pocket and understanding he wanted her to retrieve something. She reached out her hand, gently brushing his. He was shaking, whether from the cold or… what if it was trick? she thought and pulled back.

'Don't you mess me about, okay, or I will kill you,' she said, before stopping herself short. She lifted the flap of the pocket with her finger, feeling the sharp edge of paper and pulled it out.

'This?' she held it up to his face so he could see.

'Familie, please,' his voice rasped.

She strained to hear him but understood the subtleness of the situation unfolding before her eyes. The man was now dying and he was asking her to perform his last wish.

'You want me to give this to your family?'

For a brief moment his desperate, almost pleading eyes locked on hers. They looked scared and were not of the monster she thought she'd see. It was then he began to choke. His body twitched and his eyes rolled to the back of his head. Nell dropped the pocket knife which fell with a thud on the ground and she covered her mouth with her hand, shaking and crying. She looked at the folded paper in her hand and for reasons she couldn't fathom at that moment, she tucked it inside her breast pocket.

She got to her feet, gathered the parachute into a bundle and was about to run home when she heard someone shouting her name over and over.

'Nell,' a voice hailed from behind. 'Nell, step away from him…'

She turned sharply to see Greenwald and four other men in khaki running down the bank waving rifles. While the others went to check on the German, Mr. Greenwald came marching towards her, panic-stricken.

'Oh, Mr. Greenwald,' she sobbed as he got close. 'It's a German. They were right, it was a bloody German and he just went and died on me.'

'Good gracious, Nell, what were you thinking, coming up here on your own? Do you know how many bombs were dropped up here?' he said, out of concern for her safety. 'Come here,' He wrapped an arm around her. Nell could feel him shaking. She buried her face in his chest now fully understanding what may have happened to her.

'I didn't think it was true,' she lifted her head. 'You know what kids are like. They tell lies all the time.'

'You did alright, Nell but don't ever come on your own again, you hear me?'

She nodded.

'Were you on duty in town last night with Ed?' he asked.

'Yes. What a bloody mess they caused. I was just on my way home to check on my family.'

'They're alright. Is Ed okay?'

'Yes, we're fine. We had to put out a lot of bombs and rescue a bunch of men trapped in a cellar. So what are you going to do with him?' She asked, turning to face the wardens as they lifted off the German airman off the ground.

'Don't you worry about that,' Greenwald said noticing the parachute she had dropped beside her feet.

Half expecting him to give her a warning or at the very worst take it from her, he fastened his eyes on her.

'Nell, run along home, love. It's been a long bloomin' night for us all.'

She picked up the parachute, slung it over her shoulder and then walked across the hill, towards home in stunned silence. Once she got to the top of her road, she sighed with relief to see the area intact and rushed down the street to her house.

'Hello?' She dropped the parachute on the floor in the hallway and removed her coat, throwing it on the stairs. She looked into the rooms, happy to see everything was as she left it, but where was everyone? Worried, she dashed out to the back garden, hoping they were still asleep in the Anderson shelter.

'Mam?' she yelled.

The flap lifted, and Mary's head poked out. 'Here, Nell. Thank the heavens you're alright,' she cried, getting out and pulling her daughter in for a hug.

'Oh Mam, it was the worst,' she sobbed.

'We heard, Nell. I couldn't sleep for worrying about you.'

Nell pulled herself away from her mother's embrace. The face of the dead German flashed before her eyes and she looked away, towards the docks. She had to pull herself together, for everyone's sake.

'The all-clear sounded ages ago, why were you still in there?' she asked.

'Nan wouldn't come out.' She opened the flap. 'Mam, I've got to make Nell something to eat,' she said and then took Nell's arm. 'I've been worried sick about you. Dare I ask what town looks like?'

Nell paused for a moment to think, but there were no words to describe the sheer scale of devastation she saw.

'What town?'

There was nothing else she could say.

Chapter Thirteen

Exhausted, Nell picked up her coat and parachute in the hallway and walked upstairs to her room. She dumped them on her bed and then went across the hallway to the bathroom. She closed the bathroom door and locked it. Standing in front of the mirror, she pressed a trembling hand to her face that was blackened with dirt, and quietly sobbed as she dropped to the floor in a crumpled heap. Her entire body ached. There was no respite from the physical pain or the mental anguish that was crushing her skull. Flashes of images, the cries of people and the utter devastation she had witnessed flooded her at once and all she wanted was for it to go away like a bad nightmare.

She crawled across the linoleum floor and pulled herself up to sit on the edge of the bath. While she undid the buttons on her blouse, she used her free hand to turn on the tap and watched it fill to the black line her father had painted on. They were only allowed three inches of water these days, so it was impossible to keep clean when you were washing in your own filth. She allowed it to fill a few inches more and then dipped her hand in to check the temperature. Hurt followed guilt, and it didn't feel right, somehow, that she should be here, safe, when there was devastation all around her. She wriggled herself out of her jacket and trousers and kicked them aside, never wanting to see them again. The face of the German airman tagged across her mind for the millionth time since she got home, and as she slipped into the lukewarm water, a gut-wrenching sob escaped her lips. When she felt she couldn't cry anymore, she sat back against the cool tub and took a sponge and thin bar of Pears soap, and began to rub it ferociously against her skin, as if removing the dirt would somehow make the last twenty-four hours disappear.

'Nell?'

She stopped scrubbing her skin and looked up at the door. She could see her mother's outline standing behind the frosted glass.

'What?'

'I'm needed at the Community Centre, love. We're taking clothes and blankets to the people who have been bombed out. Are you alright? Do you want to talk about it?'

'No Mam, I don't want to talk about it, thanks. You go. I'll be fine.'

'Okay, I'll talk to you later then.'

'I'm at work tomorrow, Mam, so I'll see you after ARP duty.'

'You're off again?'

'There's a war on, Mam.'

She heard her mother mumble something under her breath. 'You're doing far too much, Nell.'

'Not enough it feels. See you later.'

'Take care. I'll see you later and before I forget, there's food in the oven for you. I made it before the raid went so you will have to reheat.'

'Thanks, Mam,' she yelled back, trying desperately to keep it together. The old girl didn't need her troubles to contend with. She heard her mother's footsteps going down the stairs, reached for the towel on the basin, wrapped it around her and got out of the bath thinking she'd pay Bessie a visit.

Now dressed, she bundled up the parachute and ran downstairs and out of the house. Despite the sick feeling in her stomach that the parachute gave her, she realized that she was in desperate times. She looked down at it and promised she would find his family and pass on the letter. German or not, she had seen a young man die today and nobody deserved to die alone. She went to tap on the pane of glass on Bessie's door but it was already open ajar, so she walked on through.

'Bess?'

'I'm in the kitchen, Nell.'

Bess was kneading dough on the large wooden table in the kitchen. Flour fanned out all around her, her hair, on her face, and across the floor.

'I have your wedding dress.' Nell dumped the parachute on the table and walked to the sink to fill up the kettle. She knew Bess would ask where she had got it and she wasn't sure if she wanted to answer her questions. The events of the night played around her head on a loop and the last thing she felt like talking about was finding a dying German on Kilvey Hill.

Bess wiped her hands on her apron and then looked up expectantly at Nell.

'Nell, how did you get this?' she gasped and covered her mouth. 'Were you out in that bombing last night? Is that where you got it from?'

Nell put the kettle on the stove. 'Best not to ask, but I say with your dressmaking skills we could make something out of it, what do you say?'

'I say yes please,' she squealed and did a little dance. She was about to pick it up but Nell swooped in and hit her hand out of the way.

'No, you'll get it covered in flour.' She lifted it off the table and draped it over the back of a chair. 'Do you need some help? I need something to take my mind off a few things.'

Bessie's face quickly changed from joy to concern.

'Is there something bothering you, Nell? I heard town was flattened and that there's hardly a thing left standing. And don't talk about the bombs, it was never bloody ending, wasn't it? It was so scary down that shelter, Nell, I don't know how you managed outside,' she cried and grabbed a tea-towel from the counter to wipe away her tears.

'Me? Oh, I'm fine, girl. Make us a cocoa if there's any left and I'll put this somewhere safe.' Nell turned to head upstairs, pushing back the images of the German airman lying on the ground.

' But you were on duty last night…'

Nell stopped in the doorway and turned around hoping Bess knew her well enough to know when she didn't want to talk. All the talking in the world wouldn't help her right now. She shrugged her shoulders. 'So were others. We go forward, Bess, clean up the mess, win the war and get our lives back on track.' If only it was that simple she thought, and headed upstairs to Bess's room where she lay the parachute out on the bed. When she went downstairs, she sat down and noticed an envelope poking out of Bessie's pocket on her apron. Usually, Bessie was the first to share news from abroad, so this was not like her at all.

'You've got a letter, I see?'

'Yeah,' she touched it but pulled back. 'I haven't opened it yet. It'll be the first letter I've had since I wrote to him about the baby.'

With all that had gone on lately, she felt bad for forgetting that Bess was having a rough time too. 'Oh, I'm sorry, Bess, I didn't think.'

'Don't be a silly bugger. Sooner or later I've got to get on with things. May as well start now, eh?' She took a deep breath, put the dough to the side and pulled two cups from the cupboard. 'How about we read it together?'

The kettle whistled. Nell got the tub of cocoa from the shelf and nodded, remembering her grandmother's words: someone, somewhere always has it worse.

Bessie clamped her hand around the hot mug and took a long, slow breath. 'Let's do this, shall we?' She smiled and pulled the envelope from her pocket. She started to tear it where it had been taped back after inspection but she couldn't do it and passed it over to Nell.

To my darling, Bessie,

Words cannot express how I feel right now. I am truly devastated. It's at times like these I really curse this damn war as I should be with you. As I cannot be there right now, please take comfort in my words and know that I am with you in my heart, and when I am home again, we can try once more.
I love you,
William.

A sob caught in Nell's throat. She folded the letter and passed it back to Bessie who had tears streaming down her face.

'I'm sorry, Bess.' She reached out for Bessie's hand and held it tightly.

'Knowing he knows, I can breathe a little easier,' she exhaled and tucked the letter back in in her pocket. 'I'd best crack on with the pie, it's for the Community Center,' her voice shook. 'I find that keeping busy really helps. Takes the mind off things, you know? So have you had any letters recently?'

'No, nothing for a couple of weeks now,' she replied, and then remembered the content of Alfred's last two-page letter he sent her. 'Did I tell you Alf's going in for officer training?'

'No, you didn't. Oh, that's fantastic, Nell. But it's no wonder really, he was always destined for something more.'

'Yeah,' she said, thinking that out of all the family she and Alfred were so alike, even though they were four years apart they'd always had a special bond. 'I'm proud of all of them, really…'

'I know you are Nell. Damn this,' she thumped her hand down on the table as the tears rolled down her cheeks. She wiped her tear stained eyes with the tea towel once more and got to her feet.

'You need to get out of this house for a bit. I could use a drink or two, how about it?'

'Come on then, Nell, we'll go down the Naval. If I sit here and mope anymore I'll crack up.'

'What about your pie?'

'Mam has taken quite a lot down already, and besides, I've been baking since early this morning when the all-clear went. I'll put this dough in the pantry for tomorrow as who knows what that will bloody bring.'

When they arrived at the pub, it was quieter than normal. Nell walked up to the bar and called Jack over to serve them. He was speaking to a tall, dark-haired sailor leaning on the bar, sipping on a pint. When the sailor saw Nell, he raised his glass in her direction and offered to buy them both a drink. Nell said thanks and gave him a pleasant smile in return.

Jack came over to serve them; throwing a clean white tea-towel over his shoulder. 'Hello, ladies. It's nice of you to join us. I didn't think you'd be here today, Nell, you having been on duty last night. So, tell me, is it true that the town is destroyed?' He asked, resting two hands on the bar.

'Obliterated, Jack. There's hardly a building left standing.' She replied and sat down on the bar stool that had uneven legs. Nell set one foot on the floor to stabilize it. 'So you decided to open this place regardless then?' she asked, looking around. Old man Bill and Clive the milkman were sitting at a table next to a window still covered with a black-out blind and behind the sailor, two other men whose faces were covered in dirt, looking like they had come off a shift from helping with the attacks, were throwing darts.

Jack sighed as though the weight of the world rested on his shoulders. 'What else can people do in times like these?'

Nell shrugged, nodding in agreement. After all, it was her idea to come out for a drink.

Jack got two glasses from the shelf and poured them a shot of whiskey in each. Nell raised her glass toward the sailor and downed the drink in one go.

'Did you hear about that Jerry they found on the hill this morning?' asked the sailor, who passed his glass to Jack for a refill.

Nell looked down at the empty glass thinking how she didn't want to hear any more about the damned soldier. Not today, not ever. It didn't look as though she would get a moment peace.

'Nell, you heard something didn't you?' said Bess.

Nell didn't acknowledge her and asked Jack for another drink. By far, that had been the worst thing she had witnessed of this war, and she wanted to bury it deep into her subconscious where it could never be found again. Luckily for her, the door to the bar opened, and in walked her dad followed by Mr. Greenwald.

'Just come off duty, have you lads?' asked Jack, already setting down two-pint glasses on the bar.

'Yeah, there's not much else we can do at this point,' said Greenwald. He patted Nell on the back. 'You should be home resting,' and in a quiet voice, he added, 'Jerry has been taken care of, so don't worry. If you need to talk, you know where I am.'

'Thanks.' She looked up from her drink, and saw, over Greenwald's shoulder a man about to walk into the pub. She stared long and hard at him, thinking it couldn't be who she thought. There was no possible way. When she fully realised who it was she jumped off her stool and shouted for Bess.

'It's William,' she pointed towards the door.

Bess swung around in her chair as the tall, dark-haired man wearing his khaki uniform dropped his kit bag and welcomed a screaming Bess into his open arms.

At last, Nell thought, something positive to end a disastrous day.

'How the devil are you, Will?' shouted the barman. 'We weren't expecting you home for a while according to your mother.'

Though tired looking, William flashed the wide toothy smile he'd always be known for. Even as a kid, the sight of cheeky, upbeat William would lighten anyone's mood.

'You know the war, Jack, it's bloody unpredictable at times.'

Nell rushed across the room. Bess moved aside, crying.

'You're heaven sent right now, Will.'

'How are you, Nell?' he asked, over Bessie's sobbing. He pulled her in for a hug.

'I'm alright, Will. I'm so happy to see a friendly face walk through that door if you know what I mean…'

'Yeah, I know Nell. I heard about the bombing. Is everyone safe 'round here?'

She nodded. 'Yeah, it was the town that took the biggest hit. Come on, let's get you a drink, you must need it after all your traveling.'

Nell gave Bess an excited squeeze on her arm. 'I told you he'd be home.'

'I know,' she whispered. 'I always knew he would.'

Nell could see that Bess was still in shock as she tucked her arm in his, leading him towards an empty table next to the window. She could hardly believe it herself as she returned to the bar to get her drink so she could join them. She pulled out a chair from the opposite table and sat down, happy for them both.

'I've missed you all so much especially this one,' he bent down to kiss Bess on the forehead.

'How did you get leave so early?' Bess asked, sitting down on his lap and wrapping an arm around him.

'Didn't you get my letters?' he asked, incredulously.

'What letters?'

Nell and Bess looked at each other, a quizzical expression etched across their faces. Nell thought it was odd considering how she had only read his letter about an hour ago saying he couldn't get home.

'The only letter she had is the one telling her you couldn't get back,' said Nell, happy to have a distraction from her own problems.

William's brow creased and he turned to Bess.

'I sent you one last week saying I'll be home. I actually went to your house but nobody was home and Nell's was the same. I saw tea-leaves lady and she told me she saw you come in here, with her own eyes I add, not from a teacup.'

The pub erupted into laughter.

Jack came and placed a pint on the table. 'It's on the house. Good to see you Will.' He shook his hand.

'It's good to be back for a while.'

'Perhaps I should leave you two alone,' said Nell, about to get up from her chair.

'No, don't be daft.' William looked at Bess. 'Is Nell going to be one of your bridesmaids?'

'Of course she is you silly bugger. There's no one else I'd rather have.'

'Then I hope you're up for getting married this week because I've been in touch with the vicar who has arranged it for this Saturday.'

Bessie erupted into tears and so did Nell. It was just the emotional release she needed.

With only a few days until the wedding, there was a lot to arrange. That evening, while William slept, Bess called over to Nell's house to make a start on the wedding dress. Nell knew Bess had been planning her wedding for years, so she knew what she wanted, except she didn't think she'd ever be a war bride and have to save weeks' worth of rations to make a simple cake. In the front room, lit by the glow of several candles on the mantel, Bess sat down on the sofa whilst Nell attended to the black-out blinds.

'It's okay to be happy when everyone else is suffering, isn't it, even if it's only for a little while?'

'Come on, Bess, you've had your fair share of troubles, too. Nobody in this damn war has had it easy. Here,' she handed her a veil she had been making all afternoon, 'it's your wedding and the community is looking forward to it. It has given them something positive to talk about.' She picked up the silk parachute from the sofa and held it up in front of her, wondering how she was going to cut the pattern Bess had expertly drawn. They couldn't afford any mistakes now. The material was scarce. She laid it back down on the sofa and went to get the scissors from the cupboard drawer.

'You seem haunted by something yourself if you don't mind me saying. Did you see the Jerry when you got that parachute? I mean, you don't have to talk about it if you don't want to. I just thought it may help.' She offered Nell a cigarette which she declined.

About to sit down on the sofa, Nell picked up the silk sheet draped over the back and clutched it to her chest. 'Yes, Bessie, I saw the pilot. I've seen terrible things since this war began and I didn't have to go off to fight to feel the weight of human suffering. That poor airman, German or not Bess, he didn't deserve to die. I know you may find it hard to accept with everything that has happened but he was just a kid, maybe no older than us. It's a rotten war, Bess, nobody deserves to die, especially not in those circumstances,' she sniffed back tears and flung the parachute onto the carpeted floor.

'I'm sorry. I didn't mean to upset you.'

'No, you haven't, I needed this talk, so thank you for making me get it out.'

'I hope it helped.'

As she got on with the cutting, the letter the German had given her popped into her mind. Needing to unburden herself, she sat up and pulled the letter from her breast pocket.

'He gave me this.' She held the envelope up to Bess whose mouth slacked open.

'Who did?'

'The German, who do you think?'

'What? You can't be serious.' She snatched the envelope from Nell's hands.

'I think he wanted me to give it to his family. Maybe he didn't trust anyone else to do so.'

'So are you going to?' she looked up at her questioningly.

'When I saw him lying there, I didn't see a German, Bess. I saw a human being. Of course I'm going to find a way to make sure his family gets the letter. How could I possibly deny a dying man his last wish, could you? I mean, that would be inhuman of me.'

'No, I see your point. But you should get it read by someone who can read German, just so there's nothing incriminating in it. Maybe go and see Greenwald…'

'Oh no, I'm not being nasty but the way he speaks about them, I can be almost sure it'll go straight in the bin. No, I'll speak to Edward when I get the chance.' She picked up the scissors and began cutting.

Bessie got off the sofa and held the bottom piece of material. 'Make sure you do. You don't need this trouble hanging over your head, Nell.'

'I really don't. Maybe we should just concentrate on this or you'll be wearing my gran's old thing,' she joked, not wanting to discuss things any further.

They had barely started stitching the material when the drone of the air-raid siren sounded. The next thing she heard were feet thundering down the stairs and shouts to get in the shelter.

'Put the candles out,' cried David.

Nell blew out the candles and told Bess to go ahead and get into the shelter.

'So where are you going?' asked Bess in the darkness.

'I've got to help out with the ARP. Tell Mam not to worry.'

She felt her way to the cupboard under the stairs, grabbed her helmet and jacket and left the house, hoping to find Greenwald. The moment she stood on the porch, she saw the silhouette of the Luftwaffe flying across the amber sky towards town.

'Not again.'

'Nell,' shouted Greenwald. 'We need you on fire watch duty, come on.'

'I can't believe this is happening again. What is there left for them to bloody bomb this time?'

'Well it is happening, so let's do a check on the communal shelters to make sure everyone is accounted for.'

Chapter Fourteen

'At least the rain is holding off,' said Winnie, standing by the bedroom window. 'And the bombs.' She gave a cluck of annoyance at having to mention the bombs.

For three nights there had been a series of bombings on the town but with William due to leave the following day, the wedding had to go on.

'Don't jinx the bloody weather, Mam,' said Bess sitting on a chair beside the vanity in her room.

It had taken them hours in between Nell's ARP duties but they finally managed to salvage a thing of beauty from the parachute.

Bess, who looked radiant in her dress, exhaled deeply at her mother's comment. 'And please don't wish any more bombs on us. I feel guilty as it is getting married in such circumstances.'

Nell had finished powdering Bess's face with a compact she'd borrowed from a girl at work. She stood back to appreciate her efforts.

'Don't go crying now or you'll smudge it all.'

'Oh bugger…' Winnie said.

'What is it?' asked Nell, concern in her voice.

'I can't believe the rotten swine.' Her voice was high and clear that had everyone stood at attention. 'Pigs. That's what they are. They've only now gone and left the bloody pub. There they are, look, staggering up the steps.' She pointed.

There was shock and gasps of utter disbelief all around the bedroom.

'Are you kidding now, Mam?' asked Bessie as Nell went to the window, pulling back the net curtain. Her father, William and Mr. Greenwald were walking into her house.

'My God, move over Nell, let me see…'

Nell pushed Bess back. 'It's bad luck to see the groom before the wedding. I'll go over and make them coffee, I'm sure we have some left.'

'I'll go with you,' said Mary. 'David is going to get a bloody earful for this. How could he allow it?'

Nell saw how Bess was worried, and told her not to panic or she'd ruin her make-up. 'There's not much of the stuff left, so have a drink and we'll make sure he gets to the church on time.'

She left the room hoping she wouldn't have to find someone to help prop up William at the altar and stormed across the road to her house.

'What time do you call this?' she asked, disgusted at them. William was dozing on the sofa and Mr. Greenwald was trying to get William ready.

'Oh don't you start whining, too, Mary,' David swayed and staggered into the kitchen as Mary came through the front door.

'I'll get the kettle on,' said Nell. 'Quick, I'd give him a bloody great slap in the face if I were you, Mr. Greenwald,' she smiled.

'Oh Nell, come here,' said William pushing himself up on the chair. 'I asked my old pal from the farm,' he thumbed in the direction of the hill, 'to pick Bess up in his horse and carriage. Can you make sure she's ready by 11.30?'

'Yes, I'll tell her, but you'd better hurry and sober up or she'll take one look at you and call it off.'

At eleven o'clock, Nell had managed to get the men on their way to St Stephen's church on time and went back to Bess's house.

'It's alright, they've gone to the church,' she said to Bess standing in the hallway.

'Thanks, Nell. I had visions of him passed out drunk on the sofa.'

Nell didn't tell her about the state she found them in and adjusted her veil at the back.

'William said he has a little surprise for you to take you to the church, so me and Mam will get going in a bit. Dad said he'd be honoured to give you away. He said you've spent so much time over at ours you're like a daughter to him anyway.'

'Oh really, Nell, I'd be honoured too. Hey Mam, David said he'd give me away. Can you believe it?'

Winnie appeared in the hallway wearing her lilac dress. 'That's lovely of him, thank you, Nell.' She became distracted by something out the front. 'Is that a horse I hear?'

'He hasn't gone and got me a horse and cart?' Bessie squealed and rushed to the open front door.

'That's thoughtful of him. Shame he didn't think before he went out and got drunk.' She clucked her tongue and went outside.

Bess rolled her eyes at her and Nell laughed.

'Right, I'm going to start walking to the church before I cry,' said Nell, giving Bess a kiss on the cheek. 'Good luck.'

'Oh Nell, one thing… thanks for all you've done.'

'Don't mention it.'

'See you in a minute, Winnie,' Nell brushed past her and ran down the steps and up the street. She caught the back of Edward a few yards ahead and rushed to catch up with him.

'Ed, can I have a quick word?' She yelled.

Edward turned around.

'Oh, it's you, Nell. Of course you can. So how are you after that fiasco on the hill?'

'That's what I'd like to talk to you about.'

'Oh? Well if there's anything I can do to help…'

'I haven't been entirely honest, you see, I was on the hill a little while before you lot arrived.' She could see his eyes scrutinising her. 'He wasn't dead when I arrived there and he gave me this,' she handed him the envelope. 'I think he wanted me to give it to his family. I suppose he saw something honest in me.'

'God, Nell why didn't you come to me before?'

'I thought I could handle it myself, but I honestly didn't know what to do. Could you make sure it gets where it needs to go? I'm not going to get into trouble, am I?'

He sighed deeply. 'I know someone high up in the army. I could try and contact him, but I make no promises, Nell, and no, you won't get into trouble. Relax and enjoy the rest of the day. I'll let you know what happens.' He inspected the envelope before putting it in his jacket pocket. 'Smile, Nell, we have a wedding to go to.' He offered her his arm.

'Thanks, Ed, I appreciate it.'

'Don't mention it. We'll keep it our little secret, alright.'

The church was packed when they arrived. She saw her Mam and Winnie standing outside the entrance gates with William and went to join them.

'Nell, did she like the horse?' William asked, the anxiousness visible in his face.

'She loved it. I think you may have just saved the day after this morning.'

Relieved, William nodded and pulled her in for a hug. 'Thank you, Nell. I'm really sorry about this morning. I didn't mean to give you a hard time.'

'Don't mention it.'

Someone yelled that the bride was on her way and everyone began making their way inside the church.

'Go, and good luck,' She said to William and turned around to Mam.

'She looks beautiful, doesn't she Mam?' she said as the horse and cart came around the corner.

Mary sniffed back tears. 'She does. You did a good job on that dress. Did I ever ask you where you got the material?' She looked at Nell.

Nell shrugged. She didn't feel like explaining it to her, not now. 'I just found it lying around, Mam. Oh look, there's Bess.' She pointed to the bottom of the street and went to greet the on-coming horse on the pavement. 'Don't worry, he's here and as sober as I could get him,' she said as the horse came to a stop.

'I'm surprised he managed it after this morning.' David laughed and stepped down from the carriage. He held out a hand for Bessie, who was laughing too.

'All's well that ends well, eh, Nell?'

Nell helped adjust Bess's veil. 'You look beautiful. Are you ready?' she asked.

'Absolutely, Nell.'

'So the next time we'll speak, you'll be Mrs. Evans.'

'I know, isn't it exciting, Nell? It's all I ever wanted.'

The church was packed when Nell went inside. She waved at the vicar who instructed the organist to play and walked behind her dad and Bess, smiling. David took Bess's arm as they stepped inside the church.

The vicar had only just started the vows when Nell thought she heard something outside and looked behind her.

'Dad,' she whispered. 'Dad…'

'What's the matter?' David whispered.

At that very moment the slow wail of the air-raid siren went off and the vicar stopped mid-sentence.

'Sorry, Vic,' shouted Greenwald, 'but everyone to the nearest shelter. There's one in the park, move it.'

Nell, who was sitting in the front pew, jumped to her feet, apologising as she barged into people's legs. She caught up with her mother and took hold of her arm.

'We're going to the communal shelter by the park. Don't worry Mam.'

They joined the horde as they rushed out of the doors. Once outside, Nell looked up at a sky that was thick with enemy planes.

'Stay close, Mam.' They ran across the road towards the park.

Everyone else had run, screaming, as bombs dropped from the sky and landed on the hill.

Greenwald and Nell stood at the entrance to the shelter watching and making sure everyone had got inside safely. Once she slammed the door shut there was a moment of darkness until someone lit a gas lamp at the far end of the cramped space. The flicker of light barely made a dent, but it was enough for her to make out Bess hunched over on a bench, crying.

'Is everyone okay?' Nobody hurt?' she asked, feeling her way towards Bess.

Everyone answered that they were fine and then she heard a mother sing quietly to her frightened child who was sniffling next to Bess.

Nell knelt down in front of her, pressing a hand on her knee.

'It may not be for long.'

William leaned closer to the lamp so the side of his face was visible.

'I have to go back tomorrow, Nell…'

'Well let's finish the ceremony here,' said Bess, getting to her feet.

'Are you sure?' asked Nell, surprised she didn't think of it sooner.

'Why not? This war isn't going to stop me from getting married.' Bess tugged at the vicar's arm. 'Do you think we can do the vows here, right now?'

'Uh, well… is it what you really want?'

She looked at William.

'Yes, yes it is.'

Over the drones of aircraft Bess and Will exchanged vows, and just as the vicar pronounced them husband and wife, someone had found a light-switch and the damp, cold room lit up. Winnie was sobbing into her hanky and Nell gave her a tight hug.

'It was lovely, wasn't it, Win?'

'Yeah, love. I don't suppose it matters where you marry, does it, as long as you're surrounded by family and friends. But by God, this is one story to tell the grandkids.'

It was late. Everyone had now settled down, either dozing off to sleep or sitting staring into nothingness. Bess sat holding hands with William while he rested his head, snoring on her shoulder.

Nell surveyed the room for what felt like the thousandth time. She couldn't relax and so kept checking her watch, willing for the all-clear to sound.

'I wonder what it's like out there right now,' said Wilfred, the church's caretaker as he offered anyone who was listening, a blackberry from a paper bag.

'No thanks,' said Nell when the bag pointed in her direction. She got up, and as she did, the all clear sounded.

The place erupted into cries of joy, and almost immediately everyone clamoured towards the door.

Nell undid the latch, bracing herself for what she might see when the door finally opened. She pushed the door, and a crack of daylight stung her eyes.

'Come on then, one at a time, no rushing. We don't want any accidents, do we?' She covered her eyes with the back of her hand and remarked to Bess, who had just stepped out of the shelter, that she knew how Dracula must've felt.

'Who the bloody heck is he when he's home?'

'It's a novel, Bess, don't worry…'

When the last person had left, she secured the door and walked back home with her parents, relieved to see the hill had taken the brunt of the bombing.

'Come on, Nell, we're going to miss him,' shouted David who was standing by the front door. Nell pulled on her coat and rushed down the hall. 'Okay, Dad, don't panic. He's not due for another two hours.'

'I know that, Nell, but this is a once in a lifetime opportunity. I don't want to miss it.'

Nell knew how much her father respected the Prime Minister, so when he heard that he was visiting Swansea to witness the devastation left by the Germans, she understood what it meant to him, and agreed to go along with him for company.

Standing outside the Bush, a public house, Nell and her father eagerly awaited his arrival.

'My God,' said David over the excited chatter of the large crowd, 'I can't believe you were out on the night it all happened,' he said, looking toward an empty space where a building once stood.

Nell linked his arm. 'It's all part of the service, Dad. I'm here now, so don't worry.' Images of the night flashed across her eyes and she shook them away. 'Look, Dad, there he is,' she pointed to Churchill and his large entourage. He was smoking a cigar and was wearing a long overcoat and a hat. Next to him was his wife, Clementine, in a shaggy fur coat and several bodyguards dressed in black overcoats and hats. Nell waved, feeling a sense of pride as he walked down the High Street. 'I can see why he's the man for the job,' said Nell. 'He's very stern looking, isn't he?'

A woman who was standing next to her agreed. 'Definitely, love.'

David pushed his way to the front. 'Thank you,' he shouted. Churchill put his cigar in his mouth and raised his hand, giving them the victory sign. 'Well if that don't lift our bloody spirits I don't know what will,' he said, overcome with emotion.

'The end to this war,' said an old lady standing next to him.

'That too, my love, that too,' he said. 'Come on, Nell, let's follow the crowd, shall we?'

PART FOUR

1942

Chapter Fifteen

When Nell arrived home from ARP duty, she went out the back door, just as her family emerged from another night in the shelter.

Mary held the kerosene lamp and blankets in her hand and turned around when she heard the door close.

'Thank God, you're alright. How bad was it last night?' she asked.

'They reckon there were two hundred incendiaries dropped on Birchgrove alone. We had a few casualties too.' She yawned, looking concerned at her grandmother who coughed and hacked as she made her way into the house. 'Her cough sounds bad, Mam. Is she okay?'

'I'm not sure, Nell. I'd best call the doctor, I think. That shelter is damp and cold which can't be helping her health. Do you know, I'm sure a rat ran across Gran's legs last night while I was dozing off to sleep.' She went into the kitchen and put the kettle on to boil.

Nell went in the front room to check on her gran who sat on her chair that now faced the window. Sunbeams spilled which warmed her face.

'Are you alright, Gran? Do you want me to get you anything?'

'No thank you, Nell. I just want to get some sleep if that's alright.'

'Okay. I'm going to get changed out of these clothes. Let me know if you do and I'll get it for you.'

She didn't respond. Nell took the blanket off the sofa and put it across her legs before leaving the room to get washed and changed.

There had been victories in Europe and Africa which raised the hopes of many, especially David who had just arrived home from work.

'Montgomery's Eighth Army has pushed Rommel's German Panza's toward Tunis,' he said enthusiastically to Nell who came into the kitchen for a cup of tea.

'That's fantastic, Dad. Things are looking good, but I still have shells to fill, unfortunately.' She hated her job and wished she was still working at Woolworths. 'Have you checked on Nan?'

'Yes, I have. She's a tough woman, she'll be alright.'

He went to stand by the window. Nell got on with her tea when David yelled that someone had been pilfering his vegetable patch.

'What?' she swung around.

He stormed out the door. Nell followed him out into the garden, and saw that all dad's veg had been dug up.

'What a bunch of thieving bastards.' He got on his knees and rummaged through the earth. 'Who could've done something like this?'

Florrie had come out of her house to see what the commotion was about. 'What's going on, Dai?' She looked over the fence.

'Someone has stolen Dad's veg,' said Nell. 'It must've happened overnight, obviously, but we never noticed until now.'

'You need to call the police, get the thieving scum locked up. We're all bloody hungry but we don't go nicking other people's food. Jesus. What has the world come to?'

David was too devastated to respond and went back inside the house.

Infuriated that someone could do this to her father after all the effort he put into the garden Nell decided that something had to be done about it. 'Exactly, what has it come to? I'm just going to pop down to the police station to report it.'

A few days later, Nell hadn't long come home from night duty and was lying in bed when she heard the postman's whistle and ran downstairs.

'I'll get it,' she yelled, opening the front door.

'Morning, Nell,' said James. 'Bad night last night, wasn't it?' He handed her a pile of envelopes.

'Awful, James. We had loads of bombs to put out. Even when I left they were all still working hard to make sure everyone was safe.'

'It's bloody disgusting. Oh, pardon my language, Nell, but it is. It's so terrible.'

'That's okay. This war makes me want to curse too,' she smiled weakly. 'But you're right. It's so terrible. I think I'm going to head back up there later, see if I can be of more help.'

'Well, you take care then, Nell. Hope you've got something there from your brothers,' he said, before bidding her goodbye.

Nell hoped so too and her heart leaped when she saw Francis's hedgehog scrawl across the envelope marked with kisses. She was tearing the envelope open when she overheard Edna talking. She looked up to see her standing on her doorstep talking to a young woman with a child standing by her side. Even though she could only see the back of the woman, she struck her as familiar. She looked closely at her long blonde hair thinking she knew her from somewhere, but couldn't quite place her. When the woman turned to the side, she instantly recognized her as the woman she saw with Francis at the Naval that night. The one he left with. Intrigued, she stepped back to avoid being seen and strained to hear what they were talking about. The woman cried and Nell saw Edna nervously glance up and down the street, a sign she was afraid that any of the neighbours were looking. This didn't feel right to Nell, who already had her suspicions about that night. About to head indoors, she noticed that Edna had seen her, but instead of the usual jolly good morning she'd receive, Edna quickly turned away and took the young woman by her arm, pulling her indoors.

'Strange. How very strange,' Nell whispered and was about to head indoors herself when she heard her mother yell out if there was any post. Trying to make sense of what she had seen across the road, Nell drew her attention back to the envelopes and looked again.

'I'm just checking,' she yelled back, finding three letters addressed to her mam. As she flipped the last one over, she saw there was one addressed to her from Sidney. She took the mail through to her mother, dropping the one from Francis onto the kitchen counter.

'Not going to open it?' Her mother asked, standing at the sink, washing the dishes.

'Not yet,' she replied, unsure what to do with herself. She stood by the sink, staring out of the window at the washing blowing on the line.

'What's wrong?' asked Mam.

Nell was glad her mam asked and pulled out a chair, thinking it was best to say something before it could wear her down even further.

'Oh it's nothing, Mam, well I'm hoping it isn't. No, you'll probably think I'm being silly, but...' She reached across the table, picked up the letter from Francis remembering how he never returned to the party that evening at the Naval. She promised herself she'd forget about it when he asked her to marry him and now a part of her wished she had sorted it nearer the time. 'Mam, before this drives me crazy, could I talk to you about something?'

'Of course you can, Nell? What is it?'

'Just now, while I was getting the mail I couldn't help but notice Edna's visitor. She was a young woman with a child of about two...'

'That's not really unusual is it, Nell? Who was she, anyway?'

'She's not local, and I only ever saw her here that night at the Naval talking to Francis. So, why would she be back over here, talking to Edna of all people?'

'Oh, maybe she's after Bessie?'

'I don't think so, but it's all very strange.' She pulled the letter from the envelope, surprised to see it was shorter than she expected.

Dear Nell,

It's a short letter to say I'll be home on the 14th.
Hope everything is okay.
Can't wait to see you,

Francis

She couldn't believe what she read, and so read it through quickly once more. She rose from the chair and passed her mother the letter.

'Mam, he's coming home on leave in three weeks' time.'

'Who is?'

'Francis.'

'That's fantastic, Nell. You'd better go and let Edna know if she doesn't already.' She gave her back the letter and shouted to David out the back garden the news.

'I will do Mam,' she muttered, reading it through again. She knew she had to come clean with him when he got back for the sake of her sanity. She tucked the letter in the envelope and put it in the pocket of her cardigan. 'I think Gran is having a kip in the front room. Do call a doctor for her though, I'm getting worried.'

'I've asked Florrie to call in on the doctor on her way to the shops. I expect he'll be here shortly.'

'Good. Well, I'm going to get ready for work so I'll speak to you later.'

That evening, after her shift, it had rained non-stop. She was thankful she didn't have night patrol duty and spent the night in her room listening to Vera Lynn, thinking about what it'd be like to see Francis again. What if he's changed? What if she felt differently about him? She tried to push those thoughts away, reminding herself that in less than twelve hours, he'd be home, in her arms where he belonged, but then a vision of the woman with the kid popped into her head and she felt nauseous.

When her alarm sounded, she got out of bed, happy and humming a tune to herself when she heard a gut-wrenching scream coming from the back garden. In the throes of brushing her hair, she dropped the brush and ran to her bedroom window, pulling open the black-out blinds. The first thing she saw was her mother on her knees in the garden, crying hysterically. The sack of the Anderson shelter was open wide. It could only mean one thing, she thought and she very much hoped she was wrong.

'Oh no, please no,' she cried and ran out of her room and downstairs. 'Mam, Mam, are you alright?' she shouted, and when she got to the kitchen door, her mother looked over her shoulder, her face delivering the news she feared.

'She's gone, Nell.'

Her body slumped against the door and she dropped to her haunches, covering her face with her hands. She couldn't believe it. Once she got a hold of herself, she went out into the sopping rain, walking over the boards her father had put down over the wet soil. Nell couldn't bring herself to look inside and wrapped her arms around her mother. 'Come inside the house Mam, and I'll call Dr. Fitzgerald.'

'She didn't come in last night, why didn't I check, Nell?' She said.

'Come on, Mam, you can't blame yourself,' she helped her mother to her feet just as her father came out of the back door with a look of utter confusion.

'What's happened?' he asked, piecing together the scenario in front of him. 'Don't tell me my carrots are ruined now. No, they're not bloody content with taking my potatoes, they've come back to finish the whole bloody lot…'

'Shut-up about your bloody carrots and listen,' said Mary. 'It's your mam, love. She's passed away. I'm so sorry, Dai.'

David's face crumpled with despair. He covered his face with his hands, staggering sideways into the wall. It was heartbreaking for Nell to see him like this and she went and sat with him while Mary went to the phone box.

Dr. Fitzgerald offered his condolences to the family and left the house, doffing his hat before he got into his car. David retreated to his room where he remained for the next couple of hours. Nell pulled out a chair for her mam at the kitchen table and went to put the kettle on to boil.

'I'm just going to get someone to sit with you while I go and sort out some time off work, I won't be a minute.'

'Nell, go to work, it'll take your mind off things. I'm alright here,' she replied, 'I've got lots to keep me busy.'

'No, I can go to the phone box and make a call in, I'm sure they'll understand.'

'No, it's best if you go, love. I'll be fine, besides aren't you supposed to meet Francis after work? You can't leave him waiting after all this time.'

'Are you sure, Mam?' her eyes filled with tears. With everything that had happened, she'd actually forgotten about him coming home.

'I'm sure. Anyhow, you're no good to me if you say you're making a cup of tea and forget to put the gas on.' She smiled at Nell, but Nell knew it was just for her benefit.

'Alright, I'll just go and get my coat.'

When she left the house, Edna and Florrie were walking up the steps.

'Are you off to work, because if you are we'll stay with her, Nell. It won't be a bother.'

'Thanks. Dad is in his room. I don't think he wants to be disturbed for the time being.'

'Nell, I'm sorry about Gran,' Bessie said as they walked through the factory doors.

Nell hung her coat on the hook and sighed.

'I know she was getting on in age,' she held back tears, 'but what on earth made her sleep in the shelter last night? She must've been cold – that's what probably killed her.' She pulled on her navy dungarees and scooped her hair back into a bun, 'the bloody cold.'

'She was petrified of them bombs, bless her,' Bessie tied a red scarf on her head. 'Will Francis be home later? It'd be good to see that scallywag again. The street has been quiet without him. Not sure if that's been a good thing or a bad thing.' She mused, making Nell laugh.

'Has to be a good thing, right, Bess?' she said, making her way across the factory floor to her table.

Having been given special permission to leave at six o' clock, just as it was about to get dark outside, Nell bid goodbye to Bess who was filling shells and headed to the dressing room to collect her belongings. She had spent so long dreaming of the day she'd see Francis again that she could barely believe it was now happening for real. She undid her turban and shook out her hair, giving it a sniff. She recoiled at the smell, reached into her bag for perfume and spritzed it over her hair before she finger-rolled it back with pins. Happy to get out of the stinking overalls, she took out her green dress from her bag and slipped it on. It was now showing some wear, but she didn't care. She loved the dress no matter what. She brought it close to her chest, remembering the day Alf had given it to her wrapped in fancy coloured tissue paper. It was now ready to make another memory.

She stood outside The Anchor, a pub frequented by sailors, and looked around the small crowd outside for her Francis. Men stood in suits and uniform and she noticed every so often they would glance in her direction.

'Excuse me, love. Are you waiting for anyone?' a man with a ruddy face asked.

'I'm waiting for Francis. He was meant to get off a ship that docked here this afternoon.'

There were murmurs amongst the men. Some shook their heads and shrugged their shoulders. Nell felt the anxiousness rise. What if something had happened to him?

'What did you say his name was again, lovey?' the same man asked, slurring his words.

'Francis.'

'Oh that's right, there was a Francis who just headed on home. He said his girl didn't turn up, so he left. Must've been about two minutes ago now.'

She said thank you and ran across the bridge, but her skirt was too tight on the knees and prevented her from going so fast. She slowed down when a figure carrying a kit bag slung over his shoulder appeared on the side of the road. Her heart leaped to her throat as she came to an abrupt stop on the opposite side.

'Francis?' she yelled. 'Francis, is that you?' she shouted, unsure whether to run ahead.

Under the glow of the streetlight, the man stopped and turned around.

'Nell?'

'Yes, it's me.'

He ran towards her, scooped her up into his arms and swung her around. 'There you are! I thought you'd forgotten all about me coming home.'

'Don't be daft,' she hugged him tight. 'I had to walk from the factory.'

'It's so good to see you again, Nell.' He touched her face. 'There were a few times I thought I'd never live to see this moment.'

'Well you're here now; let's not dwell on what could've been, okay?'

'You're right. So, shall we go home? Or do you want to go somewhere for a drink first?'

'We'd better get home. I know your mother has been on pins all day waiting for you.'

He offered her his arm. 'I can imagine. Her letters have been book-length,' he laughed as he pulled her tightly towards him.

They'd only got as far as the pub on the corner of the main road when Nell thought she heard a female voice call out to Francis.

Both looked at each other. Francis took Nell's hand.

'Come on, let's go.' He urged her on.

'Why? Who is she?' She looked over her shoulder and was surprised to see the girl she'd seen outside Edna's house running towards them.

'Wait, Francis.' The girl yelled. 'Your mother told me you'd be home tonight...'

'Not you. What the hell do you want, Tilly? Haven't you caused me enough problems?'

'I just want to talk, please?'

Nell was confused and wondered what was going on. She pulled her hand back and stood her ground. 'Francis, I think you'd better answer her, don't you?'

Nell could see that he was panicking and at that moment she knew her worst fears were about to be realised.

The girl ran towards them. She looked at Francis and then at Nell. 'Has he told you, love?'

'Told me what?' she said.

'Now is not the right time, Tilly.' He glared at her. 'I haven't had a chance to tell her.'

'No, no, I think it's the right time,' said Nell, shaking with anger. 'Oh, wait, let me guess. Has this got something to do with a child you conceived with her?'

Francis lowered his head. 'Nell, I said not now...'

Tilly whacked Francis on the arm. 'I think she deserves to know the truth.' She then turned to Nell. Her face softened. 'I'm sorry, love. I had no idea that you were seeing him also. I would've told you, doll, but his mother said that I shouldn't go around breaking up other people's relationships. She also said that if I told you, she'd tell everyone that Janet isn't his and she would tell him he shouldn't send home a penny for her.'

Francis reached out to Nell, but she shrugged him off. She slowly backed away from them both before she'd did something she'd regret.

'How could you lie to me for so long... how could you do this to me?' she screamed at them and then ran up the road home, shaking furiously as the ice cold rain masked her tears.

She told her mother everything as soon as she got inside which resulted in her mother storming across the road to Edna's where she spent the following couple of hours. Talking to Bess in the back garden, Nell decided she had had enough and wanted to call the relationship off for good.

'I have to move on, Bess. I don't know how, but I suppose this was never meant to be anyway. I should've listened to my gut right from the start, it would've saved me from this bloody heartache.'

'Oh come on, how were you really to know? I never would've thought he'd do something like this either.'

'The thing is, I saw them together at the Naval at Jack's anniversary party, but I wanted to be with him so much Bess, that when he asked me to marry him, I thought I could erase all my doubts and live happily ever after. God, what an idiot I've been.' She stubbed out her cigarette and took another from the pack.

'Look at it this way, at least you found out before you got married. Now you've got the rest of your life to find someone to settle with.'

'Yeah, maybe I should put it down to life experience, eh, Bess? But now I've lost a friend as well. Gosh, I've made a mess of things, haven't I?'

'No you haven't. Maybe in time, you'll be able to forgive and be friends again. But for now, you must take all the time you need to heal from this. Personally, I think you're going to be just fine, Nell.'

'Of course, I will. It's just rotten timing what with Gran's funeral too. When are we ever going to get a break, that's what I'd like to know?' She picked up her cup from the floor and drained the last of her tea.

The front door knocked and Bess went to answer it. 'I'll go, just try and calm yourself down, okay.'

'If it's him, tell him I don't want to see him right now.'

Nell pulled another cigarette out of the pack and put it in her mouth. She was patting the neighbour's dog whining behind the fence when she heard Bess come out of the back door.

'Was it him?' she asked.

'I told him you needed time on your own.'

'Thanks. Did he say anything else?'

'That he was sorry and he never meant to hurt you. He really wants to talk things over though. To be honest, Nell, I heard that Tilly is a right old slag, mind. She could be lying to him.'

'Whatever. Anyway, it's a bit late for talking things through, isn't it?'

The day of Gran's funeral, Nell spent most of her time sitting in the back garden, wanting to be alone although it was impossible, with a house full of people who came back after the service. She had been deliberately trying to avoid Francis all day who was due to leave in the morning. It was then, while leaning over the garden wall with a cup of tea in her hand, she saw him offer his condolences to her dad.

'Sorry for your loss, Nell.'

She held back the anger that welled inside her and gave a shrug of her shoulders. She hoped he'd get the message that she didn't want to talk and he'd leave her in peace, but no. He squeezed her shoulder. 'I know it's not the right time, but I just want you to know I never did anything to hurt you. I was seeing her before we got together, and no, nothing happened the night of the party either. She was harassing me for money and I had to get her out of there before you saw anything.'

Nell sniffed back her tears. Had she been so hasty and quick to judge? Did she really feel anything for him, any more than a sister would feel for her brother? She thought back to the day he came home and had to admit to herself that her feelings were not strong enough to make it work. Perhaps this was a blessing after all. She breathed deeply and turned to face him.

'It's okay.' She looked at him and saw the relief on his face. 'I forgive you, but I don't think we would work as a couple, do you?'

'You can't mean that Nell, not after all this time?' His voice cracked with emotion. There was a moment or two of silence. 'But if it's what you really feel, then I know there's nothing I can do to convince you otherwise. I'd fight for you, I would, but I love you too much and want you to be happy, even if it's without me. Can we at least still be friends?' He touched her shoulder.

Nell exhaled slowly. In times like this, she couldn't afford to lose anyone else.

'We always were and maybe that's what we should've stayed as. Friends.'

PART FIVE

1943

Chapter Sixteen

'Come on, Nell, admit it. You need a night out.' Bessie said, sitting on the bed flipping through a copy of *Brave New World*. 'How about we go to the local after we've finished work today?'

Nell sighed and looked at her reflection again in the mirror. Her usually lustrous hair was now tangled no matter how much she ran the brush through it. So many late nights with the ARP and the chemicals at the factory had also taken a toll on her skin, which now looked patchy and dry. She leaned closer to the mirror and thought she saw a wrinkle on her forehead that wasn't there yesterday. 'I suppose we could,' she replied gloomily, remembering how it had been a few years since she'd got engaged and almost a year since she had last seen Francis. 'I can't believe where the time is going, Bess. To think I almost got married to him after what he did.' She rubbed her forehead and thought about applying a bit of Pond's cold cream on it.

'I know,' she said, throwing down the book. 'I think you've had a lucky escape, Nell. Have you heard from him at all?'

'No, I haven't written to him. Not once. I don't think I'm ready to talk to him like I used to, not yet.'

'It's was so out of character, but hey here you are, young, and fancy-free to come out with me tonight.' She took a tube of lipstick from the dresser, untwisted it, and nudged Nell out of the way so she could see in the mirror. 'That's why I think we should go out for a few drinks,' she pouted and then smacked her lips together. 'We're all having a terrible time of it, aren't we? She sighed and flopped back down on the bed. 'Our men are safe, as far as we know, and we've been working our socks off the past few weeks.'

'Okay, okay…you've convinced me.'

It had been stressful, what with the shortages of food in the shops and the feeling that all they ever did was work, or clean. It never seemed to end. Sometimes she felt she was working a seven day week.

'I'm not on ARP duty tonight, so where do you want to go?'

'How about we go down the Adelphi on Wind Street? It'll make a nice change from listening to the regulars down the Naval.'

They both found it funny as one of the regulars was always proposing to Bessie.

'That sounds good to me,' said Nell, pulling on her cardigan.

'Yeah, I can't listen to old Elliot propose to me anymore. I mean, it was funny the first time, but now I think he bloody means it,' said Bess, and did the buttons up on her coat. 'Chilly out there, mind.'

'Hope we're not headed for another bad winter,' Nell said, now scratching her right arm.

'Has that rash come back?' Bessie demanded to know and took a closer look at her forearm. 'Nell, it's getting worse. You're going to have to seriously think about finding another job or at least get to the doctors.'

'I like it at the factory though. The women are fantastic. There's a real sense of camaraderie.'

Bessie groaned. 'A real sense of canaries, you mean. You know, as in the yellow birds,' she doubled over with laughter and pointed to her hair that had a tinge of yellow to it. 'I don't even have to bleach it anymore.'

Nell cried with laughter. 'It's only a matter of time before mine gets like it unless I go grey first.' They were still laughing as they made their way down the stairs.

'You're so stubborn, though, do you know that?' Bessie opened the front door.

'Of course, it's how I managed to survive that bloody bombing a few a months ago,' she replied, now serious. She thought back to February when hundreds of incendiaries were dropped on the local area. Had it not been for her quick thinking, she surely would've been crushed under the debris of a falling house. With over fifty deaths, the community was devastated. And it still hadn't recovered. Yet, despite everything that had happened, she was amazed at how everyone pulled together and did their best to carry on. No war was going to beat them down.

'Come on, or we'll miss the bus. I don't want my pay docked,' said Bess.

Standing at the bus stop on Tennant Road, Nell spotted Mr. Greenwald coming out of the bakery and waved at him. He looked up, held up a hand, and ran across the road towards them.

'I'm glad I caught you two,' he said, slightly out puff. 'There's been a small explosion at the factory. One of the women dropped a bloody great barrel of explosives, didn't you hear about it?'

As if things couldn't get much worse, thought Nell who couldn't believe what she heard. She looked at Bessie whose mouth was gaped open in shock.

'Who was she?' Bess asked.

Greenwald shrugged.

'No idea, lass, but I think it's still open for business. Bloody awful, isn't it? Take care now.' He doffed his cap and went on his way.

Nell was reeling from shock.

They took the bus to Landore and arrived outside the factory to see hundreds of workers standing outside. Smoke was billowing from the back of the building, darkening the sky so much so they couldn't tell if it was night or day.

'I can't bloody believe it,' said Bess, peering out of the window as the bus pulled up to the side of the road.

'Look at the bloody smoke. Come on, let's see if everyone is okay.' Nell leaped from her seat and got off the bus. She spotted Anne, the woman who worked along side her standing next to the supervisor having an argument.

'…someone has to take responsibility,' she yelled at him. 'Poor Louise had a child, what's going to become of the poor fella now his mother can't work?'

'I can assure you she will be taken care of,' he replied and then noticed Nell. He looked relieved to see her. 'Nell, I'm sorry to have to tell you, but there has been the most unfortunate accident. Louise,' his voice faltered and he took a tissue from the pocket of his overalls, 'her face is badly burned, Nell.'

Once it was clear to go back inside, Nell went to her workstation and got on with filling the shells.

'I think you're right, I need to get another job,' Nell said, linking Bessie's arm as they strolled down the High Street, hoping to catch the number 7 bus home before it got dark.

'Do you still fancy a drink?' asked Bessie. 'I know we said we wouldn't after what happened to Louise, but I sure as hell need one.'

Nell wasn't in the mood to go home either and agreed. 'The Adelphi is just up the road, we'll go there. I think Susan and her husband have taken it over now, so we'll be okay.'

'Susan?'

'Oh, you must remember Sue from school?' she said, thinking about the time she had bumped into her in town and invited her in for a drink if she was ever passing.

'No, should I? You were a class above me, Nell.'

'Never mind, eh Bess. Hey look, there must be a party or something going on in there,' she pointed towards the pub. 'Fancy it?'

A group of soldiers was huddled around the door, talking loudly amongst themselves. When the girls approached, the men turned heads in their direction. The short one with a cigarette between his lips stepped forward, took out his cigarette and wolf whistled. Nell wasn't impressed and raised an eyebrow at him. He seemed too had registered her annoyance as he held his hands up in defence and apologised for being brash.

'Nice evening, isn't it, ma'am?' said the tall, fair-headed soldier leaning against the wall. Like a group of vultures, they crowded around the girls as though they had never seen a woman in months.

Nell pulled Bess in close and whispered in her ear that they were American. Bess covered her mouth, stifling a giggle. They hadn't met an American before but they knew they had a base in Caswell Bay. They'd often heard they came into the town for a drink when not busy with war work but until now they have never had the pleasure of meeting one.

'Yes, it's a nice evening,' Nell replied, clapping her eyes on the tall, dark-haired stranger with striking blue eyes who was smiling at her.

They were heading into the pub when the fair-headed soldier stepped forward and tugged at Bessie's elbow.

'How about we get you girls a drink? It's the least we can do after our shocking introduction.' The soldier was tall with light blonde hair. He had a southern drawl with cute dimples. Nell noticed he had taken a shine to Bessie and so she urged her to get into the pub.

'Perhaps this isn't a good idea,' said Nell, changing her mind. Bess completely blanked her out.

'That'll be nice, thank you,' said Bessie. 'But I must warn you, I have a husband abroad…'

'That's what they all say,' the man laughed.

'She does,' said Nell, quite coldly.

'Well there's no harm in having one drink, is there?' The melodious voice belonged to the tallest of the three men standing next to the lamp post. She looked again at the handsome face and felt slightly awkward.

'Hey there, pretty lady,' he said, stepping forward. 'I'm Captain Sanders, nice to meet you.' He proffered his hand. Nell fastened her eyes on his hands and then drew her eyes upwards until she was looking into his eyes framed with dark lashes. She nearly melted. She shook his firm hand, thinking how she hadn't seen anyone so strikingly beautiful. He then turned to the fellow standing next to him. 'This is Corporal Turner, and there,' he pointed to the short guy with spectacles, 'is Captain Harland. 'We're a friendly bunch, ma'am and mean you no harm. Would it be okay if I buy you a drink?'

Nell looked for Bess but she had already gone into the pub. 'I don't think I have much choice now,' said Nell. 'But just the one, I've just got off work and I'm tired.'

'So have we, but it's our only night off for a while. So, shall we?' he gestured towards the door.

Captain Sanders put a friendly arm on Nell's shoulder and walked her into the pub. It was already heaving with soldiers and sailors.

'I've been told I don't bite,' he smiled and walked her to an empty table at the far corner by the window. 'You're safe with me,' he held out his arm as they passed the piano. Nell looked down at his arm, his sleeves rolled revealing a tattoo. She couldn't make out the wording but figured he was only being friendly and she should just relax and linked his arm.

'It's nice to have someone new to talk to,' he said as he led her through the noisy, fuggy pub. 'It's been a lonely few weeks at the base with no one else to talk to but my mates.'

'I kind of know that feeling,' she said thoughtfully as he pulled out a chair for her. She looked around for Bessie thinking she was going to join them and saw her standing at the bar laughing with her dimple-cheeked Captain.

'Is this okay for you?' he asked, taking a seat. She nervously looked over at Bessie again.

'You'll have to pardon Captain Thomas, but I can assure you that he means no harm. The boy worked all his life on his parent's farm, not a bad bone in his body,' he answered her thoughts. 'So what's your name?' he asked.

She unbuttoned her coat and draped it over the back of the chair. 'I'm Ellen, but everyone calls me Nell, nice to meet you, Captain,' she said, feeling a bit relaxed as an old man sat down at the piano and started playing one of her favourite tunes.

'That's a beautiful name. And call me Patrick, please. I get so sick of hearing Captain. So what would you like to drink?' he asked.

'A small gin, thanks.'

'A gin it is,' he smiled and went to the bar.

Nell pressed a hand to her temple. What was she doing? Nervously, she looked over her shoulder at Bessie propped beside the bar, laughing. 'Okay, just take it easy, Nell,' she said in a hushed tone. 'It's just one drink and you're not engaged to be married anymore.'

'What was that?' Captain Sanders asked as he put her drink down on the table.

'Oh, it was nothing,' she replied, her cheeks hot with embarrassment. 'So what exactly is it you do here in Swansea?'

'At the moment, I'm just unloading cargo off military trucks. I'm sure I'll be posted out in the not too distant future though. So what about you? What does a lovely looking dame like you do around here?'

Smooth talking, charming, and nice looking. She couldn't deny she felt comfortable in his company.

'Well, it's nothing terribly exciting I'm afraid. I'm not a secret agent or a spy, or...' she took a breath. 'I work in a munitions factory.' She became aware of his attentiveness while talking, which made a change from everyone she knew at her local who probably knew everyone's business before they opened their mouth. 'Although, I do ARP duty as well, so I feel like I'm doing my bit for the war effort, even if my other job is well, just adding to the despair.'

'You're an ARP warden, really? I've never met a women ARP before so I take my hat off to you, in fact, I'm in awe of all women who are doing what are essentially male jobs.' he enthused.

'That's refreshing to hear. Most men I know moan about women going out to work, stealing their jobs as they put it.'

'You guys really pull things together, you know. It's what I really love about this place. Everyone is so eager to help one another. Hitler hasn't got a fat chance in hell with people like you.'

'Swansea isn't all that great. There's nothing left of it for starters.' She couldn't help but chuckle at her remark.

'No, but the people are great here, so friendly and welcoming,' he said, catching her eye.

Nell blushed, looked down at her drink and picked up the glass. She thought maybe now would be a good time to call Bess over as she was over-doing it with her drinks and getting too familiar with the captain. As she was about to get from her seat, Captain Sander's face became anxious. He pushed his chair back and stood up. 'Pardon me, Nell,' he said and rushed around the table. Nell looked over her shoulder. Two men were having a heated conversation with an American soldier. He was short, stocky, with dark brown hair. He didn't seem fazed by the two who were now poking him in the chest, enticing him to fight. Nell noticed he had a glass of milk in his right hand and could see he didn't want any trouble.

'What's the problem, lads?' Captain Sanders asked, standing between them.

Bessie tapped Nell on the arm. 'Oh heck, the Dockers are looking to pick a fight with that

American. I almost feel embarrassed for them. He looks like he could take them all out with one punch,' she said.

Nell got up from her chair and moved towards the other side of the bar. The piano player had now stopped playing, the last note ringing out as the atmosphere in the room became tense.

'There'll be no fighting in here, boys. Take it outside,' shouted the barman.

Nell watched as one of the Dockers pulled back his fist. Captain Sanders swerved to the side to avoid being hit and tumbled backward, crashing into a table. The sergeant who didn't want any trouble was now annoyed. He ducked and administered a blow to the Docker's abdomen.

'You bastard,' he groaned, falling backwards into the bar.

'Enough, is it boys?' Captain Sanders stepped back in, creating a space between the men now standing with raised fists. 'We don't want trouble,' he said to his colleague. 'Why couldn't you just walk away?'

'Yeah, why couldn't you walk away like a baby, you American twat, coming in here, chatting up our women…'

Captain Sanders ducked as his colleague, the Sergeant, effortlessly pounded his fist into the man's face, knocking him to ground. There were shocked faces around the room, and Nell thought it was odd how Captain Sanders would find it amusing when he wanted to stop the fight from happening. She almost wanted to punch him, too.

'I'm really sorry, folks. We came here tonight for a quiet drink not looking for fights, but you should know that Rocky here,' he pointed to the Sergeant, 'is one of our best boxers. If anyone else wants to have a go, I'm sure you wouldn't mind, eh, Rock?' He smirked and patted him on his back. Furious, Nell had a few choice words to say to him, but then he went to offer to help the fallen man to his feet.

Nell saw how aggravated the men were for being mocked. She wished the Captain hadn't said what he did as she knew from experience that the silly buggers would surely try again. She decided she had had enough.

'You ought to be ashamed of yourselves,' she shouted, stepping forward, across the sticky, beer-soaked floor.

The captain turned sharply towards her, surprise etched across his face.

'We're all on the same side, you bloody imbeciles,' she yelled at the Dockers. 'So remind me how it's got anything to do with you that we're having a drink with them? We have minds of our own you know and are capable of making that decision for ourselves. Grow up, and make peace now because you just made yourselves look like a bunch of cavemen in front our allies.'

'Being told off by a woman now, Matthew,' said one of the boys standing by the bar, egging them on.

The man who took a beating looked angry for a moment, and Nell thought he was about to pick a fight with her when he broke eye contact and bowed his head with embarrassment for being told off by a woman. Though his face was hardened, he removed his cap, exchanging a glance with his mates.

'Oh come on, don't be a daft bugger,' said one of the men standing by him 'Let's apologise for fucks sake and make peace.'

The man relented, much to Nell's relief. She could see the effort it took him to admit his fault and was surprised when he proffered his hand to the American sergeant he had insulted.

'No hard feelings,' said Rocky, shaking his hand.

Nell sighed and returned to her seat.

'Come on, Bess,' she shouted to her standing by the bar, 'we should go home. So much for a quiet drink, eh?'

'But I'm enjoying myself,' groaned Bess. 'And besides, I think that Captain Sanders is smitten with you.'

Nell gave her a disapproving look, but gave in and sat down for one last drink before the walk home.

Bessie sat down next to her. 'You still amaze me, Nell, taking on a tough crowd like that. Where does your confidence come from?'

'It comes from living with three older brothers.'

Two hands gently pressed down on Nell's shoulders. She turned her head slightly to her side only to be inches from Patrick's smiling mouth.

'They should have you at the peace talks.' His lips curled into a smile. He went back over to the bar, collected the drinks and put them on the table, passing one to Bess.

'Oh our Nell is a feisty little thing. She always sticks up for those who can't do it themselves.' Bessie caught herself short and concealed a smile under her hand. Patrick laughed heartily and sat down. 'I didn't mean that *you* were incapable of defending yourselves...oh you know what I meant. Personally, I thought you fought pretty well,' said Bess, obviously flustered.

'It's okay, I know what you meant. Nell is an interesting character alright.' He fastened his eyes on Nell who was shifting uncomfortably in her seat.

'It was nothing, but they deserved it anyway,' she shrugged, slightly embarrassed. If it wasn't for that first drink she didn't think she'd have had the confidence to do what she did. She picked up her drink, thinking it was time they were heading on home. 'Bess, do you think we should be leaving, it's getting rather late and I have training tomorrow?'

Patrick leaped to his feet. 'Do you really need to go so soon? The night is just starting,' he said, and then hollered to the piano player standing by the bar to play a song. 'If you must leave then will you please have one dance with me?' He held out a hand to Nell.

Bessie made eyes at her, urging her to go for it.

'Go on, it's just a dance,' she said raising her glass with a cheeky wink of her eye.

'Okay, but just the one dance. I've been on my feet all day.' She took his hand as Glenn Miller's *That Old Black Magic* started.

Patrick swooped around the table, twirled her around and pressed a hand to the small of her back, guiding her to the empty space between the bar and the tables. He pulled her in close, swaying her from side to side.

'You're the most interesting person I've met since I got here. Do you think we could see each other again?' He whispered in her ear.

'I'll have a think about it and get back to you.' she teased.

'Do think about it, because together I think we could be an invincible force.'

Nell laughed. 'You're bold, we've only just met.'

'So? When life presents you with beautiful gifts you don't sit around and think about it, you seize the opportunity as it may be your only chance.'

'Carpe diem is what I think you mean. Seize the day?'

'That's exactly what I mean, you're catching on quick.'

She gazed into his eyes that were dark brown with flecks of gold and then traced his face, down to his smiling lips. Not another word passed between them as they danced as though they were the only people in the room. During the slow number, she drew closer, resting her head on his shoulder, catching a hint of soap and musk. He nuzzled his face against her neck and put his hand firmly around her waist. The song faded out and she broke from his embrace to a rapturous applause. She took a bow and thanked Patrick for the dance and was about to head back to her seat when he took her hand and led her to the back of the pub.

'You've got to let me see you again.'

'I think you've convinced me.'

There was a hint of a laugh in his voice. 'I have? Good,' he leaned closer, his lips inches from hers.

Nell gave into her resolve and kissed him hard on the lips. When they paused for air, Patrick took her hand and kissed the back of it.

'Shall we rejoin your friend?' he asked and looked in Bess' direction.

Bess was deep in conversation with Captain Thomas, throwing her head back with laughter 'No, leave them to talk a while. How about we go for a walk? I doubt she'll miss us.'

He held out the crook of his arm to her and they left the pub into the cool night air.

Standing on the pavement, Nell shivered and tucked her hands in her pockets.

'Are you cold?' He was about to remove his jacket for her as they walked down the High Street.

'A little, if I'm honest. Usually, I don't mind the cold.'

'Here, you need it more than I do.' He took off his jacket and draped it over her shoulders. 'I'm sorry about what happened in there, I'm still so embarrassed,' said Captain Sanders.

'Oh don't be. Just be glad I was there to stop it going any further.'

Patrick laughed heartily. 'You seem in good spirits despite all that's going on…'

'Don't let the mask fool you. Nah, I try my best to not let it get to me or at least not show those that matter to me how much it gets me down. You know the saying, keep calm…'

'…and carry on.'

'Yes, that. Shall we sit here?' she pointed to a solitary bench opposite the castle. 'Today was the worst, I have to admit. A friend of mine at work almost got blown up this afternoon.' Tears welled in her eyes. 'If I'm honest I think it hit me more than anything I've gone through since the war started.'

Patrick slipped his hand into hers.

'Don't be afraid to feel vulnerable in front of me. This war gets me down too, being miles away from home and family and not knowing if I'll ever see them again.'

Nell sniffed back the tears and wiped her eyes with her sleeve. 'It's strange. We've only just met but I feel very comfortable with you.'

'Likewise.' Patrick looked up at the sky. 'There's Cassiopeia, right there,' he pointed to a row of stars. 'My father got me into astronomy and this was the first constellation I found. Soon after that, I made the winning inning at my baseball game, so I think of her as my lucky charm.'

'That's beautiful. A friend said to me once, before the war really started that we'll see the stars again and now when I do look at them they give me hope for the future. Do you think the war will be over soon?'

'I really don't know, Nell. I kind of live day by day. It's the only way I can get through it, you know.'

'Yes, I do,' she responded, thinking she had found someone special.

The following day, Nell arrived at work for her afternoon shift and was changing into her overalls when Bess walked in and sat down on the bench next to her.

'I'm so tired. What time did we get home last night?' she yawned.

'Late. No thanks to your suggestion we stay with those Americans.'

Nell smiled to herself as she wrapped a turban around her head. She hoped to see Captain Sanders again but thought herself silly and slipped into her heavy boots.

'Was he a nice kisser then?' Bess asked. 'I want to know everything, and yes, I did see you slip out with him.' She playfully nudged her arm.

Nell was about to answer when Caitlin and Joanie from the packing shed butted in, having overhead them talking.

'Did you say Americans?' They both giggled and began changing into their normal clothes.

'Yes, we met a few last night, at the Adelphi. Why? Are you jealous?'

'It's just we heard they have a bad reputation at the barracks.'

Both Nell and Bess exchanged a glance. The twins were known for their outlandish stories.

'Well, thanks for that,' said Nell. 'But I doubt we'll ever see them again and even if we did it's no business of yours.' She folded her clothes, tucking them neatly into her bag and asked Bess if she was ready.

'Those two make me mad,' Bess said.

'I'm not really worried about them. They're just horrible and bitter. I just can't wait to finish here so I can read my letters.'

'Oh sure you are. You can't stop thinking about that American can you?'

As the girls walked to the filling sheds, Nell blushed. 'Oh alright, no I can't. He was so sweet, Bess. Do you think I'll see him again?'

'I think you will. Captain Thomas told me that Patrick was the nicest guy he'd ever met.' Bess stopped outside the shed door and turned to Nell. 'I hope this works out for you I really do.'

'Thanks. Now I want to talk to you about a fundraiser for Louise. She's going to need all the help she can get.'

It was early evening when Nell clocked out of work. She retrieved the letters she had been storing in her handbag and walked down Carmarthen Road. The day was overcast and threatened rain, and despite feeling weary and hungry, she was excited to read that Sidney had been promoted and was doing well. She smiled to herself as she read through the two-page letter, the longest he'd ever written to her during his time away. A whistling sound soon tore her away from the letter, making her flinch. She looked up at the sky expecting a horde of bombs only then to hear the excited chatter of children as they rushed to the pavement where an army truck had stopped. It was the Americans, and they were throwing sweets to the eager little hands waving in the air.

'Any gum, chum?'

'Would you like one, too, Miss Adams?'

She realised he was speaking to her and looked the familiar face in the eyes.

'If there's any going spare, Captain.' She then smiled as Patrick jumped from the truck and walked towards her.

'I never expected to see you so soon. How you doing?'

'I'm doing great. Just finished a shift at work and now walking home. What about you?'

'Me? Ah, well, you see,' his playful eyes met hers. 'I met a wonderful girl last night and spent the entire evening thinking about her and wondering if I ever would see her again. Besides, she took off pretty quickly and I never got the chance to ask her if I could take her on a date.'

She felt guilty about leaving so quickly, but when they went back to the bar his friends had plied him with more drink. He was so drunk that she'd doubted he'd even remember her anyway.

'I'm sorry about that, I wanted to speak with you before we left it's just…'

'I know,' he looked over his shoulder at his friends. 'They can be a rowdy bunch for sure, but please don't let that change your opinion of me. We got on well. I enjoyed our conversation and dancing. Please accept my apology for my behavior afterward. Here,' he handed her a bar of chocolate. 'Let's call this a peace offering,' he winked. 'I'm hoping I haven't done too much damage and you'll want to see me again.'

'Thank you,' she looked at the bar of Hershey's in her hand. 'I'd love to…'

'You would? Really?'

Nell nodded. 'Sure. I had a lovely time. Perhaps we could meet and you can tell me all about America.'

'That's great to hear. So Nell, allow me to do this properly this time. Would you like to go out for a quiet drink with me?'

Nell smiled. 'Yes, I'd love to.'

'How about tomorrow evening if you're not doing anything? I'm free from seven and I could come by and pick you up.'

'I could ask to change my day off, so, yeah, okay I'd like that. I could meet you on Tennant Road, outside the grocer's.'

'Brilliant. So I'll see you tomorrow at seven?' He asked when one of the soldiers called him over. 'One minute.' He raised a hand to them. 'I'm sorry, I'd better go.' He jerked a thumb to the truck.

'Of course, thank you for the chocolate.'

He tipped his hat and smiled at her as he got back into the truck. The kids ran back to the pavement and then the truck quickly pulled away. Nell stood amongst excited little voices and looked down at the bar of chocolate in her hand. She'd never seen anything like it before and ripped open the wrapper, a bit reluctant at first, but then took a bite out of the creamy milk chocolate.

Chapter Seventeen

It was rare for Nell and Bessie to share the same day off so both girls decided to make a day of it.

'Would you mind popping to the shops?' asked Mary, handing Nell a list. Mary had just got off from WVS work and was busy chopping carrots. 'These are the last of your dad's. Someone has been in the veg patch again and I'm bloody furious.'

'I heard,' said Bess. 'I can't believe that in times like these, people will go and steal from others.'

'Give it here, Mam.' Nell took the list and both left the house and headed down Tennant Road.

'Looking forward to your date then?' Bess said as she reached for the last tin of peaches on the shelf.

Nell blushed.

'Yeah, I am but not sure if it will happen, we didn't make firm arrangements. He's lovely. Although it feels a lot different to Francis, then I knew him well before we started seeing each other. But what would my dad say if he finds out I'm dating an American GI?' She lifted her basket to the crook of her arm, and then inspected the shopping list. She looked despairingly at the near-empty shelf in front of her.

Bess laughed and put the tin in the basket. 'Your dad will be fine, don't go worrying. From what I remember of him he was such a gentleman. Not at all what I thought the Americans would be like. He wasn't as brash as the others. Captain Sanders is lovely, Nell. You could do far worse, mind.' She gave her a wink.

Nell rolled her eyes and picked up a box of dried eggs and headed to the counter.

'Hello, Tom, how're things?' she asked, handing him the ration book.

'As well as can be. Wish I had more stock to be honest with you, Nell,' he made a sweeping gesture around the shop. 'Poor buggers are going without, but…' He leaned across the countertop and urged the girl's to come closer. 'There's a black market operating around here. So if your mam wants anything.' He tapped his nose. 'I may be able to get it for a price.'

Nell cleared her throat. The idea of cheating the system didn't sit too well for her. 'I'll let her know,' she smiled tightly and gathered up her things. The shop door opened as they were leaving. Nell stepped back to allow Greenwald inside. She turned back to Tom, about to say goodbye when she noticed how nervous he appeared.

'Come through the back,' he said to Greenwald and lifted up the counter's lid.

Curious as to why Greenwald was carrying a muslin cloth bag over his shoulder, she waited by the door to see what he would do with it.

'How's it going, Nell?' He forced a smile and he walked around the counter into Tom's living quarters.

Nell gave a polite nod of her head then left the shop, seething over what she had thought she witnessed.

'What was that about?' asked Bess as they left the shop.

'I think Greenwald is the black market operator around here. I wouldn't be surprised if he had Dad's veg in that bag.'

'No, he wouldn't do that.' Bess shook her head. 'He's done so much for the people around here with the ARP. No, I don't think it's in his nature.'

'Well, I'm not so sure. These are desperate times, Bess.'

They began walking home when Nell stopped abruptly on the pavement and grabbed

Bessie's arm.

'What is it with you?'

'Don't you hear that?' She looked up at the sky, thinking she was hearing planes. 'Come on, I think we'd better run home.' She began sprinting up the road as fast as her feet would take her when the ghostly wailing of the air-raid siren sounded, sending a bolt of fear through her.

'Nell, I can't run so fast,' cried Bess, lagging behind.

Nell turned back. Bess had stopped, holding her stomach as she tried to catch her breath.

'You've got to try harder, Bess!' She ran back, took her hand and both of them rushed up their street, up the steps and through the house, noticing the abandoned tea and cake on the table in the kitchen.

'Is that you, Nell?' cried her father, poking his head out of the shelter's flap.

'Yes, Dad,' she had just got to the shelter when the low thrum of airplanes flew overhead. Nell glanced up at the grey sky and opened her mouth in shock at the speed at which the planes darted across the bay. Bess poked her hard on the back pushing her forward.

'Sorry,' said Bess as Nell tumbled into the shelter.

Once her eyes adjusted to the dim light, she drew back in surprise to see Captain Sanders sitting on the bottom bunk. His impish, brown eyes framed with dark lashes crinkled as they met hers. She opened her mouth to speak, but nothing came out. All she could think was that he was devilishly handsome.

'I almost came looking for you,' he said. 'Your dad was getting worried here.' He stood up, stooping as the roof was too low. He offered his seat to her and she nodded with thanks as they tightly brushed past each other.

'Like sardines in a tin, eh, Nell,' Bess laughed, helping herself to a cup of tea.

Nell felt her cheeks burn with embarrassment and was thankful it was pretty dark in there so no one could see. She didn't respond to Bess but heard Patrick chuckle which was enough embarrassment for one day. 'Oh, here are your things, Mam,' she said, flustered. She passed the basket of groceries to her mother and caught Bessie's smirk in the glow of the candlelight.

'Why didn't you say you were seeing Patrick here? The poor bloke looked bloody scared when I said I had no idea about you two.'

Patrick? So now they were on first name terms. Nell didn't know what to say and looked at her mam who was now knitting with a grin on her face.

'I didn't mean to come unannounced, Nell. I thought we could go on our date a little earlier.'

'I'd love to,' she smiled.

'Also, I came by to ask you if you'd like to accompany me to the dance the barracks is putting on tomorrow evening. It's in aid of the local community. We heard about the accident at the factory you work at and we plan to give the proceeds to the woman.'

'Oh, that's so nice of you. I was only saying to Bess we ought to do something to help.'

'That's a brilliant idea,' said Bess. 'You should ask Nell to put on a show for you, she sings.'

Nell kicked Bess's foot.

'Ouch.'

'Would you Nell?' Patrick asked.

She saw her father's eyebrows raised, waiting for her answer.

'You can't refuse the lad now, Nell, not after coming all this way especially.'

A broad smile swept across her face. 'I'd love to come and sing for you, but how did you...'

'Know where you live? I saw one of the girls outside the factory. Hope you don't mind, I don't want to get anyone into trouble.'

'You don't mind, do you, Nell?' Bessie chimed in.

'No of course not. It's nice to see you again, it's a shame about the circumstances.' She pointed upwards at the shelter.

Patrick laughed.

'You're more than welcome to come along too, Bess,' said Patrick, now sitting on a chair next to Mary.

'Really? Oh, I'd love to, thanks.'

'What about me?' Florrie said with a chuckle. 'I'm not too old, mind you.'

Patrick smiled and patted her affectionately on the hand. 'If I had any more room in the jeep, I would take you along in a heartbeat, doll.' He winked at Nell, whose face flushed hotly under his stare. She leaned into the shadow so nobody would notice.

'So, I wonder when this raid will finish then.' Mary said, offering them a piece of cake. 'Hopefully not too long,' Patrick replied, taking a slice.

'So Patrick, whereabouts are you from?' asked Mary.

'Boston, Mrs Adams. I'm the eldest of three brothers. My father and my mother are both school teachers. Out of the family, I'm the first to join the military.'

'She must worry about you over here?'

'She does like any mother would really. But I know she's proud of me.'

'Like I'm proud of mine, but you never get peace from the worrying, you know. So make sure you write to her as often as you can.'

Patrick caught Nell's eye and smiled. 'I will do, Mrs. Adams. The cake is delicious by the way.'

'You don't have to be nice, sweetheart. It would taste much better with real eggs.'

It was then that Nell remembered what she had seen at the shop. 'Dad, I meant to tell you. We were at the shop not long ago, and I suspect Greenwald is the one who has been stealing from everyone.'

'Greenwald,' he scoffed. 'No, Nell, I think you're mistaken. I've known the man for years. He's honest. No, I don't believe it.'

'Well I wouldn't be so sure,' said Florrie. 'I heard he's having trouble paying rent, so you'd best go and check it out.'

'Oh good God,' said Mary. 'Poor man.'

'Poor man?' David was incredulous. 'If it's true, then the man has been stealing our food, Mary. The minute the bloody all clear goes off I'm going to sort this out once and for all.'

Patrick leaned close to Nell. 'Is it always this exciting during a raid?' he whispered.

Nell chuckled. 'It is with my family.'

Chapter Eighteen

The following afternoon, Nell headed over to Bessie's armed with her new frock and walked through the open door. She waved at Winnie dusting her dining room table and ran up the stairs to Bessie's room. She could already smell the waft of perfume before she entered.

'Hey, it's only me,' she intoned.

Bessie was sitting at her dresser, pin curling her hair. She swiveled around in her chair and a mouth full of clips.

'Alright, Nell. You're just in time to sort this disaster out,' she mumbled.

Nell laid her frock on the bed and went to help to fix her hair.

'Mam wishes she could come along,' she laughed, making a finger curl with a lock of her blonde hair.

Bess spat out the clips in her hand and offered them to Nell.

She slipped in the pin, took the head of a red flower and slipped it in place.

'It's all so exciting. I don't think I've been in such a good mood for a very long time, Nell.'

'Me neither and Patrick's a breath of fresh air. He's so well read and cultured, Bess, unlike anyone I've ever met.'

She didn't want to think of the time when he'd have to go back home when the war had ended so she decided she would make the most of the time they'd have right now. As that's all anyone really had in these unfortunate times.

'So, are you looking forward to singing in front of all those Americans?' Bess asked.

'I am, oddly enough. Patrick told me about this new dance that's everyone doing. I think he called it the jitterbug.'

'That sounds interesting. I can't wait to have a go, so as long as it doesn't require us to dance like bugs.'

Nell laughed, pinning the last of her friend's curls. 'I don't think so somehow. There, you're ready.'

Bess admired her hair in the mirror and then got up. 'Right, your turn, sit down and I'll see what I can do with this.' She lifted up Nell's long dark hair.

'I keep meaning to ask, Bess. What's up with you and Captain Thomas?'

Nell saw her blush in the mirror. 'He's just a very good friend, Nell. Nothing more. I mean, he wanted it to be, but he respects I have a husband abroad. And you know I wouldn't do anything to hurt William, don't you?'

'Of course, I know. I just wondered that's all. It's good to have friends, I guess.'

'He sits and listens to me and we just enjoy each other's company. The poor bugger is thinking he'll be deployed soon so the least I can do is be there for him.'

'That's nice, Bess. It's really nice of you. So are we done?' she asked, indicating to her hair.

'Almost. You're going to look gorgeous.'

'I don't know about that. You know they have nurses up there, don't you? I bet they look glamorous…'

'I know what you're thinking and don't be silly. Patrick only has eyes for you.'

'Yes, I know but…' She composed herself and began powdering her face. 'Yes, I'm just being silly.' She laughed.

The sight of Patrick's jeep caused a stir in the street. Many of the residents had taken to sweeping their already immaculate front steps just to get a look at the dashing American who had gone into number 39.

Nell, who had just come out of Bessie's, saw the jeep and smiled at the nosey neighbours who would no doubt be having a gossip later on over a cup of tea. It gave them something other than the war to talk about, so no harm was done.

'I suppose they'll be wondering why we're dolled up to the nines, eh, Bess?' She chuckled and crossed the road, waving at Florrie who was doing her best to pretend she didn't notice them.

When she entered her house, Patrick was standing in the hallway wearing his army uniform, talking to her mam. He immediately turned around with eyes only for her. She saw his eyes drop to her feet and work their way up, and then drew towards her and kissed her on the cheek.

'You look beautiful,' he whispered in her ear.

'Thank you.'

'Looking forward to singing? If you don't mind I've asked Lucy and a few of her nurses to join you. I've told her all about your amazing voice, Nell. She's looking forward to meeting you.'

'Lucy?'

'Don't look so nervous, Nell. You're going to be fantastic,' he then turned to Mary. 'Mrs. Adams, I've got a few things in the truck I'd like you to have. I'll go and get them.' He gave Nell a wink as he turned and left the house. Nell went out onto the porch followed by Mary. Patrick emerged with a few cans of spam and bars of chocolate in his arms and passed them to Mary who met him at the bottom of the steps.

'Here you, go Mrs. Adams, I guess it'll make up for not coming to the dance tonight.'

'Bloody hell, thank you, Patrick. We'll have a little party of our own tonight.'

'I'm so excited,' exclaimed Bess as she got into the back seat of the jeep.

Patrick opened the passenger door for Nell and helped her inside.

'I can't wait for a dance,' he winked and closed the door.

Nell turned back to Bess who was fixing her make –up in her compact mirror.

'Look at them gawping!' She laughed at Florrie climbing over her fence and across Nell's garden.

'I think Florrie is on the want again.' She pointed. 'She's already nosing in your mother's goodies.'

'Plenty more where that came from,' Patrick said as he got into the driver's seat. 'I'll drop some things around for your neighbours another day, but now ladies, we're going to party.'

'You Yanks are quite fond of your parties,' Bess said. 'Well, so I've heard.'

'What else have you heard?' he laughed. 'Yeah, we do like to enjoy ourselves. My father used to say that you've got one life, you might as well enjoy it.'

'I think that couldn't be more true these days,' said Nell.

They drove down a narrow country road. Only the beam of the headlights was visible as they made their way to the base. Patrick slowed the truck and came to a stop by high metal gates. He wound down the window when a guard appeared with a flashlight.

'Evening, Captain. Are these dames here for the party?' he asked, shining the light into the truck, almost blinding Nell. She raised a hand to her eyes.

'Yes, they're my guests for this evening.'

'Nice. Go through.'

'Dames?' laughed Nell. 'It's so funny to hear him call us that.'

Patrick laughed. 'Well, at least you're not offended.'

They approached a large arched tin barrack that was crowded with people outside the doors. Patrick parked the truck on the opposite side and got out.

'Here we are ladies. I hope you have a great time. Nell,' he said, 'I'll introduce you to the nurses okay? I'm sure you'll get on really well.'

Patrick heard someone call him and he looked up. 'I won't be a moment, doll,' he said to Nell.

Bess took Nell aside while Patrick went to speak with a group of women.

'Nurses? What's going on, Nell?'

'It's Lucy apparently…'

'Who?'

'She's a nurse here. Patrick asked if I'd sing with her and some others, so he's going to introduce me.'

'That's great. I'm looking forward to the show, Nell. Oh, I just saw Louise and Caitlin from the factory talking to some Americans. It's so nice to see Louise enjoying herself, bless her.'

'Nell,' Patrick waved her over. 'I'd like you to meet someone.'

Nervous, Nell walked up to Patrick who was standing with a tall, blonde haired woman wearing a red blouse and white skirt. She had one hand on her hip and smiled pleasantly at Nell when she approached.

'Hey, Nell,' she stuck out her hand. 'It's good to meet you, finally,' she said in a southern drawl. 'Patrick always talks about you, so I feel as if I already know you,' she laughed.

Nell felt underdressed in her presence. 'It's nice to meet you, too.'

'Why don't you come with me so I can sort you out with an outfit?'

Surprised, Nell shot Patrick a look.

'It's okay. Lucy will take care of you.' He leaned close and gave her a kiss on the cheek. 'I'll be waiting for you in the dance hall.'

'Come on, girl.' She grabbed Nell's hand. Lucy whisked her across the compound to a shed. 'This is the nurses' living quarters, hop in,' she held the door open.

Singing and laughter greeted her as she walked inside. Four other women were in various stages of dress.

'Girls, this is Nell, she's singing with us tonight so we gotta run through one of our songs, alright?'

'Hey, Nell,' said a brunette pulling a stocking on her leg. 'I'm Liz. Are you familiar with the *Boogie Woogie Bugle Boy*?'

'Andrew Sisters? Absolutely, I love them.'

'Here, Nell,' Lucy handed her a red blouse and skirt. 'We all like to look the same if you don't mind. It's part of our act.'

Nell took the clothes. 'Sure. I'll just get changed,' she looked for a private area.

Lucy laughed. 'Oh Nell, we're all the same here, honey. Just strip off where you are.'

Nell felt a little silly and took off her coat. 'So how long have you been singing?' she asked Lucy who was fixing her lipstick.

'Forever,' hailed a voice at the back of the room.

'You got that right,' replied Lucy.

Nell waved at the woman with dark, wavy hair.

'I'm Joan, by the way. We've all been singing since we got posted. It whiles the time away and keeps us all entertained. How long have you been singing?'

'Since I was a little girl. Singing is all I've ever wanted to do.'

After a little practicing session and vocal warm up, the girls headed out of the shed to the hall.

Patrick, who was standing outside the entrance held out his arm to Nell.

'You look fabulous,' he said to her.

Nell slipped hers in his and walked towards the door. Nell was excited as upbeat music she had never heard before spilled out of the door, above it a string of blue, white and red bunting. He pushed open the door and Nell gasped in surprise. Bessie nudged her arm.

'Wow I feel like I'm out of place,' she whispered in awe of the dancing taking place on the dance floor. Two women were singing and swaying their hips. Bunting flowed down the stage and across the steel roof and there were rows of tables with food.

'So what do you think?'

He took Nell's hand and gave it a squeeze. 'It's called the Swing, do you want to try?'

Before he could get her on the dance floor a tall, broad-shouldered soldier came up to him, tapping his shoulder.

'Pat, is this the woman who broke up my fight?' he asked with a cheeky grin towards Nell. Nell recognised him. 'It is.' She proffered her hand proudly.

'Well, then it is my pleasure to meet you. I'm the one they call Rocky. Apparently, you have a good right hook, want to join our boxing team?' he joked.

Nell found it amusing.

'If I didn't have so much on then I would gladly accept your invitation. You fight well, I must say.'

He doffed his hat. 'Why thank you, miss.'

'My father used to take me to the local boxing gym to watch my brothers fight. I think I might've picked up a few things,' she laughed.

'I think you could teach me a thing or two,' replied Rocky.

Patrick draped his arm around Nell's shoulder. 'I told you she was special, didn't I?' he said to Rocky.

Nell blushed and then remembered Bessie. 'Where's Bess?' she looked around the crowd on the dance floor. Bess was dancing with a short fellow, laughing as he twirled her around.

'She looks happy,' Patrick commentated, slipping his hand in Nell's. 'Are you ready to give it a go?'

'Beat you to the dance floor!' shouted Nell over the music.

'You look great in red,' Patrick said as he swung her around.

'Thanks, it's my favourite colour,' she replied, missing her step and crashing into Patrick.

They both laughed. 'I never said I could dance to new tunes,' she said, taking his hand and trying again.

Patrick smiled, looking deep into her eyes. 'We'll have plenty of time to practice after the war.'

Nell was about to answer him, but then the music stopped. Lucy pulled Nell's arm. 'Say goodbye to lover boy, we're on.'

A wave of excitement came over her as she headed towards the stage. Joan, Lucy and Liz got into their positions while Nell walked towards the microphone stand to rapturous applause and whistling.

'Thanks for inviting me tonight. This song is a firm favourite of yours, so I've heard. It's The Andrew Sisters, *Boogie Woogie Bugle Boy*.'

The music began and Nell pushed away the nervous energy she was feeling and started singing.

She was only meant to sing one song, but the crowd demanded more. After singing two more songs, Nell left the stage to find Patrick waiting for her.

'You were fantastic, Nell. They loved you.'

'Thanks.' She kissed him on the cheek. 'I really enjoyed that.'

'Nell,' said Bessie. 'That was amazing. You looked like a star.'

'She did,' Patrick agreed. 'Let's go and get another drink.'

'Okay,' replied Nell. 'But I have work tomorrow, so we must be getting home soon.'
'Don't worry, I'll get someone to drive you.'

There had been news on the radio of a few heavy bombings in London and that the Allied Forces were bombing German industrialised cities day and night in retaliation. Nell looked up at the clock above the manager's door and saw it was time for her break. She couldn't listen to any more news right now and whistled to get Bess's attention.

'Just going out for a fag, are you coming?'

Bess had just filled a shell and nodded. Her face glistened with sweat. 'I'm overdue a break, so I'll come with you but I need to nip to the loo first.'

Standing outside the factory, Nell was getting much needed fresh air when Bess came out and went to sit on the roadside and offered her a cigarette.

'I've asked if I could swap shifts tomorrow, so I won't be walking with you. You'll be alright at that time of the morning, won't you?'

'I should think so after doing ARP duty at silly hours on my own,' she stumped the ash on the floor and heard someone mockingly cough.

'I hope you're going to clean that up,' said Beryl with a laugh. She sat down next to the girls on the curb and took a newspaper out of her handbag and showed them the front headline.

'Poor buggers, eh?' said Beryl. 'I have cousins that live in Walthamstow. My mother has been trying to reach them for the past few days with no luck. I'm getting quite worried now.'

'Sorry to hear that, Beryl. Try to remain positive, okay,' replied Nell, putting a comforting hand on her arm. 'They could've made their way to a shelter and have no way of contacting you. Don't lose hope, girl.'

Beryl smiled weakly and wiped her tears with the sleeve of her shirt. 'Thanks, Nell.'

'Anytime, love.'

'Girls, come quick,' shouted Elsie.

They all looked up expectantly when the low drone of the air raid sounded.

Nell threw her cigarette on the floor, stumping it out with her boot.

'What the hell is going on?' She stood up, looking in the direction of the docks. She shielded her eyes from the sun and to her surprise saw an enemy plane flying low in their direction. Elsie yelled to the girls to get to the communal shelter, but Nell knew they had no chance of making it. Across the road was a small woodland and she called for the girls to follow her.

'Are you sure, Nell?' cried Bess.

'Of course, but quickly before they see you.'

The girls huddled under bracken. Nell could feel Beryl shaking beside her and wrapped an arm around the girl's shoulder. 'It's going to be okay,' she whispered as the sound of a bomb landed.

They all covered their ears.

'That sounded like it was the Hafod,' said Bess.

'My mother lives there.' cried Beryl about to leave.

Nell pulled her back. 'Don't be ridiculous, the all-clear hasn't sounded yet.'

Beryl took off down the road, heading towards the Hafod where clouds of smoke billowed into the sky, eclipsing the daytime.

'My God, we can't let her go.' Nell looked at Bess whose eyes were round like saucers.

'Don't you think of going after her, alright?'

'I'll be okay, don't panic.'

Nell took off after her. She could make her out running under the railway bridge when she heard a whistling sound grow near until she realised it was behind her. The next thing she knew, she was hurtled a few feet in the air, landing several yards up the road. An excruciating pain in her ankle and arm rendered her motionless.

She hadn't been able to work for weeks and was increasingly getting fed up with being stuck at home. She heard that Beryl and her mother were fine and so with the aid of her grandmother's walking stick, she hobbled over to Bessie's who decided a trip to the Naval was in order.

'Can't keep yourself out of strife, can you?' Jack laughed as he handed her a drink.

'I always seem to get caught up in things, don't I?'

'I was starting to think you were invincible up 'til this point.' He nodded towards her leg. 'I don't know, Nell, I'm starting to wonder if it's you they need to stop this bloody war.'

'I would gladly try, Jack.' She laughed and went to join Bessie at the table. She took out a few letters she had received and passed them to Bess. 'It's all happening abroad, too,' she said when her father walked into the pub with Greenwald.

'Alright, Dad?' she asked.

He waved as he went to the bar.

'Not even he's got a lot to say the past few days.' She turned to Bess. 'Perhaps we should've gone out with the Americans, this place is as dead as the cemetery.'

'We could always ask them if they fancy a night out to the pictures in the week if you're up for it?'

'Splendid idea.'

It was evening when they left the pub. As Nell hobbled down the steps outside the pub, she heard the pub door opening, and a faint clanging on the piano. The rowdy, drunken laughter belonging to the locals spilled out. She recognised one of the voices as that of her father.

'Dad, is that you?' she asked, squinting hard to see in the darkness.

'Yes, Nell, wait up,' he slurred.

'Oh, Dad, how many have you had?'

'Nell, I don't want you to go off panicking because I know what you're like, so listen to me. If you had the news that one of your sons has been injured; wouldn't you go out and get drunk, hm?'

Nell's heart leaped to her throat.

'Oh my God. Who is it, Dad? What's happened? Are they okay?'

'Didn't I tell you not to panic,' he stopped walking now and grabbed hold of Nell's arm to stop him from swaying. 'I didn't tell you earlier as you're only now feeling better yourself, but you ought to know. It's Alf. His plane was shot down near Hamburg. Thankfully one of ours got to him in time, or...I don't want to think what would've happened.'

'Nevermind the what ifs. When is he coming home?'

Nell knew her personal hell was just beginning. The agonising feeling of loss was already tearing her apart. If only she could stay strong for just a while longer...just a little bit.

'Not sure yet, but he's fine. Well, truthfully, I don't know what his injuries are exactly, but he's alive and that's all that ruddy matters.'

'Yes, Dad, that's all that matters. Come on, then, let's get you home for a cup of tea to sober you up.'

'Do we have any of that coffee left?'

'Not sure. If I can find any, you can have it.'

'Thanks, love. You're one in a million.' He said as they walked up Jersey Terrace. 'Nell, I don't know who is in the worst state right now. Me or you with that bloody leg.'

Nell laughed out loud and helped him find his way up the steps.

'Watch for the doorstep, now there you go.'

The light was on in the front room. Mary put down her knitting and got up from the chair by the fire.

'Oh Dai for heaven sake, you didn't have to go and get drunk.' She looked at Nell. 'Did he tell you about Alf?'

'Yes, Mam,' she gave her a hug while her father flopped down on the sofa and began dozing off. They both looked at each and laughed.

Mary had tears in her eyes.

'Come on, Mam, everything is going to be alright. I'll go and pop the kettle on.' She went to the kitchen and lit the gas stove.

Chapter Nineteen

Nell arrived home from a walk to the shops on Tennant Road. She only managed to get a few pieces of bacon, barely enough to feed her father, but it was better than nothing. As she entered the hallway Mary called to her from the kitchen with the exciting news that Alf had been discharged from the military hospital and should be home by the end of the week. Elated at the news, Nell dumped the shopping bag on the table and threw her arms around her mam who was now crying with happiness, but it was soon short-lived as that familiar drawn-out wail sounded, scaring them both senseless. They looked at each other wondering if what they were hearing was real.

'Why now? We don't have a raid for ages and we get two in the space of a couple of days?' Mary threw her hands up in the air. 'The food is going to be bloody ruined now,' she said turning off the stove.

'I'll sort it, Mam. Go to the shelter.'

Florrie shouted from the back garden that they needed to get a move on as there were snipers about. Nell took the Woolton pie out of the oven and shoved the bacon into the pantry while Mary rushed out the door, armed with her teapot and cigarettes. After checking that the front door was closed, Nell shut the back door behind her, ignoring the planes flying above and dashed across the garden to the shelter.

'I'm so glad I got home when I did,' she said breathlessly and sat down on the lower bunk. 'Do you think Dad's going to be alright out there on fire watch?'

'Now you know how we feel when you are out on ARP duty. Of course he'll be fine, try not to worry because it worries me enough. But oh God, why now? My nerves are shot enough as it is.'

Nell apologised and sat with her back against the tin wall, hands resting on her chest. She listened to her mother quietly crying then the sound of someone screaming and banging outside of a nearby back door jolted her upright.

'What's going on?' Mary jumped to her feet.

Nell went out of the shelter to check and saw Florrie dashing across her garden. There were no aircrafts over-head now, thankfully, but the banging and screaming continued until Florrie managed to yank the tight-fitting door and as she did so, Winnie tumbled outside.

'It's Bess, oh my God, they got Bess.' A gut-wrenching sob escaped her lips. She continued to scream, clenching onto her apron until she couldn't stand anymore and dropped to her knees.

Nell ran to the back gate and dashed to Florrie's garden and once there she held Winnie tightly, hoping that what she had just heard wasn't true.

'What about Bess?' Nell's voice shook as she knelt down beside Winnie's trembling body.

'She's dead, my lovely girl is dead,' she screamed. 'They killed her! The bloody bastards killed her.'

The words whirled around Nell's head. How could Bess be dead? She was at work and wasn't due home until this evening. No, this had to be a mistake.

Mary, who had followed close behind her daughter, comforted Winnie and Nell got to her feet, pacing the garden. 'I'm going over to Greenwald's, I'll be back as soon as I can,' she said, hoping to get the facts from him. She stepped out of Florrie's front door but, when she got to the bottom of the steps, she saw Greenwald and Edward walking up the street. The grim expressions on their faces already answered her questions. She rushed to meet them as they approached her house.

'What's happened? Winnie is out there saying that Bess is dead, please, for the love of God, tell me it's not true?' she cried, 'Tell me it's not true.' She begged Edward as Greenwald took them inside.

Edward shook his head. 'She got caught by one of those snipers on Tennant Road…'

'No!' she sobbed burying her face into Edward's chest.

'Sorry Nell,' his voice trembled.

'You've got to be mistaken, it can't have been her, she's at work. She traded someone an afternoon shift.'

'Nell, let's get you into the shelter, there's still a raid on, come on.' They took her gently by the arm and led her out of the back door. There was another guttural scream from the next garden but Nell didn't respond to it. It became almost background noise in her head as her focus was still on the words she was thinking, Bess is dead. She's not coming back.

Edward guided her towards the shelter, helped her inside and poured her a glass of water. She didn't take it and picked up her gran's blanket draped over the chair, clinging to it for comfort.

'Nell, stay calm and don't move from here, you hear me? I'll be back as soon as I can.'

Her gaze fastened on Edward's eyes but she couldn't speak. He touched her lightly on her face and got up to leave.

Now she found herself sitting alone in the darkness with tears running down her cheeks. It was hard to think that Bess was no longer in this world. No, she couldn't accept it, never would.

PART SIX

1944

Chapter Twenty

'It's a beautiful day,' said Nell as she carried a tray of cups of tea out into the back garden. Winnie and Edna were sitting chatting to her mother about organising a summer fete so they could raise money for the school.

'Come and join us for a natter, Nell,' said Winnie, patting the seat of an empty chair next to her.

She put the empty tray down next to Edna who was basking in the glorious June sunshine when the conversation turned to their sons.

'I have a letter from Alf,' Mary said to Nell. 'He said he has been discharged from the hospital but it has to be post-phoned for some reason. I think there must be something big brewing I can feel it in my bones.'

Nell felt the whistle in her pocket and smiled.

'And I had one from Francis the other day, too. Did I tell you?' Edna threw an apologetic look at Nell. 'Oh I'm sorry, Nell…'

'Don't mind me. We're still friends and that's what counts at the end of the day.'

Edna had a look of relief on her face and took a sip of her tea.

'I've been saving my rations,' said Winnie. 'When this bloody war is over, this street will know about it. I've even got the bunting ready. I tell a lie, actually. I had it ready in the summer of 1940.'

Everyone laughed.

Nell didn't want to quash their hopes and kept her thoughts to herself. The back door opened, and her father walked out with a cheesy grin on his face. Nell was surprised to see Patrick follow behind. His eyes came alive when he saw Nell who jumped to her feet at the sight of him. He gave Nell a kiss on her cheek. The women whooped and cheered deliberately trying to embarrass her.

'Oh shut-up you lot, haven't you got anything better to do?' she chuckled.

'Look who I found on the way home,' David said. 'Good lad offered me a lift from the shops on Tennant Road.'

'Hello. It's nice to see everyone. Enjoying the sunshine, I see?' Patrick doffed his cap.

'Any spare Americans at the base, Captain?' Winnie laughed.

'I'll see if I can find someone for you,' he laughed, nodding to the gifts he had in his hand. 'I know it's not much but I have a few packets of nylons if you'd like them?' He handed one each to Edna, Winnie, and Mary.

'Like them?' screeched Edna, 'Hand them bloody over.'

'It's like bloomin' Christmas,' Winnie said and got up from her seat to give him a hug. 'You've got a fine fellow here, Nell.'

Nell snaked an arm around Patrick's waist and rested her head on his chest. 'He's brilliant isn't he, I'm very lucky.'

'I've got something special for you in the car,' he whispered in her ear. 'But I was wondering if you fancy the cinema later?'

Nell took his hand, leading him into the kitchen while they all chatted excitedly over their new stockings.

'I'd love to go, be nice to get out for a bit. You didn't have to give them anything, you know. You're too kind.'

He shrugged.

'Why not? You have to admit, it's nice to see a smile on someone's face these days.'

'Don't I know it? My brother was meant to come home but something has come up and he can't. It's just disappointments after disappointments lately.'

Patrick didn't say anything. She noticed his far-away look. She didn't want to ask what bothered him, the war was full of secrets and she was sure he'd tell her in time.

They strolled through town, passing blocked off streets and signs for bus diversions. The empty spaces between buildings were still full of rubble from the Blitz, which made her feel emotional. She turned her head from the wreckage and nestled her head on Patrick's shoulder. He held her tightly as if he knew what she was feeling.

'I've organized a picnic for us later on. Do you have any idea where we could go?'

'There's a place down the Gower we could go, not far from the RAF base.'

'Nice. I'd like to see a bit more of Wales one day, but…' He held back. 'Nothing, it's nothing,' he reassured her and planted a kiss on her forehead. 'Let's get to the pictures before we miss the news.'

Nell felt anxious. What could he mean he would like to see more of Wales one day? What was he insinuating? No more was said and she thought maybe it was a slip of the tongue.

They walked along Oxford Street where a small queue had already formed along the wall. Rain began to fall heavily and Patrick took off his jacket, holding it up over their heads. A kind of giddy energy came over Nell, who felt the weight of the war slip from her already heavily burdened shoulders.

'I'm glad you came by today.' She pressed herself closer to his body. 'I've sort of missed you,' she said, reaching up on tiptoe and planted a kiss on his lips.

'I've missed you, too. You're all I think about, Nell.'

The romantic moment was caught short when he walked into a puddle.

'Damn, you get enough rain here, don't you?'

Nell doubled over with laughter.

'So you don't get rain in the States, then?' she asked as they joined the back of the queue.

'Of course, we have plenty in Boston where I'm from. Before I left for the United Kingdom, I lived with my parents and three brothers. I was meant to attend university, but I really wanted to be in the military. Naturally, it didn't go down well with parents who I think that I told you, are both teachers.'

'A least you had a choice. Not many did.'

'For which I'm thankful.' He hugged her tightly.

The doors to the theatre opened, and soon they were out of the rain. At the box office, Patrick bought two tickets and took her hand as he guided her into the auditorium. A man standing next to the entrance turned to look at Nell as she passed.

'Excuse me? Miss Adams, isn't it?'

Nell didn't hear him at first. Patrick directed her attention to the man she recognized as Henry Wilder, the promoter she met at Woolworths.

'Yes, it is.'

'Well, there's a face I'll never forget,' he said, shaking her hand enthusiastically.

'It's nice to see you again, Mr. Wilder. How are you?' she said, genuinely glad to see him.

'Very well, thank you. You never did call me, did you?'

'No, I didn't…'

'I've been in London since we met, putting on musicals. It's a surprise to see this place still standing after the Blitz.'

'It's a surprise to see anything standing,' she said thinking back to those three nights.

'Anyway, I'd still love the chance to work with you, if you're interested. I have a musical I'd like you to audition for?' he took a card from his pocket. 'Call me, okay,' he looked up at Patrick. 'It's very nice to meet you, lad. Make sure she calls me, okay.'

'I will do.'

When Henry Wilder went back to the people he was talking with, Patrick had a look of surprise on his face.

'You didn't tell me you had a shot of singing professionally?'

'Once upon a time, I did. But really, I used to sing in the local pub. I'm hardly what you'd call professional.'

'But you are obviously good enough to get this guy's attention, so what's stopping you? After the success at our base with Lucy and the girls.'

'Not much right now…'

'Then you'll call him and do the audition for me?'

'Yes, yes, if it stops you from going on,' she said, urging him to the auditorium. 'We're going to miss the news if you don't hurry.'

Patrick guided her to the second row from the back, taking the two end seats as the Pathe newsreel began. They hadn't sat down for much more than five minutes when the usher came running down the corridor.

'The sirens have sounded! There's an air-raid shelter, up to you. You can stay or take cover.'

Patrick wrapped an arm around her and held her close. 'Do you want to stay?' he asked as everyone left out theatre.

Nell spotted a glint his eyes.

'Why not?' Nell looked around. 'It seems like we have the place to ourselves.'

Patrick ran a finger along her cheek, eliciting a shiver through her body. He drew close until their lips met. 'Are you sure?'

Nell nodded. 'Absolutely.'

The all-clear sounded a little while later and Patrick sat up and adjusted his jacket. Nell took out her compact and re-applied her lipstick.

'We should go,' he stroked her hair and pressed a kiss to her cheek as people began returning to their seats.

The cool breeze blew across their faces as they stepped outside. A man smoking a cigarette told them that it was a false alarm but they didn't want to go back inside.

'I don't want this day to end,' he said, taking Nell's hand. 'Seeing as it's still daytime and we have a few hours until I'm due back, what do you say we go for a drive?'

'Need you ask?' she smiled.

Later that afternoon, as the sun was low in the sky they arrived at Rhosilli Beach. Patrick pulled the jeep into a parking space that overlooked the vast ocean and sandy beach that stretched around the cliff.

Nell sighed, taking in the views. 'I haven't been here in forever.'

'We drove down here once when we first came to Wales. It's so beautiful.' Patrick's eyes swept the panoramic views of Rhossili beach and reached for Nell's hand.

'Is there something wrong?' She asked, softly.

Patrick shook his head, his eyes still fixed on the view ahead.

'No. I've been thinking of home the last few days. I miss it a lot.'

'I'm sorry.'

'It's quite alright. I'm not usually the sentimental type.' About to say something else, he stopped and smiled. 'Come on, let's find a spot to sit down.' He got out of the jeep, but Nell wasn't convinced that everything was as okay he wanted her to believe. Something bothered him she could tell. The question was whether she wanted to find out.

Patrick went to the back of the jeep and took out a basket. 'Come on my little Welsh goddess, we have the entire place to ourselves, so sing me a song. '

Nell laughed.

'Didn't you hear me sing enough at the party?'

He put the basket down on the grass and then put his hands on her hips, pulling her in close.

'You can't be serious. I love your voice…' He looked intently into her eyes. 'I love you.' He cupped her face in his hands.

'I love you too.' She wrapped her arms around him.

'I always knew you did. So how about that song? And to make it a challenge for you, sing it in Welsh.' He smiled.

Nell playfully thumped him on the arm. 'I'm too embarrassed.'

'No you're not, you just don't love me enough.' He winked, taking her hand and twirling her around.

'I do too. Oh alright then, but I only know one song in Welsh, and I'm not even sure if I can remember all the words. I was never any good at Welsh at school.' She brushed a strand of hair away from her face.

'Nell, I'm shocked you don't know your mother tongue,' he joked. 'Yes, and why don't you southerners speak Welsh anyhow?'

Nell shrugged. 'No idea. Do you want the song or not?'

Patrick took off his overcoat and spread it on the grass.

'One minute while I get comfortable,' he laughed cheekily and sat down.

Nell breathed deeply and focused on the horizon. She couldn't look at Patrick as she sang, but as the words came out, so did the tears. She thought about all the men fighting on the sea, land, and air, giving special thought to her brothers and friends. When the song ended she felt Patrick's arms wrap around her.

No words were spoken between them for a little while as they held each other, soaking in the moment.

'That was beautiful,' he whispered.

They then sat down on the grassy bank overlooking the Bay, sharing the large picnic of American treats and a flask of tea. Patrick, who had spent the last few minutes in silence, smoothed her hair and then turned her around to face him. 'Nell, my love, do you fancy a little walk?' He asked in a quiet, calm voice. He stood up and held out his hand.

Nell gazed up at him and got to her feet, dusting the sand from her polka dot frock. 'You seemed miles away,' she said.

'I'll soon be miles away, Nell…' He said sadly as they strolled hand in hand.

She felt her heart beat rapidly. She didn't think this would happen again, and so squeezed his hand tight. She followed him onto the gravel coastal path bordered with hawthorn. Suddenly Patrick dropped down on one knee.

'Life is short, Nell. I love you with all my heart.' His voice graveled with emotion. 'This afternoon has been really special to me so it breaks my heart to have to tell you I am leaving quite soon. I'm being deployed overseas.'

Tears began to fill her eyes. She couldn't believe what she was hearing.

'Why? What's going on?'

'I can't really say much at this point, sorry. You'll soon hear about it…'

'But… no, you can't go now. I've had a war full of goodbyes and I'll be damned if I say another goodbye to someone I love.' Her voice ebbed, and she bent her head forward, tears splashing onto her cheeks.

'I didn't say this was a goodbye,' he held her tight. 'I will be back for you and we will build a life together if that's what you want as well?'

'Of course, that's what I want.'

'So this leads me to the reason I brought you here today… I want to marry you, tomorrow if you'll have me?'

She burst into yet more tears. 'Yes, yes I will marry you, I'd do it tomorrow if we could,' and she threw her arms around him.

'We could do. There's nothing stopping us.'

Nell stared down at the crashing waves against the rocks for a moment and then pulled back.

'Yes, let's get married in the morning, if we can.'

When she got home, she called out to her parents asking them to come into the front room.

'What's going on?' asked David, covered in dirt from the back garden.

'Mam, Dad I'm getting married. Tomorrow! Do I get your blessings?'

At first, they were shocked, standing in stunned silence.

'Did I hear right, Nell? Did you say you're getting married in the morning? Well who the bloody hell to?' David said, holding his pipe halfway to his mouth.

Mary dug her elbow into his side and gave him a glare.

'You know who, the American boy, Patrick.' She then turned her attention to Nell. 'What's the rush love, are you…'

Nell laughed. 'No Mam, I'm not expecting. He's leaving soon and I know in my heart I want to marry him. Do I get your blessings? Please. This means a lot to me.'

'Well you've got my blessing,' said David.

'And mine love,' said Mary. 'Well, I suppose I've got a lot to organise. I'd better go and ask the vicar if he has an hour to spare tomorrow morning.'

'Thank you, both of you, I'll call Patrick inside. He's been waiting in the jeep.' Nell dashed out the front and waved him inside the house. 'They said yes!' She squealed on the porch. She took his hand and pulled him into the living room.

'I hear congratulations are in order.' David said, shaking his hand.

'Thank you. I know it seems rather rushed, but it's what we both want and I can assure you, Nell will be taken care of.'

'I have no doubt.' David sucked on his pipe and then indicated for him to sit down. 'She said you are off somewhere soon. Where are you going?'

Nell shook her head at her mother who was also rolling her eyes at David. 'You can't leave the war out of anything, can you? Look, I think we need to get organised, we'll need the help, eh, love?'

'Yes, Mam. I'm so excited.'

Mary and Nell left the house, leaving the men to talk.

There was chaos in the house the following morning. Mary had managed to persuade the vicar, who had already spoken with Patrick a few days ago to marry them at the last minute and was now busy sewing Nell into her old wedding dress. Vera Lynn played on the radio, which Nell was singing along to, when Edna and Florrie rushed through the house with a bunch of fresh flowers and a small cake they had managed to make by donating their precious, rationed eggs.

'Only the best for you, Nell,' Edna set it down on the table.

'Now we need something old and something blue,' said Florrie, looking around the room.

'I have something borrowed.' Nell held up Alf's whistle. 'It's my lucky charm.'

'Here, I have something old,' said Edna, taking off her ring.

'And the flower in the bunch I brought is blue. So there we are, you're all set,' said Florrie.

'Yeah, it looks like I'm all set then.' She got up and walked towards the mirror hanging above the fireplace to check on her makeup.

'Doesn't she make a beautiful bride, eh David?' Mary was almost in tears.

'Beautiful,' he said fixing his tie. 'I thought we could go down the Naval for a drink later on? Do you fancy that, Nell?'

Nell smiled. 'That sounds fine, Dad.'

'Right, you'd better get upstairs,' said Mary, 'just until everyone arrives.'

Nell lifted up her dress, and as she passed the front door she heard a commotion of engines outside. 'They're here, Mam, where are my flowers?' she panicked, running up the stairs to her room.

'I'll get them, go while I get everyone inside.'

She anxiously paced the floor in her room while she listened to Patrick's friend's greeted her mother at the door.

'At least he turned up, eh?' Emily joked, poking her head around the bedroom door. 'Here are your flowers,' she handed her a bunch of roses her father had grown in the front garden and the flowers from Florrie. 'Your mam said to come down, and your father will walk you into the front room, okay, Nell? By the way, you look wonderful – see you downstairs.' Emily left, closing the door behind her.

Nell nodded, feeling a tightness in her chest. She exhaled and turned to her dressing table mirror. 'Let's do this!'

She left the room, walked across the landing and down the stairs and saw a few American soldiers gathered in the hallway. She was surprised to see that there was hardly any room left to maneuver either. They gave her a salute as she passed. It made her smile and she mouthed a thank you back. David was on the verge of tears.

'I'm proud of you, Nell,' he said and offered her his arm.

She linked her father's arm as they walked into the living room. Mary stood next to Edna, Emily and Florrie who were all wiping away tears with tissues.

Patrick was in his army uniform and turned to face her when she stood next to him. He smiled, whispering that she looked beautiful.

Chapter Twenty One

It was almost as if the world had stopped spinning. It was the anniversary of Bess's death and Nell was finding it difficult to cope. The following day, the sunshine pooled through her windows basking her face with a warm glow. She lay in bed where she had been since the previous supper time and pulled the cover over her head, hoping that by the time she woke none of the bad stuff would have happened and Bess would do her usual of knocking the door to go to work and Patrick wouldn't be leaving. She cried herself into another deep sleep and woke hours later to her mother tapping her on the shoulder.

'Nell, Nell...'

She stirred awake and opened her blurry eyes to see her mam staring down at her.

'What is it?' she asked, dozing off again.

'Patrick has come to see you. Now please get up, Nell.'

She opened both her eyes at the mention of his name.

'Patrick is here? Oh I can't let him see me like this,' she cried, and sniffed back tears.

Mary rolled her eyes and was about to leave the room but turned back when she got to the door. 'Staying in bed won't solve a thing you know. Bess is gone Nell and no amount of staying in bed will bring her back. I'm sorry. I don't mean to be harsh. We all loved her, but you must get a firm grip on reality. Life has to go on, sweetheart.'

'Tell him I'll be there in few minutes.'

'Okay and I've put a bowl of hot water over there for you to have a swill.'

'Thanks, Mam.'

Mary closed the door behind her as she left. Nell thought she really needed to make the effort to get back to the real world. It's what Bess would've wanted. She pushed herself up, taking a moment to gage her thoughts.

'Keep calm and carry on, eh Bess?'

She pushed the cover back and precariously reached a foot out of the warm blanket onto the rug and stood up. As she did so she caught her reflection in the mirror. Her face was ghostly white and her hair was matted. Part of her couldn't be bothered to make too much of an effort, so she went over to her dresser, pulled open the top drawer and rummaged through her clothes.

'Nell, I've put the kettle on.' Her mother called up the stairs.

'Alright, Mam I won't be a moment,' she shouted back, pulling out a blouse and skirt. After a quick wash, she got dressed, brushed her hair until the knots were loose and thought bugger it, it is the best I can manage given the circumstances.

She walked across the landing and had just mounted the top step when she heard chatter from the front room. Patrick came out of the living room, rushing up the stairs towards her.

'I'm so sorry I woke you.' He pulled her in for a hug. Nell relaxed into his body, grateful for his strong arms around her. 'I just had to see you. If there was a way I could've got out of that meeting last night...'

'You don't have to apologise. I haven't forgotten there's a war on. Anyway, I've missed you,' she whispered, caressing his face.

'Oh Nell, why didn't you get someone to contact me? I would've been here straight away, you know that. But why didn't you tell me how sad you were that Bess is not here to share our happiness?'

'I should've, I'm sorry. I can't believe she's gone, you know. And now you're leaving as well,' she sobbed on his shoulder.

He ran his hands through her hair and then gently placed a kiss on her forehead. 'You know

I'm going to come back for you. Come on, let's go for a drive, spend some time together.'

She hesitated a moment.

'I miss her so much, Patrick…'

'I know, love. Bessie was a real trooper. I know Captain Thomas is still heartbroken. He really thought the world of her too.'

'We all did and thanks for coming by today, I really appreciate it.'

'Hey, you're my wife, where else would I rather be.' He kissed her on the lips.

'Would you like a drink before we go?'

'I think a tea would be nice.'

While she waited for the kettle to finish boiling, Patrick stood at the side of her. He had one arm resting on the counter watching her as she scooped the tea leaves out of the tin and into the teapot. She could feel his eyes on her, watching her every movement.

'I didn't know making tea could be so interesting?' she said.

'It is when you do it.' He stroked her arm.

All she wanted was for him to take her far away from this place as possible but then she remembered how this was his last day in Wales. A hard knot settled in her heart, shooting spasms of pain through her body. She handed him a cup of steaming hot tea.

'I can't believe it's your last day here.'

She turned to the window, covering her face with her hands.

Patrick put down his cup. 'Come on, we need to make the most of it.' He wrapped an arm around her shoulders. 'How about we go and see a film? It'll be my treat. Or we could go for a long drive if you want. I've packed a blanket and a few treats I've managed to salvage from the canteen. God, Nell I want to spend as much time with you as I can.'

His words sent a shiver through her. What could he mean "as he can"? Was he scared of not coming back to her? Where was his confidence when she needed it the most?

'Where would you like to go? I don't care as long I'm with you.'

'Shall we recreate our first proper date and have a picnic down the Gower? Come here,' he moved closer, gently turning her to face him. 'You have nothing to worry about I promise. I'm going to come back to you.'

Nell smiled tightly. 'I know. Alf is due back today, too.' She picked up her handbag from the kitchen table. 'He made me the same promise when he left.'

Patrick lay out a blanket over tussocks of grass and sat down, cuddling up to Nell as the warm summer's breeze brushed their skin. Over the barbed wire fencing that separated the beach from the footpath were hundreds of ships. Nell had never seen anything like it. A plane flew overhead with three white rings on its wings, heading south.

'I've never seen so many ships in my life, it's actually making me nervous looking at them.'

'How do you mean?'

'To have so many congregated here must mean something big is happening. Do you think the war will end soon?'

'I really hope so, Nell. All I think about these days is what sort of life I'll have without it having happened. I would not have met you and that makes our troubles bearable.' He looked at her. 'I can't wait for us to start our new life and have kids.'

'Neither can I.' She rested her head on his shoulder. 'I hope it won't be too long.'

She recognised that faraway look he had as he stared across the Bay. Her mind went back to the day she and Francis sat on the beach when he told her had joined the Navy. Now her husband was leaving and the sadness engulfed her.

'Do you know where they're going?'

'God knows, but I suppose I'll find out soon enough. Anyway, enough of the war, this is supposed to be our date.'

It was late when they got home. Patrick walked her into the house which was lively and full of chatter. It was then Nell saw the bare feet of a man who was sitting on a chair from the hallway, his body concealed by the wall. She wondered who had come to visit and slowly entered, thinking it couldn't be Alf, not yet. They weren't expecting him until late this evening after all. As she entered the living room, she saw the happy smiles on her parent's faces and almost instantly the tension fell away from her shoulders.

'Is that my favourite sister?' Alf asked.

Alf's smiling face beamed back at her.

'Oh it is you, Alf. It's you, you're home.' She took a moment to allow it all to sink in. The left side of his face was now pinky flesh, but he still had that sparkle in his eyes. He was still her Alf.

'Have you got my whistle?' He pushed himself up from the chair.

'I can't believe it…' she flung her arms around him. 'I've missed you so much.'

'I've missed you too, Nell. Thanks for writing to me and keeping me sane.'

Nell pulled back from the embrace.

'What happened to you?' she asked in a low voice.

'My plane got shot down. I guess I'm lucky to escape with a few burns, but aside from that I'm okay.' He looked up at Patrick standing in the doorway. 'So who's this?' he asked, moving to greet him.

'Alf, I'd like you to meet my husband, Patrick. Patrick this is my brother. One of my brothers, I should say.'

'What she meant to say is that I'm the favourite one.' Alf joked and shook Patrick's hand.

'Hey, don't be so silly,' said Nell. 'There is no favouritism.'

'I won't tell if you won't,' Alf said.

'It's an honour to meet you, Captain,' Patrick said.

'Likewise. I knew a few Yanks at the hospital, some became good friends of mine.'

'And here's your whistle.' Nell reached into her handbag and presented him with their lucky charm. 'I told you I'd keep it safe for when you got back, and now it's yours again.'

'I heard it has kept you safe a few times. I still can't believe you walked into a burning building.' He shook his head at her, laughing.

'Patrick is being deployed tomorrow,' David chimed in.

'You're shipping out tomorrow?' Alf said to Patrick. 'I can't say I envy you mate, so here,' he passed the whistle to Patrick. 'Just make sure you come back for my sister, won't you?'

'Thank you. And of course I will.'

'Right, come on, I don't know about you lot but I could do with a couple of drinks. Does anyone fancy going down the Naval?' He looked for everyone's approval.

'One last dance before I knock off for the night,' yelled Greenwald, from his seat at the piano. A slow number started, and those who were able, made it onto the dancefloor.

Patrick pushed back his chair. 'Nell. Dance with me?'

Alf raised his glass to them both.

She slipped her hand in his and took to the floor.

'You'll be careful out there won't you?'

'You know I will. I have your brother's lucky whistle now, don't I?' He made her laugh.

'I'm going to miss that smile of yours.'

'You'll see it again soon enough, I promise'

'Nell, when I'm gone I want you to do me a favour.' He looked down at her. 'I want you to sing again, follow your dreams.'

'I'm always singing.'

'Yes, when nobody's around. Promise me you'll contact that theatre guy and do something for yourself for a change.'

'Okay, I promise.'

Most of the evening until the early hours were spent talking, until Patrick decided he had to leave because of his early start. After a heartfelt goodbye to the family, he took Nell outside, alone.

'I'm going to miss you very much. I wish you didn't have to go.'

He ran his fingers through her curls and kissed her forehead. Nell could hear his quiet sobs as she clung tightly to him.

'I wish I didn't either.'

A car horn tooted. Patrick looked over Nell's shoulder. 'It's my ride. Nell, I love you with all my heart, you hear. We've had a pretty good time and when I'm back we'll have more.' He patted his trouser pockets. 'Here, before I forget, I want you to have this.' He unfolded a piece of paper. 'This is my address back in the States. I've told my family all about you and they promised they'd write to you also. But if anything should happen to me…'

'Don't say that.' She snapped. 'Please, don't say that,' she begged through tear filled eyes.

'Let's be realistic, Nell. I don't know where I'm going, or what I'm about to walk into. Please contact them if anything should happen. They will help you in any way they can.'

'I promise I'll do that for you, but just make sure that you come home so I don't have to contact them with awful news.'

Patrick exhaled deeply. 'I really have to leave now.'

'Shall I come and see you off tomorrow?'

He thought about it for a second or two and shook his head. 'No, one goodbye is enough and I'd rather remember you here, in happier times.'

'But…'

'No, no buts,' he said wrapping his arms around her. 'Before you know it the war will be over and when that day comes, you stand on that porch of yours and watch me walking down that street. I'll be the man you met but in civvies and carrying the biggest bunch of roses I can get my hands on.'

Nell smiled. 'I love you. I don't know what I would've done over the past year without you.'

'Me neither. You've made this war bearable, that's for sure.' He laughed.

Patrick took her hand and walked her to the waiting car. He opened the passenger door and asked the driver to give him a moment. He turned to Nell and kissed her hard on the lips.

'Write to me, and please don't forget me.'

Nell closed her eyes and gently caressed his face. 'I'll be here waiting for you.'

Patrick got into the car and as it drove off, Nell stood on the pavement quietly sobbing.

'I love you, Nell,' Patrick shouted.

'Sis?'

She heard Alf's voice and turned around, wiping away her tears with the sleeve of her cardigan.

'Come here.' He hugged her tight. 'It'll be alright,' he whispered. 'It's all going to be alright.'

The sun had finally risen. She sat with Alf in the back garden sipping on a hot cup of tea. He was despondent and more lost in his thoughts than earlier so Nell nudged his arm with her elbow.

'Silly question but are you okay?'

'I'm home out of the worst of it, I should be happy, shouldn't I? But I don't know Nell. The flashbacks don't stop. I don't know if I'm worse off now than when the plane crashed. God, that sounded selfish, didn't it? A lot of my friends never made it back home.'

'It's not selfish at all. You have every right to feel the way you do.'

'War changes people. I didn't imagine I'd end up feeling like this.' He broke eye contact with the wall and looked at her. 'And not just physically either,' he pointed to his burn. 'I mean, who's going to love me like this Nell?' he sobbed onto her shoulder.

'Plenty of women,' she nudged his arm again just as Emily walked across next door's garden with a basket of washing.

'Are you alright, Nell?' she asked, throwing a sopping wet towel over the line.

'Not really. Have you met my brother, Alf?' she asked, turning back to him. He lowered his head as Emily walked toward the fence. Emily stuck her hand out over the slats.

'Nice to meet you.'

Nell saw that Alf reluctantly approached Emily's outstretched hand. It was obvious to Nell that he was embarrassed about his face.

'I've heard a lot about you,' Emily said.

Alf smiled nervously. 'Nell likes to spin the odd tale. What has she told you?'

'Good things, so don't worry.'

Nell left them alone while they continued chatting and went back inside the house. She dropped down on the sofa, took a cushion, and held it tightly to her chest. David switched on the radio, walked silently towards his chair and sat down.

'Tired?' He asked Nell.

'Yes, Dad. I'm exhausted.'

Chapter Twenty Two

It had been a long evening only made worse by the knowledge that the following day wouldn't be better. After being woken around one o' clock with the disturbing screams of her brother reliving his own worst nightmares, Nell sat on the back doorstep in the morning chill, taking comfort from her last cigarette.

'What was the name of that poor boy he was calling out to?' asked Mary handing Nell a mug of hot tea.

She exhaled, blowing puffs of smoke. 'Billy. Poor Billy. I daren't mention it to him. Maybe he will come and talk to us when he's ready.'

Mary had gone into check on him several times through the night and once, Nell sat on the edge of his bed watching him writhe, sweat and cry for almost two hours until he settled down at 4 a.m. Not able to sleep, she had spent the time thinking about her husband and what hell he was about to experience.

'Is it horrible to say that I wished the sun wouldn't rise just for today?' asked Nell, thoughtfully. She was too numb to cry and too tired to feel anything. 'I mean if we could put a pause on the day, so I don't have to say goodbye to the man I love.'

'It's perfectly natural what you're feeling. Look, your dad is off down the docks in a bit, why don't you go and see if you can find Patrick?'

Nell shifted around on the doorstep so she faced her mother sitting at the table pouring herself another tea from the pot.

'I could, couldn't I? Even if I can only catch a glimpse of him it would be worth it?'

Mary, whose eyes were tired with dark circles under them, stared intently at Nell. 'You must take every chance you get. Go, get dressed.'

With fervor, Nell jumped from the doorstep, put her mug on the table and ran upstairs calling her dad.

'Dad,' she bumped into him on the landing.

'What is it?' he asked, pulling on his waistcoat.

'Mam said I could come with you to the docks to see if I can find Patrick.'

David shook his head. 'I don't know, Nell…security is tight.'

'Please Dad, just give me this, please…'

'Get dressed, but there are no guarantees you'll even see him.'

The sun rose higher in the sky. She ripped down the blinds, slinging them across the room. She had done nothing but think of Patrick all night and no, she couldn't wait at home while he sailed to who knew where. She had to see him one more time despite his instructions that she was to stay home.

'Nell, come here,' hailed David from downstairs.

'What is it?' she shouted down from her room. She had just got dressed and was about to put on her shoes when she understood the urgency in his voice. She ran down the stairs, her heart pounding madly.

David was standing in the front garden, looking in the direction of the docks.

'What is it, Dad?' she said, and as she stepped out, she looked at the Bay and saw a convoy of ships turning around, heading out of the channel.

'I've got to go, Dad,' she ran down the steps and up the street to the bus stop, but decided once she got there that she'd be quicker walking.

When she arrived at the gated entrance to the docks, a man stepped forward out of a small hut.

'Where are you going, lady?'

'I want to see my husband. He was leaving today to somewhere, I don't know…please, let me in to see if I can find him?' she banged the gates. 'I just want one minute with him, please.'

The man's aggravated expression became soft.

'I'm afraid everyone has gone, miss. I'm not privy to what has happened, but I've heard something big is brewing and we'll soon hear about it.'

'That's what everyone keeps saying, but nobody is giving guarantees for their return. Are they?' she screamed. 'Are they?' she screamed again. 'I hate this bloody war, I hate it.' She whacked the gate once again, hurting her hand.

Defeated, she tucked her hand under her armpit and began to walk aimlessly home through near-deserted streets. Most people weren't even awake yet, but Nell had already had enough and thought she'd go home to bed where she could sleep and not think about things for a while.

Chapter Twenty Three

Nell said goodbye to her colleagues at the entrance of the factory and started to walk home in the early morning light. She had reached the crossroad when her eyes blurred, and she lost her balance. Kneeling down on the curb, she felt lifeless, and vomited onto the roadside. There wasn't anyone around, and she wiped her mouth with the sleeve of her coat then sat down on the corner wall of a shop for a while, thinking she must've caught a stomach bug. After some moments, she got to her feet and walked the rest of the way home, clutching her stomach.

'Mam,' she shouted as she got in the house.

Despite the early hour, Mary was already awake, pacing the front room with a letter in her hand.

'Mam?'

Mary looked up at her daughter, her thoughts interrupted.

'Oh, Nell, I won't be sorry to see the end of this bloody war now. Don't you think we've had quite enough?' Mary didn't like cussing, so Nell knew something major must've been written in the letter to cause it. 'This letter is a month old, and only now it arrived, can you believe that?'

'Well, what does it say?'

'Both boys are on the same ship. You know how that worries me, Nell.' She stopped talking long enough to notice Nell's peaky face.

'What's wrong, love?'

'Oh don't mind me, I think I have a stomach bug, so I'm going to bed. Try not to worry too much about the boys, okay? They are fine.'

Nell couldn't stand on her feet much longer and headed upstairs to her room.

She hadn't realised she'd slept through to the evening, having only woken as she heard children laughing from downstairs. She got up and dressed thinking she'd go down and join the family.

Emily was standing at the foot of the stairs. 'Are you alright, Nell?'

'I've been better, thanks.' She felt better than she had but didn't think she was up to going to work in the morning. 'What are those two little buggers up to?' she asked with a nod to the youngest playing with a toy airplane.

'Your mam is looking after them for a little while. Alf and I are going down the Naval for a couple of drinks. Why don't you join us?'

'No,' Nell waved her hand. The thought of alcohol only made her feel more nauseous. 'You two go and have a good time, I'm sure I've got a book or two here I can read to these two. It'll calm them down,' she smiled, with a look at the eldest.

'Thanks, Nell.'

'Yes, thanks, Nell,' said Alf who had got his coat from under the stair cupboard.

'It's nice to see you going out if I'm honest.'

'Trust me, I wouldn't be if I didn't have a beautiful face to stare at all night.'

Emily blushed. 'Oh hush, you.'

Nell thought it was sweet, the way their friendship had blossomed and wished them a nice time. 'Kids, how about I'll read you something fun?'

Relieved they agreed and sat silently on the sofa. She settled between them and opened her copy of *The Five on A Treasure Island* she had got from the library. 'Hope you're ready for an adventure, kids? I sure am.'

It was almost nine o' clock when Nell heard the front door creak open. She had just put a blanket over the boys who were fast asleep on the sofa when Alf and Emily walked into the room with huge grins on their faces.

'I see you two have had a nice time.'

'We did and thanks for taking care of them, Nell.'

Emily went to wake the boys but Nell swooped in saying that they were alright to stay the night, as, after all, she was only next door.

'It took me ages to get them to settle. They're so hyper, aren't they?'

'Are you sure? Well, I'll get them early, as I'm on the afternoon shift.'

'Yeah, of course, they're alright. I must say this has been the nicest evening I've had in a long time.'

'Kept you busy, I see,' Emily nodded to the books piled on the chair.

'They did, and now I think I've got a sore throat coming on.'

'Nell, you're the best.' Emily hugged her. 'I don't know what I'd do without you. Well if it's okay with you then, I'm going to get to bed, goodnight. Like I said I'll get them early in the morning.'

Emily gave the kids a kiss on their cheeks and left the room with Alf. Nell was exhausted and sat back on the chair, pulling a blanket around her shoulders. After a few moments, the door opened again and Alf came back into the living room.

'Thanks for tonight, Nell. She's lovely and she doesn't care about my scars. Am I lucky or what?'

'Very.' She yawned and felt queasy again. 'Sorry, I need an early night, I think. See you in the morning.'

'Goodnight.'

The morning came and so did the post. While making the boys breakfast, Nell waited with anticipation to see if a letter had come from Patrick. She was spreading the last of the dripping over the toast when David came into the kitchen sifting through a pile of envelopes.

'Looks like most of these have got delayed. Your mother will be happy,' he said, sorting them into a pile on the table.

Unable to take her eyes from the letters, she passed the children their breakfast on a plate and asked her father if there was anything for her. There was a moment's silence as he looked through them all again then shook his head.

'Sorry love, it's mostly from the boys to your mam.'

She felt the knot in her stomach tighten once again and then the bile rise up her throat. She covered her mouth and dashed to the door, flung it open and vomited outside, next to the drain.

David shouted for Mary to come quickly.

'Are you alright Aunty Nell?' asked Dylan, standing on the door step.

Nell wiped her mouth with her apron and nodded. 'Of course, it's just a stupid stomach bug. Go inside and eat your breakfast.' She heaved again, straining her throat, but nothing came out.

'Let's get you back to bed, love.' Mary started to help her inside the house, but she shrugged her off and ran upstairs to the bathroom. She had never felt so awful. Mary came into the bathroom and pulled her hair back from her face.

'I'll ask Emily to tell the manager you're not well, shall I?'

'Thanks, Mam.'

'How long have you been like this?'

Nell thought for a moment. She'd been feeling under the weather for a while but thought nothing of it. 'On and off for about a week.'

'I think you need to go to the doctors, love.'

'Why?' she asked, making her way to her room. 'It's just a stomach bug.' She lifted her bedcovers and got into bed. 'I'll be alright in the morning, please don't fuss.'

'I don't think you're going to be alright in the morning, Nell. I'm willing to bet all the money in my purse that you're pregnant.'

Her mam was right. She was still in shock as she left the doctor's surgery, and despite feeling nervous about the idea of being six weeks pregnant, she thought she'd go into work to explain to them that she could no longer work there as her doctor had instructed it. On her way to the bus stop in the light rain shower, she heard Emily's voice calling her from the opposite side of the road. She was walking with an older woman Nell didn't recognise.

'Where are you off to, Nell?' She waved.

Surprised to see her, Nell waved back and crossed the road.

'I was just on my way to work. I need to tell them I won't be able to go in anymore.' She then gave a pleasant smile to the older woman fussing with her scarf.

'Oh sorry, Nell, this is my aunty, Lynn. She's visiting us this weekend.' She turned to Lynn. 'Aunty Lynn, this Nell who I was telling you about.'

'Hello, love, Emily speaks very highly of you.'

'That's a relief to hear.'

They accompanied each other to the bus stop.

'So what do you mean you won't be going into work anymore?' Emily asked, turning to face her.

Nell knew she'd ask. 'Well, I have some exciting news. I'm pregnant.'

'You're what?' Emily squealed. 'That's wonderful Nell. So we won't be seeing you at the factory anymore then?'

'No, that's where I'm headed now. I thought it would be best to tell them in person. Where are the kids by the way?'

'Don't worry about going to the factory if you're not feeling up to it. I'll tell them when I start at six. You get home and rest. I left the kids with Alf because I'm going to see a lady about renting a house. I think it's time we gave Florrie a break, you know. The kids need their own room now. And I don't know if Alf told you, but he's moving in with us too.'

'Really? That's great news, Em. I'm glad he's getting his life together. I'm sure Florrie doesn't mind having you though.'

'I know, but it'll be nice to have somewhere of my own. Anyway, I'm so excited for you. You're going to be a great mam, I just know it. The boys absolutely adore you.'

'Thanks. I had a feeling I was pregnant so I wrote to Patrick last night to tell him the news. I hope he's going to be okay with it. '

'Are you kidding? He's going to be really happy Nell.'

'There's the bus,' said Nell, taking her purse out of her bag.

'If you don't mind me saying so, love,' said Lynn. 'You're still looking a little peaky. Why don't you let Emily go and tell them for you?'

'Would you mind, Em?'

'Of course not, I've already told you. Tell you what, when I get home we'll have a proper celebration.'

'That will be nice.' Nell said. 'It was nice to meet you,' she said to Lynn. 'Pop around later for some tea.'

Nell had only got a few feet away when she remembered the letter she had to post to Patrick. 'Could you do me a favour, Em, and pop this in the postbox, I don't want it to miss the next post.'

'Of course, Nell, hand it over.'

'Thanks, I'd better go home and tell Mam that she was right.'

Over the course of the next few weeks, Nell looked after Emily's boys while she was at work. It gave her something to do now that she wasn't able to work at the factory.

The growing bump meant she couldn't squeeze a button in its hole. She pulled the white, patterned material as far as it would go, but as soon as she managed to squeeze the button in the hole, it popped open. Frustrated, and tired of being pregnant, she tore off the blouse and put on a loose fitting dress instead. She took herself down to the front room. No sooner had she got comfortable on the sofa, she heard the sound of an expensive engine roaring outside, and she went to the window to look. In the frosty gloom of the early January morning, a black car had parked outside her house. She waited to see which house they were visiting when the car door opened and she saw a man wearing a military hat emerge.

'Mam...' Her breath shuddered, thinking that officers don't turn up at people's houses for biscuits and bloody tea. The tall, elegant figure, American, judging by the uniform, looked up at the house and then re-checked the paper in his hand.

'Please not here...'

He walked up the steps and removed his cap. Her father dashed down the hall and intercepted the officials. As the men spoke, Nell heard her name.

Clutching her swollen belly, she quickly left her vantage point and went into the hall.

'Ma'am.' The officer greeted her with a weak smile which didn't put her at ease.

'Is it Patrick?'

'Mrs Sanders. I've been asked to come and give you a message in person. Patrick has been missing in action for quite a few days now.'

'You can't be serious,' she burst out crying. 'I mean, you may as well have come with a telegram telling me that my husband is dead.'

The officer stepped forward and put a comforting hand on her arm. 'I'm very sorry for bringing you this news. I really am, Mrs. Sanders.'

'What's going on?' asked Emily racing up the steps. She had just finished work and was collecting the boys for their tea. She brushed past the officer to Nell.

'It's Patrick. He's been missing in action for days. Oh, Emily what if he doesn't come back at all?' She clasped her hand over her mouth as hot tears streamed down her face. 'He said he'd come back for me,' she cried onto Emily's shoulder. 'I can't lose him, I just can't.'

David thanked the officer who shook his head in sorrow as he returned to his car.

'Come on, love. Go and make yourself comfortable on the sofa and I'll make the tea.'

'It's all going to be okay, Nell.' Emily walked her into the front room. 'Now you must sit down, you've got a little one to look after, you know.' She rubbed Nell's belly.

Nell nodded. 'I know. It's just so hard though. It's the thought of him being lost, who knows how far away and me being stuck here. It's hard, Em, really hard. This whole damn war has been so hard.' She covered her hands over her face. 'When is it going to end?'

PART SEVEN

1945

Chapter Twenty Four

It was early morning. Nell heaved herself out of bed and made her way downstairs. She hadn't slept much because of the baby kicking her sides all night, so thought she'd get up and start the breakfast. The rest of the house was asleep, even Alf was snoring soundly in his room as she passed.

Since he'd been home, he had had many restless nights. Nell realised that last night was the first one in which she hadn't heard him screaming in his sleep. She mouthed "thanks" and shivered as she walked down the stairs. The fire had gone out and the house was chilly, but with her belly being so large, she couldn't bend down to light it, so decided to wait for her father.

In a basket beside the kitchen door, she rummaged for her thick, woolly cardigan, sniffed it and then put it on. Once she had filled the kettle and lit the stove, she snuck a cigarette from the pack in her mother's apron pocket and went outside.

Everything outside was covered with frost, which glistened in the early morning light. As she puffed away, staring blankly at the snow pile banked up against the shelter, a faint sound broke the silence. Nell took the cigarette out of her mouth, blowing smoke and heard it again. This time it was louder and she couldn't be ignored. She looked around the garden but none of the neighbours were out. She focused on the sound and realised that they were sobs which seemed to be coming from the back lane. She picked up the sweeping brush that was propped against the wall, and she carefully walked across the icy garden to see what was wrong. She slid the bolt on the back gate and then cautiously pushed it open, surprised to find Brenda, the woman she slightly feared because of her apparent ability to see into the future couching against the wall with her hands covering her face.

'Brenda, what is the matter?' she asked.

Brenda removed her red, cold chilblained hands from her face and looked up at Nell.

'Just had awful news, my lovely…'

'Do you want to come in for a cup of tea?' she asked, holding the back door open. 'It's freezing out here, for God's sake, you'll catch your death.'

'Would you mind, Nell? Is Mary here?'

'Yes, Mam is inside, come through and I'll get her.' Nell took Brenda into the living room and offered her a blanket from the back of the sofa. 'You'll want to wrap that around you, okay? I'm just going to get Mam, one second,' she said and went upstairs, but Mary had just got up and was walking down the landing.

'What is it, Nell? Is it the baby?'

'No Mam. It's Brenda. I found her crying in the back lane. Come and talk to her, will you? She said something about bad news.'

'No, please don't say that. I really don't want to hear it, not today.'

Nell made them all a cup of tea and took them through to the front room.

'Here you go,' she said putting the tray down on the table. She took a seat next to Mary who sat slumped in stunned silence. Nell had an idea that news was about Brenda's son. He was her only family.

Brenda reached a hand out of the blanket, her hands shaking as she picked up her cup. She slurped on her tea. 'It's my Alan. His plane was shot down over Germany. I had a telegram early this morning.'

Mary immediately leaned across the sofa to comfort her before they both broke down. The tears rolled down Nell's cheeks too as she remembered the day she last saw him.

Brenda sniffed back the tears and opened her handbag; producing the few precious photos she possessed. She passed one over to Nell, who smiled when she saw it. Alan was her age but never hung around with her and her friends. She couldn't believe it.

Alf came downstairs and walked into the room having heard the commotion.

'Don't tell me the bastards got Alan!' he scowled standing in the door frame. Nell nodded and offered him her seat.

For the next hour, he spoke with reverence about Alan and his flying abilities. It turned out they had crossed each other's path several times at the NAFFI. Nell listened intently to his stories, bursting with pride.

Brenda took comfort from his words and had calmed down enough to ask for another cup of tea – if her mam could spare the tea leaves.

Nell went to refresh the pot, and Alf followed behind while Mary continued to comfort Brenda.

'She's not such a scary old bat after all, is she?' Nell said as she scooped a heap of tea into the pot.

Alf laughed.

'I'm not so sure. She used to scare me and poor Alan enough when we were kids.'

Putting the kettle on to boil again, Nell felt a twinge in her back and had to sit down.

'Are you alright sis? Let me do that for you,' he said, hobbling to the stove.

'What a pair we are,' Nell laughed, but started to feel awful. Her due date wasn't until early March.

'Take it easy for a bit, I'll take their tea in then I have to go and see the kids.'

'Are things going okay?'

'I'd say that they are going more than okay. I love her and I love the kids as though they were my own. Don't tell Mam yet, but I've asked her to marry me.'

'Have you really? I must say, it's nice to see you happy, oh gosh…' She felt the stab in her back again and pushed herself up from the chair.

'Do you want me to call Mam?'

'No, it's fine. I've had aches and pains most days, I can deal with it. Here, give me the tea and I'll take it in. It's best if I keep myself busy.'

She took the pot and more milk into the front room and settled the tray on the table. Brenda had already finished her cup of tea and just as she was about to put it on the table, she lifted her cup and glanced inside.

'What is it, Brenda?' asked Mary.

'I don't like what I see here, love.'

'Oh, come on Brenda, surely it can't be bad news all the time…'

Despite her fear, Nell was interested and sat down on the sofa. 'What do you see?'

Brenda sighed heavily. 'I see someone drowning.'

'Who?' Mary whispered.

'There are two men here, but I can't see which one is drowned. They're stationed abroad, that's all I know.'

'I hope you don't mean our boys?'

'Mary, I don't know who it is, honestly. But then again, I don't think anybody ever believes a word I say anyway.'

'I hope in this instance you're way off the mark, my love. Come on, drink your tea, you're too drained to be reading the tea leaves.' Mary sighed and gave Nell a look to say she couldn't take anymore. Nell felt the same.

The following day, Nell made her way to Port Tennant road, hoping to make the next post - she had a couple of letters to send to Sidney and Edward telling them all about the comings and goings at Jersey Terrace. As she put the letters in the postbox, she felt a sharp stab in her lower back. She ignored it and joined the queue outside Tom's shop where she heard a couple of old women mention that there was a limited supply of sausages available without the use of coupons. The queue soon moved forward and she was able to get inside the shop, feeling that she ought to get home, but as it was her father's birthday in a couple of days she wanted to give him a surprise.

'Are you alright, Nell? You look mighty awful if you don't mind me saying so,' said Tom wiping the tins on a shelf.

'I'll be glad when this baby comes now. I can barely walk.'

'As Mrs. Hill always used to say, it'll be worth it when the little 'un arrives. Now, what can I do you for?'

'I heard you have sausages available.'

He frowned at her for a second, wondering how she knew. He went to the back of the counter and presented her with a package in brown paper.

'I've kept some back for my special customers,' he winked. 'Don't go blabbering now, will you? I'll get besieged. Anyhow, have you had any news about your husband?'

'No, Tom. I just don't know what to think anymore.' As she opened her bag to get her purse, she felt the stabbing increase. She reached a hand out and grabbed hold of the counter's surface.

'Nell, I'm no expert but I think you want to get yourself home.'

'God, that hurt,' she bent clutching her belly, feeling as though she was going to be sick. A few seconds later the feeling subsided and she slammed down the money, grabbed the package and headed for the door as fast as she could.

'Thanks,' she said as she left the shop.

The walk back to the house was extremely painful. She thought she was going to have the baby on the pavement but was determined to make it home.

'Nell, are you alright there?' Greenwald yelled, standing on his front doorstep.

'No, get my mam.'

Greenwald rushed over the road, put his arm around her and helped walk her up the steps to the front door.

'Mary, get out here!' he yelled.

'Oh my God, I feel it coming.'

As they reached the top step, Nell felt water gush from between her legs.

'Mam,' she screamed. 'Mam, the baby is coming.' She dropped the package on the floor and Winnie, who had heard the shouts, came rushing over the road to her aide.

'Good God, girl, let's get you inside. I'll take over from here, Greenwald, thank you.' She put an arm around Nell and pushed open the door. 'Mary, Nell is having the baby.' she shouted helping Nell into the front room.

Mary came running up the hallway from the kitchen.

'Win, call the midwife would you?'

'I'm on it.' She said and left the house.

'Mam, it really hurts!' Nell cried, clutching her belly.

Mary helped her onto the sofa and undid her daughter's coat. 'You're going to be fine, my girl, just fine. I'm going to take your underwear off and see how far gone you are, alright?'

Nell nodded, feeling a pain sear down her belly. 'Mam, it's coming now, I feel it.'

'I don't think we can wait until the midwife is here, I can see its head already, so give me some pushes when I tell you.'

Nell felt the need to push and at the second one, there was a strange noise and Nell had a feeling of release. 'You did it, Nell. You have a beautiful daughter!' cried Mary as she lifted the baby onto the new mother's bosom and pressed a kiss on her daughter's sticky forehead.

'Look at your daughter, Nell, isn't she beautiful?'

Nell cried tears of joy. 'Hello, little Bess,' she cried. 'I'm calling her Bess after Bessie. What do you think?'

'I think it's perfect, just perfect.'

Winnie stood on her front porch instructing Edna where to place the coloured bunting on her window. Nell laughed at the pair, more so because the war wasn't officially over yet.

'Is it wise to get ahead of yourselves, ladies?'

'No, just getting excited, Nell. I feel it in my water. I have a pantry full of goodies I've been saving for the street party too. How is the little one?'

'She's keeping me busy.'

The baby cried so she went indoors to check on her and then brought her back out into the warmth of the sunshine. Just as she got there, the postman walked up the steps and handed her a bunch of envelopes.

'Mam, we've got mail from the boys!' she yelled and tore open the one that was addressed to her.

Dear Nell,

You've probably heard about William by now. It was quite a shock especially since I only saw him hours before his ship went down. My shipmates and I had gone to a bar in NYC and met with a sailor who told us there was another Welsh lad in a bar not far from the docks. So on our way back, we called in to find William sipping on a pint. He was in good spirits that night and spoke fondly and at length of Bessie. As he knew that I was due to arrive in

Liverpool on the 10th May, he gave me a bracelet he had bought for her and asked if we'd give it to Edna instead. Anyhow, we had got back to our ship, the SS Myrtlebank and not very long later, a torpedo had attacked his ship, sinking it and killing everyone on board.

It was the worst day of the war for me. To stand on a docked ship and watch a fellow sailor sink in the depths of the Atlantic Ocean with no way of saving him will stay with me for as long as I live. I sincerely hope he is with Bessie now. This war has taken so many lives. I hope it's true that an end is in sight.

Look forward to seeing you all soon,
All my love
Edward.

'Bloody hell. I can't take much more of this.' Mary cried, blowing her nose into her apron. David put a strong arm around her and pulled her in close. 'Now, come on, love. It'll be over before we know it, and yes I know it won't bring everyone back.'

Nell had heard enough, picked up the baby who was lying on the sofa and put her in the pram. 'I need some fresh air, Mam. I'll be back in a little while.'

'Leave Bessie here if you want,' Mary said.

'Are you sure?'

'Yes. She's fine.' She scooped her up from the pram, blowing raspberries at her. Bessie giggled. 'Go on, she's company for me.'

Nell gave Bessie a kiss and then pulled on her cardigan before stepping out into a warm day. As she made her way along the street, a familiar voice called out from behind.

'Nell, is that you?'

She turned around to see Francis running down the street towards her. He had a child in tow holding his hand.

'I didn't know you came home?' Nell said, surprised to see him. She didn't hold any resentment for the past and knelt down to say hello to the child.

'This is a good friend of mine, Jess. Her name is Nell, you can say hello.'

'It's very nice to meet you,' Nell smiled and then looked up at Francis.

'Your daughter is lovely. You must be very proud.'

Francis didn't reply for a moment then asked Jess to go and join the other children playing on the street.

'She isn't my biological daughter, Nell. I did write and tell you, did you not get my letter?'

Nell was taken aback. 'No,' she said, stunned to hear about a letter that hadn't arrived, one of how many? She wondered. 'What do you mean she's not your biological daughter?'

'Come sit down a minute,' he pointed to the wall where they always used to sit. 'I dated her mother up until a month before I had the nerve to ask you out. It wasn't the most amicable of splits because I found out last year she had been dating someone else. I learnt last year that Jess was the product of their relationship and when he left her she ran back to me. I'm no longer with her mother, but I'll always treat Jess as my daughter.'

Nell was saddened to hear this. She knew that if it hadn't been for the lies Tily had manufactured, maybe she and Francis would've married.

'I'm sorry to hear that, I really am. I think it's commendable that you treat the child as your own. But you didn't say how you came to be home from the Navy?'

'I only got back a few days ago and asked my Mam to keep quiet.' He raised his left hand. Three fingers were missing. 'Lost them when a bomb went off.'

'Oh dear God, Francis, I'm sorry.' She touched his arm. 'That reminds me, did you hear about William? His ship sank. We had a letter this morning.'

'Good God, no. Didn't his mother move away after your Bess arrived?'

'She did. It seems like our past has been wiped out. There's nothing left for me here anymore...'

'Mam told me about your husband. Have you heard anything yet?'

Nell shook her head.

'Nothing. I'll be glad when the official announcement goes out so I can plan on what to do next.'

'You're not the only one. Mam is leaving the street soon, so I'm helping her pack. She's decided to move to West Wales with her sister.'

'Oh. We haven't seen nor heard from Edna in a while. I'll tell Mam when I see her.'

'Please do, Nell, so, I guess this is a goodbye from me, too, as I'll be going with her.'

'You're going too?'

'Yeah, I'll hopefully find some work on the docks. Look, I'm sorry about everything that happened between us.' He stepped forward, putting a hand on her shoulder. 'No matter what, I still love you, Nell...you'll always be my friend.'

'Honestly, Francis there's no need to apologise now. That was before, it's in the past. We can't hold grudges in times like these. They're so precious.'

'I'm happy to hear that, I really am. I've never forgiven myself for not being open and honest with you from the start. Anyway, I'd best be off. You take care, alright.'

'Stay in touch, won't you?'

Nell held back the tears that were threatening to fall. She longed to tell him that she still loved him too, but only as a friend. Besides, he was leaving now, so maybe she didn't have a right to say anything at all.

'Of course I will.' He gave her a peck on the cheek and looked longingly into her eyes for a few seconds before he crossed the road with his child in tow.

Over the weeks that followed, Nell's heart ached with the loss of everyone, even Francis, but she wouldn't really admit to it or talk about it with anyone. The day was bright with sunshine, not a cloud in the sky. Strolling home with Bessie in the pram, she saw Mr. Greenwald standing outside Tom's and went to say hello.

'And how are you, love?' Greenwald asked while taking a look at Bessie snoring in the pram.

'As well as one can be. I must say, I do miss the ARP. Are you doing much these days?'

'Not really, Nell. Not since I fell off a ruddy ladder and did my back in.'

Tom appeared at the shop door.

'Have you heard, you two,' he said, excitedly, 'Hitler is dead. The bastard is dead!'

Greenwald let slip a laugh. 'Been on the drink again, eh, Tom?'

'What? Are you being serious?' Nell almost shouted.

'It was just on the wireless, honest to God.'

Nell covered her mouth in shock. There was a rush of excitement building inside her as she realised that this could be the end of the bloody war.

'Oh my God, I'd best get home to tell Mam. I'll see you later.' She waved at them both, and then ran up the street, not stopping until she got to her house. Her dad was sitting on the front porch smoking his pipe and rose to his feet when he saw her.

'What's got into you?' he asked, full of concern.

'He's dead. Hitler is dead, Dad.' She gasped for breath.

'You bloody what?' He almost dropped his pipe.

'Come on, help me with the pram and then switch on the wireless.'

'Come off it. It's probably a bloody wind up by the Germans.'

They went into the front room and gathered around the radio. Nell picked up Bessie because she was crying and held her tightly as the news reporter announced that Hitler had committed suicide. David took a tissue from his pocket and covered his face. Nell heard his gentle sobs just as Alf came bursting into the house declaring the news that they had already heard.

'Hitler is dead!'

Chapter Twenty Five

'Why don't you come to Brecon with us?' Emily asked Nell. 'It'll be a nice day out for Bess, too.'

Nell wrung out the last of the washing, stood up and leaned against the garden fence. She wiped her sweaty forehead with her apron and gratefully accepted the glass of water Emily offered her. 'Thanks, but some of the girls from the factory are popping over later with some things for Bess.'

'That's right, you did say. I hope I get to see them later.'

Nell latched on to Emily's good mood and wondered if there was something she wasn't telling her.

'What's with all the smiles today? And don't say it's because the sun is shining for once.'

'I'm expecting. I found out yesterday,' she beamed.

'That's wonderful – I'm going to be an aunt!'

'That's good news number one. The other is that my ex-has moved to Cork. So I won't be bothered by him again, I hope.'

'That must be a relief. Hey, come on over and have a cup of tea to celebrate,' Nell pushed Bess's pram to the back door, out of direct sunlight.

Later that afternoon, while Nell was washing Bess in the sink, the door knocked. She called out to her father to answer it, but he didn't hear.

'Come on, you,' she said to Bess as she wrapped her in a towel.

Standing on the doorstep were Caitlin and Louise from the factory.

'Oh look at her,' Caitlin, cooed taking Bess into her arms.

'It's so nice to see you both.' Nell gave them each a hug and invited them into the front room.

'And you,' said Louise, taking a seat.

Nell thought she seemed so much like her old self, before she was horribly burned in the accident at the factory.

'I'll make us some tea.'

Caitlin balanced Bess on her knee, making funny faces at her. 'Thank you, Nell.'

It was then that Nell remembered they were out of tea leaves and had to reuse the ones from earlier. While she poured water into the kettle, Louise joined her in the kitchen.

'So how is everything with you?' asked Nell.

'Things are good, Nell. I managed to get myself a job at the local grocer's. It's more than half of what I was used to at the factory but it's something.'

Nell put three cups on the counter. 'Anything is better than nothing these days.'

'That's true. So has there been news about your husband?'

Nell handed her a cup. 'No. Not a word. I feel like I'm in limbo most days. Thankfully I have Bess, or I don't know what I'd do.'

Louise gave her a sympathetic look. 'I knew there was something I had to give you,' she said.

They went back into the living room and Louise went straight to her handbag. 'Do you remember at the dance the Americans put on, I got to talking to a nice fella, Private Lowe?'

Nell thought back. 'I remember; blonde hair with dimples. Aw, he was cute. Didn't he ask you to dance?'

'Yes, several times,' she blushed. 'We became pen pals we did.' She fished around her bag and then produced a photograph. 'I hope it's alright to give you this.' She held a photograph out for Nell to take. 'He sent it last week. It's him and Patrick before he...,' she became flustered, stumbled over her words and picked up her cup of tea.

'It's alright, Louise.' She looked at the photograph of a smiling Patrick standing next to Private Lowe. 'Thank you for showing me this.' She choked back tears. 'It's nice to see him smiling.'

'You can keep it if you want.'

'Oh can I? Thank you so much,' she bent down towards Bess. 'Look, there's your dada.'

'What do you think about the war coming to an end soon?' Caitlin said, handing Bess back to Nell.

'My Dad seems to think there's something cooking up.'

Louise held out her hands to take Bess. 'There is something brewing for sure and I for one will be glad to see the back of this nightmare.'

'Wouldn't we all,' Caitlin agreed.

Emily, Alf and the kids came home looking refreshed and happy.

'Hello, girls,' Emily gave both her colleagues a hug and introduced them to Alf who shook their hands. 'I suppose you heard the news, Nell.' He asked, walking out into the kitchen. Nell followed.

'You mean about the baby? Oh yes, it's excellent news. I was delighted when Emily told me earlier. Are you pleased?'

'Yes, and very happy. So, today we've decided to get married as soon as possible. No point hanging around.'

Nell heard a commotion at the door. 'Dad, what's going on?' she asked watching him make a beeline for the front room.

'Come and listen...'

Nell and Alf followed her dad and watched as he turned on the radio. Normal programmes were announced as being momentarily interrupted.

'I think Bess wants you.' Louise passed her to Nell.

'Oh hello, I didn't realise we had guests,' said David. 'Nice to meet you both.'

There was an air of something major taking place and Nell hoped it was the news they all been longing to hear.

Yesterday morning at 02.41 a.m. at General Eisenhower's Headquarters, General Jodl, the representative of German High Command, and Grand Admiral Doenitz, the designated Head of the German state signed the act of unconditional surrender...

Cheers and screams of joy erupted around the room.

'I had a bloody feeling.' David spun around and then covered his face with his hands.

Caitlin and Anne began jumping and whooping. Nell joined the girls, but not so high because of the baby in her arms, trying rapidly to come to terms with the news that the war was finally over.

'We were only saying...' Louise said.

'I know. Isn't this amazing?'

The front door burst open and Mary, Florrie and Edna ran down the hallway crying tears of happiness.

'Is it really over? Did I hear right?' Florrie was overcome with emotion and pulled Nell in for a hug.

'Yes, Flo, it's all over.' She looked at Bess and held her tight, whispering in her ear that she loved her.

'I think it's time for a little celebration,' David declared and went to the cabinet and brought out a bottles of champagne he'd saved and popped the cork.

'I think I'm going to open that tin of peaches!' Mary exclaimed. 'I just hope this means our boys will be home soon.'

The next day, Nell returned home from a walk with Bessie and arrived, slightly out of breath, at the top of her road. A row of tables covered in fresh white linen, were laden with food and strings of colourful bunting hung from the immaculately clean windows. Everyone was out on the street, dancing, singing, and drinking. She figured at least one part of her nightmare was over.

'Hey, Nell, how's the little one?' Greenwald stooped down to tickle Bess's chin.

'She's fine, thanks for asking.'

He handed her a drink in a mug. 'Get that down you, girl. I just want to say how proud I am that I had you on my team. We did good Nell.'

Nell took the drink. 'Yes, we did,' she smiled, coming over tingly with goose-bumps. She didn't feel like reminiscing, and drank the remaining liquid and handed him back the mug.

'I'll speak to you later, alright? I'd best go and help Mam.'

She walked across the road, pushing the pram, and saw her father sitting on the front step with a newspaper up to his face. The headline read:

VE DAY

Overcome with yet more emotion, her eyes filled with tears. Her father lowered the paper with a broad smile on his face.

'It feels good to actually read it, eh, Nell?'

'Yes it does,' she picked Bessie up and ran up the steps, throwing her arm around him. 'I don't want to spoil everyone's fun but, oh Dad, I still haven't heard anything about Patrick. I will feel rotten if I join the celebrations when I don't even know where my husband is.'

'Give it time, Nell, give it time. I'm sure you'll hear something soon.'

She nodded, wiping her tears with the sleeve of her cardigan and spun around when she heard kids emulating the sound of aircraft.

'Not you two,' she said to Charles and Jimmy running down the street. 'It's lovely to see you back home again.'

'Hello Mrs. Sanders,' said Charles. 'Mammy said you got married. Is that your little girl?'

'It is. Say hello to Bessie.'

She was glad to see them back and held Bessie's arm up and waved at them. Bessie chuckled.

'Didn't your mam move a while ago?'

'Yes, miss. We live down the Mumbles now. We came back to see everyone.'

'How nice,' she looked up and saw their mother, Sally, waving at her from Florrie's front step.

'I bet you're glad they're home,' Nell said.

'Absolutely, Nell. I missed them so much.'

As everyone in the street busied themselves with the preparations for the day, Nell thought that life on Jersey Terrace was returning back to normal.

That evening, when the last of the neighbours had gone indoors, Nell stood on the front doorstep surrounded by streamers and stray bunting that wound around her feet. Looking in the direction of the docks, silent tears ran down her cheeks. She had resigned herself to the fact that Patrick was lost in action and she'd probably never see him again. But oh how she wished to see him walk up the street towards her house and into her arms one more time.

'Are you okay, love?' asked Emily stepping outside of the porch holding a plate of cake. She pressed her hand on Nell's arm as a sign of comfort and concern.

'It's not really over for me yet.'

'Really?'

'Patrick's gone, practically everyone I loved has gone.' She shrugged. 'The war took everything I loved.'

'Not everyone, Nell. You have Bess and you have us. You'll never be alone, I promise.' Emily handed her the plate with a large slice of cake. 'Here, I saved you the last bit before the kids wolfed it down. You know, no matter what you think, you also deserve to celebrate the end of the war. You did an awful lot for this community – more than you may ever know.'

Nell appreciated the sentiment and clutched the plate of cake in her shaking hands.

'Thank you. I can't celebrate until I know what's happened to my husband. But even then, unless the news is good, I don't know how life can ever return to normal for me. I am not sure what normal is anymore, or what it might be.'

Chapter Twenty Six

The war had been over for a week now, but life still carried on pretty much the same, especially for Nell. She was fed up of waiting for news about Patrick, of being stuck in an uncertain future. She rolled over on the bed, thinking, and looking out of the window at the stars that twinkled in the clear night sky when she heard the chimes of the clock in the front room striking the half hour. Her alarm clock showed it was 5.30. Bessie began whimpering in her cot.

'I'm coming, Bess.'

She pushed the covers off and swung her legs out of the bed. 'There, there, little one, I'm coming,' she reached down, smiling at the child who was bathed in moonlight. 'And what's wrong with you?' She lifted her out, comforting her on her shoulder. 'Missing Daddy, are you?' she whispered as she stood by the window. 'Mummy is. An awful lot.'

A light went on in a neighbour's house, lighting up their garden. Would she eventually get used to such a sight? 'And now we slowly return back to normality. Whatever that is these days.' She gave Bess a kiss and went downstairs. She had planned to take Bess to the beach today for some fresh air.

'You're up early,' said Mary. She was about to take Bess from Nell when there was a knock at the door. 'Give her breakfast, love. I'll get it.'

While she went to answer it, Nell fed Bessie her milk from a bottle. She could hear the muffled conversation and looked down the passage to see who it might be at such an early hour.

'Nell, come here,' Mary shouted.

Nell went into the living room, propped Bessie on the sofa, and went to see why her mother had caused such a commotion.

Florrie was on the doorstep in her nightgown. 'There's been a phone call for you from the States. You can come in and take it if you want.'

Nell felt a rush of excitement. She had written to her in-laws and gave them Florrie's number as she was the only person in the street to own a telephone. 'I wonder what they want?' she cried.

'Go on, go and see what they want, go.' Mary ushered her out of the door.

She started sobbing as she ran out of the door, and across the front garden. The receiver had been put on the wooden table in the hallway and she snatched up.

'Hello… Hello.'

After a delay, a rather quiet, gentle voice at the other end introduced herself as Lorraine Sanders. 'I'm sorry I haven't called before now. It's been a difficult time as you know...'

She expected it to be Patrick and was bitterly disappointed that it was his mother.

'Yes, it hasn't been much fun here either, Mrs. Sanders.'

'I appreciate that, Nell. I can call you Nell, can't I?'

'Of course, Mrs…'

'Call me Lorraine, dear. We're family now. I thought I'd give you a call to say that we have been working with the army to find Patrick but there hasn't been any luck yet. They say he may have been captured and put in a,' she paused. Was she crying? Thought Nell. 'P.O.W camp.'

'My worst fear was that he was dead… Not that a POW camp is much better. ' She closed her eyes, wishing it could've been better news.

'I don't want you to worry now you have a little one to look after. How is my granddaughter anyway?'

'She's growing up fast. Looks a lot like Patrick, too.'

'I'd love to meet her one day, but until then I will keep in touch either by phone or mail. If there's anything we can do for you, don't hesitate to ask us.'

'Thank you, thank so much. Thank you for calling and take care.'

'You too. Goodbye, dear.'

'Well?' said Florrie standing in the hallway waiting for an update from Nell. 'What did they say?'

Nell exhaled, thinking she had to be thankful it wasn't really bad news. 'It was his mother. She said she'd keep me posted if they hear anything about Patrick.'

'Oh I am sorry, love. I was really hoping this would be the good news you wanted.'

Nell gave a shrug of her shoulders. 'I've not given up hope, Flo. Thanks for taking the call and coming in to get me.' She left the house and crossed the garden to her mother who was waiting for her in the hallway, holding Bess.

'Nothing?' she said.

Nell shook her head, holding out her hands to Bess. 'Not yet, Mam.'

A week after the emotional phone call, Nell was strolling down Wind Street with Bessie in her pram, alone with thoughts of the summer of 1939. It seemed like a lifetime ago, the day her youth had been wiped by the declaration of war. The gaping hole between two buildings reduced to rubble, stirred images of the night of the Blitz and the insanity she had witnessed. She didn't feel sad anymore, just bitter in knowing how different her life and that of many others might've been. Trying to refocus her mind on the present, a vaguely familiar voice called her from across the street.

'Is it Nell Adams?'

She looked long and hard at the woman standing on the road.

'Yes.'

The tall, elegantly dressed woman waited for the traffic to slow before she hurried across the road to Nell.

'Don't you remember me? It's Sarah from Woolies.'

'Oh my, I'm sorry, I didn't recognise you. You look wonderful.'

'Thank you, so do you, and I see a new addition to the family here,' she said and fussed with Bessie in the pram.

'So how have you been? You look really well.'

'Oh, I left Woolworths ages ago to sign up for the Land Army. Best thing I ever did. That's how I met my husband,' she said. 'Are you married, Nell?'

'Yes, he's an American army captain.' She replied, not wanting to go into too much detail about him missing in action. The last thing she wanted today was sympathy.

'That's lovely, Nell. I'm so happy things turned out alright for you. I've always wondered what happened to you, you know.'

A man started yelling after Sarah and she turned to look.

'Mr. Wilder?' Nell said, remembering him from the day at the Woolworth's fundraiser.

'You know each other?' said Sarah, surprised. 'This is my boss now. I'm his secretary.'

'Are you? Well, I don't know him personally. He offered me a chance to sing at the Empire many years ago. I never took him up on the offer. In fact, he asked me twice.' She thought about the day when Patrick took her to the cinema.

'You never did, did you? I always thought you were meant to be a star, Nell.'

Mr. Wilder joined them on the pavement.

'Good gracious, I remember you singing at Woolworths. You didn't get in touch with me even when I asked you the second time.'

'No, I'm sorry, I didn't. I suppose you could say that the war got in the way.' Nell laughed.

'Well the war is over,' he put a friendly hand on her shoulder. 'You should come by next week. I have a new play that requires a leading female singer...'

'Do you really mean that? Gosh, I...'

She looked at Sarah who was beaming. 'Go for it Nell, you deserve it.'

'Then alright, I will. I think I'd better get practicing,' she replied excited at the new future that was maybe opening up for her.

'And is this your little one?' Mr. Wilder took a look at Bess in the pram. 'Did you ever marry that American lad I saw you with?'

Nell smiled. 'I did Mr. Wilder,' she said proudly.

'Well, I look forward to meeting you next week.' He turned to Sarah. 'Do you have any of my business cards?'

'Yes, I do,' she searched through her bag and handed Nell a small card.

'Thanks, I'll see you all next week then.'

'You do that, Nell, and we should arrange a day out. It'll be nice to catch up after all this time.'

'Most definitely. It's been great to see you again.'

They said their goodbyes and Nell felt like she was walking on air when she pushed the pram up the High Street. She looked again at Wilder's card, and deciding to make a conscious effort to call in the morning. With the warm breeze blowing through her hair, and lightness in her step, she felt that her old self was close to re-emerging. 'It's just you and me now Bess,' she said, and gazed lovingly at her daughter. 'And we're going to make the most of our tomorrows that's for sure. It's what Daddy would've wanted.' She forced back her tears.

Bess began to whimper.

'It's okay, little one, we're just going to the market for Nanny,' she checked on her baby, tucking in her blanket. 'And then we'll go home for supper, yes?'

Eventually, Bess settled down and they made their way to the open market. As she was browsing the vegetable stall, she felt a tap on her shoulder. She spun around, wondering who else she'd meet today and was alarmed to see Emily who she hadn't long left home.

'I didn't know you were coming or I would've waited for you.' She was about to tell Emily the news about her audition when Emily took both her shoulders.

'He's alive, Nell...'

Nell didn't immediately connect with what she was hearing at first and then, slowly, it sank in, word for word. 'He's alive? You mean...' Her lips quivered. 'My Patrick has been found alive?'

Emily nodded. 'Yes, Nell. A phone call came for you just as you left.' She too also choked back tears. 'I had to come and find you, I just had to. My God, Nell, isn't this the greatest news?'

Overcome with shock, she reached out for the handle of the pram and knelt down next to Bess. 'Daddy's home, little one...' She could hardly believe the words she spoke, but in that instant, she felt a peace within her which she hadn't known for a long time. For Nell, Bess and Patrick the war was finally over.

Printed in Great Britain
by Amazon